Late Bloomer

by

Barbara Lohr

Purple Egret Press

Purple Egret Press
Savannah, Georgia 31411

Cover Art: The Killion Group
Editing: The Editing Hall

Print ISBN: 978-1-945523-05-2
Digital ISBN: 978-1-945523-04-5

For past students and colleagues, thank you for those eight short years. Teaching is such a gratifying career—one that I remember fondly, although I don't recall a Brody in room 207!

Chapter 1

The plane landed on the tarmac, jolting Carolyn awake. Hot and sweaty, she rubbed the crick in her neck. Then she lifted the shade to the noon sun blasting Albuquerque. Against the New Mexico horizon, the Cristo de Sangre Mountains formed a blue ridge. *Mountains.* Her stomach took a sickening dive. Heights terrified her so she'd had the shade down the entire trip. Back on solid ground, she couldn't wait to see her grandmother.

Puffs of reddish Albuquerque earth rose as the jet settled. Chatter broke out and passengers climbed from their seats, shaking out cramped legs. Carolyn had to get out of here. Just like high places, crowds had never been her thing. Leaping up, she cracked her head on an overhead bin.

Pain shot from her neck. And for what? Passengers crammed the aisles, grabbing bags and making calls. She wasn't going anywhere soon. Dragging her tote from under her seat, Carolyn slung it over her shoulder. The cabin became too warm for her quilted jacket, and she rubbed eyes gritty from the dry air. Soon she'd be in Mama V's back yard with a glass of lemonade. The thought eased her neck pain. All she had to do was get the rental car and drive about an hour to Santa Fe.

As the rows ahead emptied, she edged her way up the aisle. The thin wail of a child brought her to a stop. A baby strapped across her chest, a young mother struggled with a booster seat. Behind her a toddler whined.

"Here let me take that chair." When Carolyn held out a hand, the girl smiled.

"Thank you." She probably wasn't even thirty, younger than Carolyn. With a grateful smile, she handed the seat over and reached back for her little boy. The tyke regarded Carolyn with suspicion, as if she might run off with his carseat. "Come on, Weldon." The mother coaxed him and he took her hand.

How brave to travel with two kids.

Brave and lucky.

Booster seat bumping against her leg, Carolyn imagined she was the mother as she thanked the smiling flight attendants. Contentment settled over her. Didn't she just wish. Together, the four of them tromped up the ramp to a handsome young man who stood waiting.

"Daddy, Daddy!" Weldon nearly knocked Carolyn over trying to reach his father.

Arms outstretched, the father in cargo pants and a T-shirt sized up the situation and took the carseat. "Hey, thanks for helping my wife."

"No problem." With a wave, she left the young family. The pretending was over.

But that was okay. Someday. For now, she was here. Walking quickly past shops with colorful clothing and leather goods, she skidded to a halt to buy a key chain shaped like a cactus. Her first souvenir this trip. Carolyn loved visiting her grandmother. Santa Fe always felt like another country.

Ducking into a restroom, she splashed water on her face and slicked her brownish hair back. Too bad she hadn't had time to lighten it before this trip. Why bother with lipstick or eye liner?

Later. Right now she wanted to get her luggage, pick up her rental car and be on her way. Zipping back out onto the concourse, she took off. When she reached the baggage claim area, passengers crowded around chute D. No suitcases had tumbled out yet. She angled into a spot close to the conveyor belt and dug out her phone.

"I've landed," she said when her grandmother picked up.

"Oh, sweetheart. You're here!"

Carolyn smiled. Mama V always sounded overjoyed by life. Even her broken hip hadn't changed that. "Just landed. Still no luggage."

"Take your time, sweetheart," her grandmother said. "No need to hurry. Lots of traffic on that busy highway. We have a whole week. Are you hungry?"

"Not really," she lied. All she'd eaten since leaving Gull Harbor were two bags of peanuts on the plane.

"I'll have something waiting. How I wish you didn't have to rent a car when I have one right here. You should have let me drive down to get you."

Mama V on the highway? Horrifying and not possible. "Not necessary. You broke your hip, remember?"

Her grandmother chuckled. "That was three months ago. I think you'll be, well, surprised." Her voice dropped mysteriously.

"You're still recovering. Isn't that what Dr. Lewis told us when I was there at Christmas?" Her grandmother could be so stubborn. A bell rang and the conveyor belt started with a lurch. People surged forward. "Got to go. See you in about an hour."

"I'll be painting out in front of the gallery."

Following Grandpa Winston's death five years ago, her grandmother had surprised them all by relocating to Santa Fe. "I'm up for a change," she'd said. Painting had been her hobby but buying the gallery? Another surprise, one Carolyn's parents viewed skeptically. She'd been painting up a storm since then, equally amazing. Carolyn was so proud of her. But a bad fall from a stepladder last Christmas had landed her grandmother in the hospital with a broken hip.

"If you're painting outside, be sure to wear a hat and use sun block." Funny how roles changed with age. Tucking her phone into her slacks, Carolyn edged toward the luggage falling topsy-turvy onto the carousel. She was searching for her pink luggage tag when a tall man stepped in front of her. No way could she see around those shoulders.

"Uh, excuse me." Squeezing past him, she regained her spot. A gazillion black bags came spinning out but she spotted hers right away. After years of use, she knew that bag like the back of her hand. Although she couldn't see the handle—the big galoot kept horning in—her pink tag was attached.

But as she reached out to snag it, the idiot lifted her bag off like it was a box of tissue. After hours on the plane and waiting in Atlanta for her connection, Carolyn's patience was wearing thin. Her temples throbbed when he started to walk away.

"Excuse me." She tugged on his leather jacket.

"Yes?" He swung weary eyes her way.

"You have my bag." She pointed.

"Really?" He looked down at the suitcase as if he expected it to talk.

"Yes, that's mine. You've made a mistake."

"Ah, huh. Well, let's check." He slapped the bag down on its side.

Violation heated the air. The kind that involved pink bikini panties and pushup bras. "Stop!" Bending, she flattened one hand on her bag.

He ran a hand through inky black hair. "Look, I don't want to walk away with all your stuff. We're not the same size." Was he grinning as he bent over, jeans tight on muscled thighs?

Standing up, she waited.

Two zips and the bag opened. Shiny black boxers caught the overhead lighting. Her stomach clenched. Several pair were rolled neatly next to a leather shaving kit. He'd done an excellent job packing. Shaking out a pair of what were obviously his shorts, he offered them. "Yours?"

By now, other passengers were staring. "Of course not. Sorry, I thought for sure the bag had a pink tag."

The man threw her a cocky grin. "Ma'am, trust me. This bag has no pink tag. Satisfied?"

"Yes. Look, I said I'm sorry."

With one decisive movement, he'd zipped up his bag.

Stumbling back, Carolyn felt her hands tingle. She could almost feel the soft, satiny fabric...along with other stuff that definitely might not be soft.

Like all English teachers, she was cursed with a wild imagination.

"Mercy," she murmured with a shake of her head.

His boots stepped closer. This guy was one tall drink of water. And he was darkly handsome. Classic features. The kind you'd find on a heath or storming a castle. *His Hotness.* She liked to make up names for people, as if they were in a book. Yep, definitely His Hotness.

"Hey, you're not going to faint or anything? You all right, ma'am?"

Her mother was a ma'am. Her grandmother was a ma'am. Carolyn was...well, what was she? She sure as heck wasn't a Mrs. and at thirty-two, she was getting too old to be a Miss.

Then his brilliant blue eyes narrowed. "Wait a minute. Aren't you Miss Knight?"

Her head snapped up. "Why yes. Yes, I am."

"You taught at Gull Harbor High School, right?" He rocked back in his western boots.

"I did. I *do.*" She squinted. In the past ten years, she'd taught so many gawky teenagers. His Hotness definitely wasn't one of them.

"Brody." He arched a thumb into his chest. "Brody Wolf."

"Brody?" She thought back. The linebacker who never tied his gym shoes? When he breezed into class late, girls immediately lost interest in plot structure. Their eyes followed him to the back row. Women to Brody Wolf were like fruit flies to ripe peaches.

"You taught me how to write a thesis sentence." Shrugging, he gave her a sheepish grin. "Well, you tried anyway."

"Did you ever use it?" Sometimes she wondered. Was all the stuff she tried to drill into their party-hearty minds ever retained?

"Nope, probably not." And he chuckled.

"So, in college you got all your term papers from the Internet?"

Silence was his only answer. His Hotness, now her former student, moved closer.

"You flunked me that first semester of my senior year." How amazing that he could smile about it.

"Did I?" Enough polite chatter. She wanted to be in her rental car heading for Santa Fe. His wife was probably waiting for him out front. "Sorry about the bag."

Her eyes swung back to the conveyor belt. The metal plates clanked and her beat-up black bag circled, its pink tag giving her an angry eye.

Brody's glance followed hers. "Let me get that for you."

"No, really, I..."

He hefted it off as if it didn't weigh forty-nine and a half pounds. She'd weighed it at home. Even left her favorite clogs behind so she didn't have to pay extra. Their hands sparked when they both grabbed the handle. "Dry air." She shook out her tingling fingers. He regarded her silently, flexing his hand.

"Well, nice seeing you again, Brody. Gotta run." She turned to leave.

"You too, Miss Knight." With a final wave, he grabbed his bag and was off.

Thank God she could leave that embarrassment behind. As she trekked toward the exit, Carolyn's running shoes squeaked on the tile floor. She couldn't get away fast enough. Picking up the pace, she maneuvered around other passengers. Why did she feel so rattled? This wasn't the first time she'd run into a former student. She just hadn't yet run into one who was, well, so hot.

Made her feel old. Like she should have been wearing makeup.

Outside the air felt dry but mild. Shrugging off her quilted jacket, she tied the sleeves through the handle of her suitcase. Was she overheated or just excited? She tugged on her turtleneck. Spring was arriving in New Mexico. The sun burned bright but the air held a cool edge, perfect for sleeping with the window open. Trotting to the shuttle sign, she got there in time to watch the small bus pull away with a final puff of diesel fuel. *Perfect. Just perfect.*

"You renting a car, Miss Knight?" His Hotness came up beside her, his chin level with her forehead. Dark stubble dusted his chin and cheeks. Not a bad look, but not a look he'd had in high school. "Miss Knight" was having a hard time adjusting.

"Yes, I have a car reservation." How long before the next shuttle? "I'm visiting my grandmother in Santa Fe. She lives up there."

His jaw shifted, like he'd made a decision. "Look, I live in Santa Fe. I'll be glad to take you to your grandmother's. My car's right there in the lot." He jerked a finger over his shoulder.

The thought of one hour with His Hotness made her uncomfortable. "That's not necessary. After all I barely..."

His eyebrows lifted. Carolyn bit her lip. The unspoken words hung between them. *I barely know you.* And she didn't. Not *this* Brody Wolf.

Back then he was the class clown who took up too much time. That was her first year teaching, and her seating charts had to be constantly changed because of him. Brody wouldn't shut up. Wherever she put him, the girls talked to him. It was so annoying. Finally, she surrounded him with guys. Didn't help a bit.

That first year was exhausting. She spent her weekends planning next week's lessons or grading papers. No grading on the curve for her. Oh, no. An A was an A. It meant something. And, as in Brody's case, an F was an F.

But when it came to girls? Brody aced it. His locker was right across from room 207. She'd see them waiting for him, freshening their lipstick and mascara. When he finally arrived, they struck a pose against his metal locker, like they wanted to crawl inside and take him with them.

And now? Brody Wolf could have become an ax murderer, for all she knew. What was he doing in Santa Fe instead of Michigan?

"Come on, Miss Knight." His lips formed her name with an impish smile, and he crossed the T with his tongue. "Let me take you to your grandma's house. I won't bite. We can catch up. It's just me. Brody." Shrugging innocently, he grinned, the naughty but nice boy who'd helped with her audiovisuals.

What was wrong with her? Carolyn could save a heap of money

by using her grandmother's car. "Well, why not? Thanks, Brody."

"Follow me." Didn't even wait for an answer. Just moved those hips like Tatum Channing and struck out for the parking garage. Laughing, he crossed three lanes of traffic by holding up a hand. She scurried after him.

Carolyn felt so darned tired, she could hardly see straight. Maybe Brody would do all the talking. Tell her about his four children and beautiful wife. She could zone out along the highway. Take a nap.

Thinking back, Carolyn smiled. He'd hardly been her star student. Had he even read the Cliff Notes for *Wuthering Heights?*

Well, hello. He may not have read the book but he'd *become* the book. Brody Wolf had grown up to *be* Heathcliff. His Hotness without the heath.

The breeze played with his dark hair and more than one woman gave him a second look. Brody took on the dim, cool parking garage as if he owned it. For him, walking involved shoulders, hips and shaggy hair that wouldn't stay put. The boy oozed rugged masculinity.

Boy? Or man. She was really having trouble. Carolyn patted her snarled hair and tried to keep up.

But Brody didn't seem concerned about his looks, not with those worn boots, time-softened leather jacket and faded jeans. He wore coolness casually, except for the glasses. His aviator sunglasses added mystery, like he'd just flown in from Morocco or Caracas, with no time to shave. Her imagination ran riot and she almost giggled. Feelings that were definitely not academic rippled through her.

Lordy, it was hot in here.

And she recognized her wandering thoughts on the faces of the women they passed. They probably assumed Carolyn was his mother or older sister. Working on losing her grin, she tightened her lips. Her suitcase made a racket behind her on the concrete. Could be her imagination again but she could swear the wheels were warbling, *His Hotness, His Hotness, His Hotness.*

Her palms were sweaty by the time they reached a black SUV. Brody popped the hatch open and turned. "Here we go."

Back on her I-don't-really-know-you craze, she glanced inside for bodies. Nothing.

Unaware of her surveillance, Brody stowed away both suitcases. Then he reached inside for a Stetson. That bad hat completed the picture. The rakish angle didn't hurt and neither did the brown feather band.

She gulped. *This* Brody Wolf *was* a total stranger.

Opening the passenger door, he grinned. The weathered leather jacket hung open over a black shirt, releasing a manly scent. Her knees almost buckled.

Snap out of it, Miss Knight.

When it came to men, she'd been on a starvation diet.

"What?" Peering at her over the tops of those badass sunglasses, he held the door wider. "You're thinking that my mother taught me well? She did. I open doors for women."

"Right. Well, good." Carolyn couldn't remember a thing about his family. Heck, right now she barely knew her own name.

Didn't she pride herself on taking a personal interest in her students? But not one like this. Not a man who was six foot three or taller. She climbed inside. Brody closed the door and walked around the back. She smoothed her hair, pinched her cheeks and licked her lips. How ridiculous. Why, he was old enough to be her… How old was Brody anyway? Math eluded her. Settling herself in the bucket seat that smelled intoxicatingly like his jacket, she needed air. Cool air. Frigid, even.

Brody jumped in and started the SUV. "All right now. Let's get to it."

Yeah, let's. She slapped a hand over her mouth and hoped she hadn't said that out loud.

The engine rumbled. "Man, it's hot in here. Let's get this air working." He punched some buttons. She had a thing for men with long, tapered fingers. And this was a new revelation.

Along with a blast of air, music came on. Bone-melting blues. The kind of music that had you taking off your clothes before you knew what happened. Fingers moving with competence, he turned down the sound and turned up the air. "You can adjust your own vents."

"Right. Okay. Thanks." Knobs had never presented this much of a challenge. She fumbled until cold air performed dermabrasion on her face.

"So you're visiting your grandmother?" he said as they headed for the highway. A broad New Mexico sky with a tin sun blinded her. Carolyn rooted around in her bag for sunglasses and jammed them on her face.

"Sure am. Oh, my gosh. Will you just look at this traffic?" Getting a lift from Brody was looking better with every honked horn along Hwy 25.

"You come here a lot, Miss Knight?" His eyes swept her bare left hand, now clutching her tote. She eased the bag to the floor and grabbed the door handle.

"Now I do. My grandmother had a bad fall last Christmas. Broke her hip. Luckily, it was just before winter break so I could come out. She's been in rehab ever since. Now I'm just checking up on her." Her words rattled out like melting ice cubes.

"That's sweet. You still teaching at Gull Harbor?"

"Of course." She hated the stilted tone of her voice.

"No ring on that left hand?" Brody always had an impudent streak.

"No, I'm-I'm not married." *Not that it's any business of yours.* His question made her bold. "I suppose by now you have a house full of kids and a two-car garage?"

The square chin shifted.

What has gotten into me? "Sorry. That's none of my business."

Full lips set in a thin line, Brody seemed to agree. "No, it's not," he finally said. Then his smile twisted. "You've gotten kind of sassy, Miss Knight. I don't remember that about you."

Her face flamed. But just when Carolyn thought her cheeks must look like ripe tomatoes, he laughed. Roared, actually. She had to laugh along, the way she had when he brought a bullfrog into class. The darn thing croaked throughout seventh period. Took about forty minutes before she realized the sound was coming from Brody's pocket and not outside.

He settled back in his seat and moved into the left-hand lane. The SUV shot forward. Good lord, the boy had a heavy foot. They zipped past slower cars and at least three trucks. She'd watched the Indy 500 once in a sports bar with a man whose name she couldn't remember. The race had felt just like this. Pressing both feet against the floorboards, Carolyn tightened her hold on the door handle.

"You probably don't remember much about me. It was so long ago." She tried to make conversation.

"You were a good teacher. I bought a ton of Cliff Notes that year. Wasn't going to let you down." To her surprise, a blush worked its way up his right cheek.

"Thank you, I guess. I'm surprised that you remember."

"Trust me. You weren't a teacher any guy would forget."

Really? Pleasure and embarrassment twisted through her. How pathetic was this? "Who were the other kids in your class? Do you keep up with them?"

"You're trying to place me." Glancing in the rearview mirror, she saw his mock look of surprise. "You really don't remember?"

"I've taught for ten years, Brody." The pert tone was there, as if she were defending her career. Details came floating back like a sheaf of pink tardy slips. "But sure I remember you. I think you set the school record for detentions."

"Yeah, I had trouble getting to class on time." His grin widened. "Could never remember which books to bring."

"All you needed was a folder with all your Cliff Notes."

They laughed together. He eased up on the accelerator. "Have I changed much? You didn't seem to recognize me at first."

"You're well, taller. Broader." *Stronger, hotter.* "I remember when you broke your leg senior year. All the girls signed the cast."

"*You* signed it," he reminded her. "The other guys were jealous."

"I felt sorry for you." She turned so she could see him better. "You played so many sports."

"Coach Teegarden was so mad." He shook his head. "That stupid accident."

"You were important to the team, as I recall." Like a major player.

"And I didn't even break it in a game." His carefree laugh felt unsettling. "I jumped from the jetty up in St. Joe and landed on the rocks. What an idiot. Could have killed myself."

"I never knew that part." Teenage boys. Those details were chilling.

"I was crazy stupid back then."

"But that's all changed, right?" She was enjoying the teasing. Liked watching that ruddy pink stain his cheeks.

"God, I sure hope so." That gravelly chuckle massaged her tight neck. He glanced down at her wrinkled khaki slacks. "You've changed too. Kind of miss the miniskirt, though."

Well, that nailed it. Brought her past into focus. Miniskirts. When she'd graduated from college and taken her first teaching job, her college wardrobe came with her. "Miniskirts and boots. Turtlenecks with beaded necklaces."

"That's right," he said with approval. "Short skirts and earrings that swayed when you moved. The guys loved it. When you walked down the aisle, we'd drop our pens to check out the landscape."

"Brody Wolf!" she yelped, squeezing her knees together.

"Hey, don't worry, Miss Knight. We couldn't see much."

"That's so reassuring."

His lazy side-look sent shivers into areas she always thought were private.

"Your hair was long back then. You'd get so frustrated, always pushing it behind your shoulders. It was cute." In the rear view mirror, he was eyeing her braid, or what was left of it.

"I should have dressed more sensibly."

"Now, that would've been a real shame." The last two words came out low and slow.

Carolyn swallowed hard. This ride was turning into an education.

The traffic flowed heavy and fast. She was glad to be a passenger until Brody passed a double Federal Express truck. Instinctively, she leaned in from the door. "Don't these trucks make you nervous? Passing them seems so dangerous. But I don't, of course. I always stay in the right-hand lane."

Brody erupted into laughter. "No way. Must take you forever to get someplace. You've got to pass those trucks."

Her stomach swirled. Maybe it was a good thing she hadn't eaten. They left the white and blue truck behind. "Sure is a lot of traffic for a Saturday. Gets busier every time I come. Were there always homes out here?"

By now, they were in between the two cities. He glanced out, bruising the landscape with a frown. "This area keeps growing."

"You don't sound happy."

"I liked Santa Fe better before everyone discovered the Land of Enchantment." The sarcasm wasn't lost on her.

For a while, they traveled in silence. Crossing her khaki-clad legs, she smoothed the wrinkled fabric. When had she stopped wearing those short skirts? Her legs had always been one of her best features, or so people said. How embarrassing that the boys had talked about her. Her slacks with elastic waistbands probably weren't the subject of any teen-age conversations these days.

"Penny for your thoughts."

She jumped. "Just trying to remember how it was back then." *When I was young and naive.* "So you went on to college?"

"I did. Yes, ma'am." He nodded, suddenly solemn. "Even graduated. So you're divorced?"

"No. I'm not divorced. You get one more question, Brody Wolf." Lack of sleep was making her testy.

"Whoa." He chuckled. "Now you *do* sound like a teacher."

Really? Oh, when would they get there? She folded her arms over her elasticized waistband. His laugh died. "Sorry. I can't understand why you're single."

"Neither can I." Now, why would she admit that?

"But I bet a lot of guys were interested." His forehead puckered the way it had when she explained the difference between a literary hero and an anti-hero.

Gazing out the window, she studied the dry, reddish brown

earth. "My mother says my standards are too high."

"Really? Is that even possible?"

The open honesty of the question caught her unaware. "You got me."

Next to them, another truck decided to give them a run for their money. For a few terrifying moments, they seemed stalled next to the great lumbering beast. God, how she hated this. Squeezing her eyes shut, she leaned away from the door again. This time she pressed her head right into his shoulder.

He cupped her head with his hand. "Hey, you okay?"

"Eyes on the road, Brody," she barked. "Hands on the wheel." If he kept this up, they'd wind up in a dusty ditch, some huge truck on top of them. She just knew it.

"Geez, your hair is soft." With one final pat, he pulled his hand away. Stepping on the gas, Brody left the truck behind. She peeled away from his shoulder.

"You're safe with me, Miss Knight," he said softly.

"Am I?" Carolyn felt as if she were tottering, like one of the amazing rock formations in the distance.

"Of course you are." And he pulled into the right-hand lane.

Their speed slowed. So did her racing mind. "How about you? Is your family still in Gull Harbor?"

"My younger brother Braydon works the family winery in Paw Paw now that my grandparents are gone." The teasing was gone. "My mother and stepfather retired to Florida."

"A winery?" The Michigan wineries were favorite tourist destinations. "Why didn't you go to school in Paw Paw?"

"My grandparents kept a place on Lake Michigan. That established residency for Braydon and me. They had my mom convinced Gull Harbor schools were better. Turned out there were some advantages." He flashed a smile her way.

Was Brody flirting with her?

Get a grip, Carolyn.

"So did your wife live out here? Santa Fe is a long haul from Michigan." *Now who was fishing for information?*

"I'm not married," he said crisply. "Not married. Not divorced. No children that I know of, to my mother's disgust."

A sudden sense of kinship caught her by surprise. "I know that feeling. Every time my mother calls, she asks me if I'm seeing someone." Then she stopped. Usually she was so private.

"And the answer would be?"

She must be imagining the seductive tone in his voice. "No, of course not." Carolyn shifted uncomfortably. Hot sunlight beat down through her window.

"*Of course?* Why in the world not?"

They were driving under an overpass bearing turquoise and earth brown designs. "Oh, look! Don't you love it?"

"You're changing the subject." Peering over the rim of his aviator glasses, he caught her eyes in the mirror.

Her mouth felt too dry for words. They passed a sign that said Santa Fe 19. *Thank God.* This catching up stuff with His Hotness was getting to her.

"Overpasses like that are why I'm here," Brody said. "No way did I want work in a big, crowded city."

"I understand." She had first-hand knowledge of gritty winds tunneling through tall city buildings.

"Where are you from, Miss Knight?"

"Chicago."

He did a slow whistle. "That's a big city all right."

"A little too big. Traffic gets worse every year." Her parents had escaped all that with their high-rise condo along Lake Shore Drive. The luxurious building loomed high above the city, smugly secure. How she grew to hate that long, silent elevator ride.

"I understand." His head swiveled from one side of the highway to the other. "I need plenty of room. Open spaces."

"Eyes front and center please." His head jerked and she dropped her head into one hand. "I am so sorry. After all, you're not my student anymore."

"No, I'm not." Looking ticked off, he pinned her with an accusing glance then returned to driving.

"It's just that I haven't seen you in years. Do you ever come back to the class reunions?"

"No, but I would have if I thought you were going to be there."

A funny prickling started in her chest. "You're teasing again. So what do you do in Santa Fe?"

"I'm an architect. I design and build houses."

"Whoa. Impressive. I love the adobe houses out here. They make me feel like I'm in another country."

His smile widened. "Me too."

Brody had broken out of the mold. Guys like Cole Campbell and Finn Wheeler stayed in Gull Harbor for a number of reasons, mostly family. Not Brody, apparently. "I'm proud of you, Brody."

His smile slipped. What had she said?

"Thank you, Miss Knight. Then I finally get an A?"

"No, that's not it." Geesh, when did he get so sensitive? "I mean, so many students come back to Gull Harbor, which isn't a bad thing. Did you know Cole Campbell?"

His forehead furrowed. "Name's not familiar."

"He may have graduated before you. Cole's involved in construction in Gull Harbor. Married to a woman I know."

"Gull Harbor was so small. Can't be much construction going on there."

"Things are changing."

For a few miles, they traveled without talking. He turned up the music and she tried to relax. The long day had drained her but she couldn't nod off. Brody was about as relaxing as a double-shot espresso.

In between Albuquerque and Santa Fe, the land stretched flat on either side of the highway. Small pines and gigantic cacti patterned the reddish brown earth. From time to time, a cluster of squat adobe homes would crop up. "So do you build houses out here?"

He shook his head. "Not like these. Nothing wrong with them, but I specialize in custom homes up in the hills."

"You mean hills like Canyon Road in Santa Fe?"

"More remote than that," Brody said. The tension had eased. "Do you like Canyon Road?"

"My grandmother has an art gallery there. She lives in a casita out back."

"Lucky you." The saucy grin was back. "Cool area."

"I wish I could visit her more often." Her hair had escaped the braid and Carolyn twisted a length of it around her finger.

"Why don't you?"

"Too busy, I guess." Was she a slave to her schedule? But the cost was a factor. Although her parents always offered money, she hadn't gone to college to remain dependent on her folks.

Cars passed them. Were they creeping along? Brody was staying in the right hand lane. "You don't have to slow down for me."

The only sound was the whirring of tires and Billy Holiday crooning seductively. "I'm enjoying the ride," he finally offered in a low, husky voice that could have melted the North Pole. She opened her window.

"Are you warm? I can turn the air higher." One hand went to the console.

Carolyn breathed in. "Just need a little fresh air."

How pathetic was it that being with Brody revved her up? Her life was so drab that a ride with him served as high entertainment. A sign for Cerrillos Road came up but he wasn't slowing down. "You don't take Cerrillos Road?"

"It's faster staying on the highway. Do you want to drive up Cerrillos?" He was already taking the turnoff.

"Thanks. I just like to see everything again." She didn't feel tired anymore. "Is Jackalope's still there?"

"That junk pile? Yeah." But he smiled, as if he loved the rambling collection of buildings too.

The past hour had been fun. She liked Brody.

"Oh look! There it is!" She clapped her hands. Brody slowed down as they passed Jackalope's. "You can buy anything there."

He chuckled. "Right. And you might actually use some of it."

"Maybe this time I'll get a chance to visit. Christmas was so rushed, getting my grandmother set up and everything." She watched Jackalope's recede as they passed it.

"How long are you staying?"

"Only a week."

Santa Fe looked just like it had when she left in January. Adobe buildings stretched out along the road, merchandise displayed out front. But now trees were beginning to green up. The wisteria in her grandmother's yard might be in bloom. "Have you built any homes in the Canyon Road area?"

"One or two." Brody looked preoccupied as he shifted gears. "Mostly I work outside of town."

The poor guy must be tired of her chatter.

Probably can't wait to unload me.

When they came to Canyon Road, Brody turned up the narrow street. She'd never tire of the galleries and shops. Many of them were former homes with blue shutters and doors, another Santa Fe trait. Saturday tourists wandered up the sidewalks, gawking and stopping. "Right up ahead." She pointed to the low adobe wall that held a turquoise sign with the word *Vera's* scrolled in white.

"Pretty place." Ducking his head, Brody peered over the steering wheel. "I've probably driven past here a hundred times."

As they drew closer, she noticed her grandmother's purple sun hat bobbing beyond the wall. She often sang or hummed while she painted.

Brody pulled up and parked. "That your grandmother?"

"Yep, sure is." She couldn't help the pride in her voice. After Grandpa passed away, Mama V had created a new life in Santa Fe. Not many women could do that, especially at her age.

Brody came around. Carolyn jumped out and stretched. "Wonder where her walker is."

Mama V had turned, setting her palette on a bench. Her lime green skirt swirled in the breeze and a loose, flowered coat billowed around her. At Christmas, she'd worn her hair long. Now it was short and pushed up in sassy peaks.

"Mama V!" Waving, Carolyn smiled to imagine what her mother would think of this new Bohemian look. Pendleton plaid had been Mama V's uniform in Chicago.

Brody trailed through the open gate behind her.

"Darling!" Mama V opened her arms.

Dipping below the brim of her grandmother's hat, Carolyn gave her a tight hug. "Look at you! But where's your walker?"

"Oh, walker, smalker. I don't bother with that." Hands on Carolyn's shoulders, her grandmother pushed back and studied her. "So glad to see you, darling!"

Then her faded blue eyes swung to Brody and sharpened.

Sweeping off his hat, he extended a hand. "Brody Wolf. Delighted to meet you, ma'am."

"Well, my goodness." Grandma's eyes circled between the two of them. "Me too."

Carolyn flushed. Oh, no. She had to set things straight. "Brody, this is my grandmother, Vera Stanford. Brody's a former student. We ran into each other at the airport."

Her grandmother's head took a girlish tilt. "Why, how fascinating."

Chapter 2

Fascinating? Oh, no. Carolyn had to set Mama V straight right now. "Isn't it amazing? Our suitcases got mixed up. So nice that His H—. Brody offered me a ride." Then she clamped her lips shut. Good grief, she'd almost let His Hotness slip out.

But her grandmother wasn't listening. Instead, she circled the poor man like a barracuda about to take the first bite. Where the heck was her walker? But Mama V was hardly limping as she continued to study Brody.

He seemed to enjoy the attention. "Nice gallery you've got here, ma'am."

Mama V glanced back at the long, low structure with a pleased smile. "Thank you. We're growing. I suppose I could paint inside my studio but with a day like this? It's much more interesting outside." Brushing back a wisp of silver hair that had escaped her hat, she left a blue trail on her cheek.

"Brody probably has to get going. Could I get my bag out of your SUV, please?"

Carolyn was charging back to retrieve it herself when Brody caught her arm. Sensation sizzled through her. "I'll take care of it. You visit with your grandmother."

Before she could protest, he'd sprinted to the road with long, muscled legs that could evade a lineman to sack their quarterback. Her grandmother wiggled her brows at Carolyn. "So. Handsome," she mouthed.

Carolyn didn't want her grandmother getting ideas, but Mama V ignored her. She only had eyes for His Hotness. Carolyn dreaded the conversation sure to come once Brody drove away.

"Here you go." He set the suitcase next to her.

She stuck out a hand. "So nice to see you again. Can't thank you enough for your hotness...*help*. Your help." Carolyn dropped her eyes to his boots.

Brody engulfed her hand in both of his. "No trouble at all. Glad I ran into you, Miss Knight."

What did a melted hand look like? She pulled her hand away and studied it. His eyes twinkled. Like he'd asked her for another bathroom pass and she'd given in. Again.

"Miss Right? Did you say *Miss Right*?" Mama V inched closer.

"No, Brody called me Miss *Knight*, like he did back at school." Order had always been her strong point. But his impish expression tempted her to ditch decorum. "After an hour in the car together, I guess he can call me Carolyn."

Brody looked pleased. Her grandmother's lips formed a pink O. "Now I get it. And what were you two doing for one hour?" Her shoulders squeezed together.

"No. No. Not *that*." Carolyn waved her hands, as if she wanted to erase those words. But she couldn't. They hung in the air, provocative and permanent. Wearing a wide grin, Brody was enjoying this. "I'm sure Brody is anxious to get home."

His eyes found hers. "Not really...Carolyn." On his lips, her name sounded sensual. She melted into a puddle.

Mama V had a bad case of the giggles. Carolyn reached for her suitcase handle to steady herself. "Well, my grandmother and I have things to do. Good-bye, Brody. Nice seeing you. Catching up and all that." *Basking in your hotness.*

Smile brightening, Brody said, "Look, maybe we should have lunch this week. Do you have time?"

"Oh, well." Carolyn stubbed the toe of her shoe in the walkway. "I expect to be very busy. Helping my grandmother and everything."

"Oh, sweetie, I told you. I don't need that much help," her grandmother piped up.

"I could show you around." Brody's laser blue eyes gleamed.

"That's very kind." Her lips felt frozen.

"Great." He put his hat back in place. "See you later, Miss Knight. I mean, Carolyn."

There it was again. The softening of her name. Did women swoon in the real world?

"And so great to meet you, Mama V."

Her grandmother practically shimmered with delight as she wiggled her fingertips at him.

What had just happened here? Lunch with a former student wasn't on her agenda. Carolyn's grandmother didn't bother to hide her giggles. But how nice to hear her laugh after all she'd been through last Christmas.

Whistling, Brody sauntered around the back of his SUV. That cocky confidence sure brought back high school. She could almost smell that tiled hallway and her smile faded. Confusion descended like a biblical cloud of gnats.

The afternoon sun shone through the aspens as Brody drove away. Her long skirt swirling around her ankles, Mama V took her elbow. "Let's get you settled. Wendy's inside taking care of the gallery. You must be starving." Together they walked down the small alley leading to her casita. Carolyn trundled the suitcase behind her on the unpaved walk.

With every step, she struggled to clear her head of His Hotness. The sight of her grandmother's tiny house drowsing in the sun helped. The confusion of the past hour vanished. Contentment washed over her in soothing waves. Why didn't she come more often? Sure, Gull Harbor kept a slower pace. But this place was beautiful. And here her grandmother fussed over her in a way her mother never had.

The blue gate in the low adobe wall creaked when Mama V pushed it open. "Come on, sweetheart. I think you need a soak in that new tub I had installed."

"You changed your tub? What was wrong with the old one?"

Her grandmother lifted her shoulders. "Too small."

"Too small for you?" Carolyn laughed. Her grandmother seemed to get smaller every visit. Taking out a key, Mama V opened the door. If she didn't lock it, tourists might wander in, mistaking the house for another gallery.

Inside, the living room felt casually comfortable. Cushions

provided dashes of brilliant colors on the rattan furniture. The rounded kiva fireplace in the corner showed signs of use, a pile of logs stacked next to it with the pleasant smell of wood lingering in the air. Everything in the room felt so earthy. Natural. Simple. So unlike the slick black and grey decor of her parents' condo. Past the kitchen area, french doors led outside to the back garden.

Carolyn was hanging up her jacket when her grandmother turned. "So, what's up with this Brody?"

"Nothing." Was her nose growing?

Sitting down on the sofa, Mama V motioned for Carolyn to do the same. Knees wobbly, she sank. "Really, we were both grabbing our luggage at the same time. He must have been on my flight, but I never noticed him."

"You didn't notice *him*?"

Carolyn totally understood her grandmother's amazement. His Hotness would be a hard guy to miss. "Brody must have been sitting up front. Probably arrived late and was the first to leave." And she smiled. That would fit. "Years ago, I taught him. But that's all in the past"

"Ah, hah." Arms crossed over her flowered smock, Mama V cackled. "That's not what I saw."

Memories unfolded in her mind like pages of a yearbook. "He was always acting up. That was my first year teaching, and I had my hands full."

"Boys are always late bloomers."

"Maybe. Still, I could have done just fine without all Brody's jokes at my expense." She wouldn't go into the pencil dropping.

"He probably liked you. Wanted your attention."

"Oh, no. It wasn't like that." *Or was it?* "Anyway, I was Miss Knight to him. And I still am."

"Oh, Carolyn." Mama V did a pretty good imitation of Brody's voice, giving her name a sultry twist. "I don't think so, honey."

What had gotten into her? "Really, Mama V, I'm here to *help* you."

Her grandmother propped sandaled feet up on the leather hassock. "Help me what? Help me paint?"

"No, I'm going to cook and clean. Make sure things are shipshape." But glancing around, Carolyn noticed everything looked pretty tidy.

Her grandmother waved a hand. "Oh, Ana helps with that. Comes once a week."

"How *is* your hip?" She looked around. "Not even a cane?"

"Don't need one. My physical therapist was great." She flexed pink-tipped toes. "I worked at it, and well, here I am."

Amazing. "Are you still doing your therapy?"

"Nope." Mama V shrugged. "Through with all that."

"Oh. Well." Carolyn stared down at her sensible walking shoes.

"Don't look so disappointed, dear."

"But why didn't you tell me?"

Mama V leveled a look at her one and only grandchild. "Would you still have come?"

She had a point. The visit might not have been as urgent. "I just want to, you know, be here for you."

"Because your mother isn't?"

She gulped. "Exactly." Her grandmother could see right through her.

"Carolyn, I came to terms with that a long time ago. Your mother and father are busy in Chicago. I'm willing to send checks to their foundations, fund raisers and galas. But I don't want to attend."

"Neither do I." She chuckled. "You're so generous."

Another wave of the hand. "Whatever. I'm here because I don't want that life."

"You were always there for me, Mama V." Those weekends with her grandparents had meant so much. Stories at bedtime. Cocoa with marshmallows. Cuddling up to watch *Jungle Book* or *Peter Pan*. "It was always so peaceful at your house. That's what I love about Gull Harbor. The peace and quiet."

A head toss met that remark. "But sweetheart, I'm in my seventies. You're still so young, and you've hidden yourself in a small beach town."

Carolyn sat upright. "But I love the lake and my girlfriends. And I like my job."

"I know. But you're hiding out there. Ten years and no husband?"

This was something new and it hurt. "Maybe I don't want to be married."

"You don't?" Her grandmother's brows lifted. "Why not?"

"Maybe marriage doesn't appeal to me."

Her grandmother's features softened. "Not every couple has a marriage like your parents."

Biting her lip, she couldn't even go there. Her parents hadn't weathered a storm. They'd survived a tsunami.

"Your grandfather and I were always very happy together."

"I know." Carolyn smiled, remembering their private jokes and secret hugs. Her grandparents had adored each other. If only every marriage was like theirs. They'd golfed at the club, played bridge and even joined a cooking class together. How she'd laughed when her grandfather tried to teach her how to separate an egg. The yolks were everywhere and the butcher block, sticky with egg whites. Her grandmother had laughed hysterically.

"You're beautiful and smart, so why don't you have a beau?"

The old-fashioned term made Carolyn smile.

"Oh, okay. A hot man." Her grandmother put the last two words in quotes with her fingers.

"Like His Hotness?" She felt a heat flash just saying that name.

"Perfect. Is that what you call Brody?"

Shaking her head, she tried to let that name go. "I don't call him anything, Mama V. He's just a boy who was a problem student."

How the heck did Brody change into His Hotness? "I'm too busy to search or whatever it is people do." When she thought of plopping herself on a bar stool at the Mangy Mutt and trying to make conversation with the beach bums and boat owners who frequented the place, her stomach turned queasy.

"Busy." Her grandmother's glance pierced her with eyes that saw everything. "Doing what?"

"Teaching." Her voice rose. "My career means a lot to me."

"I know it does, sweetheart, but there's more to life than work."

"And I've made friends. In fact, I have a book group." She smiled, thinking of Diana and Phoebe. They were the three in the group who hadn't grown up in Gull Harbor, which made bonding easier.

Her grandmother heaved a sigh. "Oh, dear. Are you reading about romance instead of having one?"

The conversation began to feel like an argument, and tears prickled in Carolyn's eyes. She didn't want to cross swords with Mama V the way she did with her mother.

Thank goodness, her grandmother must have felt it too. Shifting her feet from the hassock, she stood. And then Carolyn saw it. Getting up required effort. Mama V turned sideways and pushed up with her hands.

"Oh sweetheart, I'm butting in where I don't belong." She glanced at the clock on the wall. "Almost two o'clock and you must be starving."

Carolyn's stomach growled as if it agreed.

"The usual?" her grandmother asked, walking into the kitchen area.

"Yep, I'll get out the peanut butter."

Working together at the counter, Carolyn helped her grandmother assemble the peanut butter and orange marmalade sandwiches they both adored. An unopened bag of cheese curls sat waiting. Ice cubes clinked in the glasses when her grandmother filled them with lemonade laced with tea. They both settled at the rough-hewn table.

Carolyn was so relieved to be here. Apparently, her

grandmother wanted to appear independent. Fine with her. Mama V must have worked really hard on her rehabilitation.

When she'd licked every bit of marmalade from her fingers and finished the cheese curls, she pushed back. "I'm full as a tick." One of her grandfather's favorite phrases.

Mama V smiled. "Better?"

"Still a little tired."

"You know where your room is. I'll just tidy up the kitchen." Carolyn started to protest but her grandmother waved her away. "Skedaddle now."

She wasn't going to argue and took her suitcase down the hallway to the bedrooms. A roomy bathroom stood at the end of the hall, with a guestroom opening to the right and her grandmother's room on the left. The casita was small and cozy. At night she could almost hear her grandmother's light snoring. Somehow that was comforting.

Eager to get settled in, Carolyn swung her suitcase up on the bed. After shaking out her sensible cotton knit dress, she tucked tops and pants in the dresser drawers. The carved headboard of a queen size bed stood between two windows, and a skylight allowed extra light. At night she loved to stare up at the stars pinned to a sky skewing toward turquoise. A comforting sense of peace fell over her. She'd have her special week with Mama V.

Grabbing her makeup bag, she took it into the bathroom. The soaking tub her grandmother had mentioned was something else. It stood in front of the window and had a lovely high back. A small footstool was pulled up and a new grab rail was on the wall next to the tub.

She sniffed. No familiar lavender scent. No, a strange, new smell circled in the air. Had Mama V changed her perfume? Maybe a friend had spent the night, leaving a trail of her fragrance. Next to her grandmother's pink electric toothbrush sat another one in olive green. Aw, Mama V was so thoughtful about the little things. Picking up her gift, she pressed the button and watched it vibrate.

For a second she was tempted to try it out, but right now she needed a nap. She'd just stow her things away. Yanking open the drawer she'd always used, she stared at a man's shaver, alongside toothpaste for sensitive teeth.

What was this? Her mind carefully sorted through some sensible options. Maybe her grandmother used this to shave her legs, although she'd never seen or heard her do that. Casting a glance at the closed door, Carolyn slowly pulled the drawer out to see what was in the back. No, these blue pills and some kind of hair wax did *not* belong to her grandmother.

Her heart pounded. This was really none of her business. And yet it was. How long since her visit? Three months ago nothing had been in this drawer. She set her pink cosmetic bag in a corner of the counter. Then she washed her face and hands, dried them on a fluffy white guest towel and walked back into the kitchen.

Her grandmother looked up from the newspaper. "Everything all right, sweetheart?" How could Carolyn have missed the violet eye shadow or the cream rouge on the apples of her grandmother's cheeks? And what had happened to the fine lines around her lips? Was she having them injected? "Thought you needed a nap after your long trip."

Uncertainty churned in Carolyn's stomach. She perched next to her grandmother, who folded the newspaper and reached for her lemonade. Every family had boundaries. Was Carolyn about to breach one? "So, what have you been doing lately, Mama V?"

Her grandmother's eyes turned mischievous. "Oh, busy with the gallery, mostly. I'm making more friends. You know, people on Canyon Road." A dreamy expression drifted across her face.

"A lot of women in these shops, I suppose?"

"Both women and men." Mama V's voice softened on the last word.

"Really? Are there any single men in Santa Fe?" *Men who like to brush their teeth at your house?*

Dipping her finger into the lemonade, her grandmother slowly nudged an ice cube. "You'd be surprised. It's amazing how many men come out here in their retirement years."

"Do they? Probably the ranch type, right? Like Brody."

"Oh, some are very cultivated. Cultured." There was that blissful expression again.

Heck with it, she was diving right in. "Anyone in particular?"

Her grandmother's lips tilted into a shockingly naughty smile. A smile Carolyn had never seen before. When she tried to phrase another question, nothing came out of her mouth.

Mama V twirled a wisp of her new, sassy hair-do. "Well, I've met a man I kind of like. Howard. Howard Haynes." The name was released with reverence. Carolyn looked at her grandmother in disbelief. She just hadn't seen this coming.

"Sweetheart, I'd like you to meet him," Mama V offered.

"And I'd like to meet him too. Maybe lunch someday while I'm here." Her one-week vacation was beginning to feel crowded.

"How about dinner tonight? Howard offered to take us to Geronimo's."

Geronimo's. Probably the most expensive restaurant in Santa Fe. A place where you had to make reservations in advance. "So it's that serious?"

Her grandmother burst into laughter. "Don't be silly. Howard's a widower with a jewelry shop a little way down the hill. You probably passed it."

"Sounds nice." She wasn't about to pee in her grandmother's pool, as her friend Phoebe would say. But dinner tonight? Right now, she felt like curling up on the sofa for some girl talk. Maybe take a book to bed early. That's what the two of them used to do when she visited. But Mama V looked downright dithery with excitement. Carolyn couldn't say no.

And she wanted to meet this man who kept personal items at her grandmother's. After all, wasn't that her family duty? "Sure, whatever you say."

"Terrific." Her grandmother patted her hand. "Now, about taking that nap? I've got some work to do down at the gallery."

Nodding, Carolyn gulped. "Okay." She'd been dismissed. A million questions chattered in her head, but she'd been handed off to nap.

Retreating to the guest room, she longed for the uncomplicated past with her stately white-haired grandfather. Now she had to deal with this. First Brody and now Howard what's-his-name. Ripping the rubber band from her unkempt braid, she sank onto the queen size bed and sniffed. Nope, no smell of lavender linen. Opening a window, she inhaled the clear scent of the desert with a hint of wisteria. The gnarly vines outside the window must be coming into bloom. Maybe everything would be all right. Sinking onto the bed, she pulled up the comforter, closed her eyes and tried to block out what she'd found in the bathroom.

Some time later, she shook herself from a dream that left her sweaty.

Brody. The dream had been about him. His Hotness. Sitting bolt upright, she fought the urge to touch her body in the places he'd explored in that dream. What was this? She pulled her knees up into her chest. The dream felt disturbing but in a wildly exciting way. Releasing her knees, she fell back onto the bed.

But it had just been a dream. When her heart rate returned to normal, she slipped on her flip-flops and ventured out to the small back yard and sat down. The iron bench was warm on her back, and the sun filtered through the aspen trees above, just greening up. Everything looked the same, but it wasn't.

Feeling a little like Alice in Wonderland, she wondered if she'd fallen down a rabbit hole into an alternate reality. She'd never liked that story. Little Red Riding Hood was a lot more predictable.

This trip wasn't going according to plan.

Chapter 3

Howard Haynes sure talked a lot. Carolyn's head pounded as she faced her grandmother and Howard across the crisp white tablecloth at Geronimo's. The way Mama V gazed at this guy made Carolyn look away. He sure didn't measure up to her grandfather. And his son Alan? He wasn't "tripping her trigger," as her friend Phoebe would say. To be fair, a lot of women would find him attractive in his navy blazer and subdued ways. When she'd realized there would be four of them tonight, Carolyn didn't want to hurt her grandmother's feelings. "Sure. That sounds nice."

But it wasn't nice at all. She hadn't come here to be fixed up.

The past five years had been hard for Mama V. After her husband's death, she wasn't the same. Her smile didn't reach her eyes. This move to Santa Fe and a new artistic life had been a total surprise, one her mother had questioned. Mama V shut her down with a simple, "Well now it's my life, sweetheart, isn't it?"

Watching Mama V and Howard exchange secretive glances, Carolyn felt change rumbling her way. Again. This wasn't the same grandmother she'd rushed to help in late December. Carolyn squirmed in the straight-backed chair. The dinner stretched in front of her, a slow progression of courses and conversation. She almost did a face plant in the plate of fancy butters.

But maybe it was worth it to see Mama V's faded blue eyes sparkle in the low light. Her joy had returned. Still, Carolyn felt wary. Howard had been droning on about what to look for in a luxury car for at least ten minutes. Sure, she'd love a car that parked itself. Maybe she'd put that on her next Christmas list. Right up there with a trip around the world. Even Alan was beginning to look bored, his complacent smile fraying at the corners.

"What looks good to you, Carolyn?" her grandmother asked, studying the menu.

"Order anything you like." Howard knew a lot was riding on this visit.

Mama V tapped one finger to her raspberry lips. "That salmon sure looks good."

Salmon had always been her favorite. Howard turned. "Now, now Vera. You know what we talked about."

"Oh, you're right." Mama V closed the menu with a sigh. "The tenderloin it is."

In the past, Carolyn and Mama V had bonded over grilled salmon. Clearly, that had changed. Carolyn's grip tightened on the menu.

Mama V leaned toward her. "Howard is teaching me to appreciate beef. You know, to avoid frailty. Lean beef."

"Frailty?" She snorted. Her grandmother was a long way from frail, although she'd had that fall from a step stool.

Giggling, her grandmother squinched up her shoulders. "I've decided to live dangerously with very lean meats to give me muscle mass." Holding out an arm, she formed a muscle.

"That's my girl." Howard and Mama V exchanged a syrupy look that made Carolyn gag.

Alan caught Carolyn's eyes and smiled. What did he think of all this?

"I'll have the salmon." She set the menu aside. Awake since four that morning, she was fading fast. It might be eight o'clock here but her body was calling it ten. Anxious to get this show on the road, she plucked at the ruffle on her pink blouse. Both the blouse and the khaki skirt could have used pressing but she didn't have time.

"How about you, son?" Howard asked.

Alan set the menu aside. "Strip steak for me. Baked potato. Green beans." Yep, nothing out of the ordinary there. Alan seemed like a solid guy. Thinning hair, a little paunch and shoulders beginning to slump. Nice looking, in a quiet kind of way. Maybe early forties. Probably the age she should be considering for herself.

That is, if images of Brody didn't keep popping up. She kept seeing him stride through the parking garage while the 007 theme played in her mind.

But back to Alan. Were her grandmother and Howard playing cupid? Carolyn took a sip of her chardonnay. Any man his age probably had at least one divorce and some children tucked away in his past, a back story waiting to be revealed.

Her vision blurred and she blinked. That year her Christmas cards had arrived with photos of children. Almost all the girls she knew at St Mary's were safely married. Sure, she'd dated Jeff Cunningham at Notre Dame. But when he mentioned marriage their senior year, she'd wanted to wait. After he went on to Harvard law school, the relationship had cooled. He'd met Allison. Sometimes she wondered. Why had she held back? Jeff was such a nice guy. Now all she met were men like Alan, a little worn around the edges.

And then there was Brody. Her heart kicked up. She sucked in a deep breath.

Howard continued to study the menu. "Appetizers, anyone ? Lobster bisque. Doesn't that sound good?"

Why not? Wasn't this a vacation? She glanced at the menu again. "Cauliflower bisque for me."

Her grandmother ordered the same as Howard. In an eerie way, they were acting like a couple. Why hadn't Carolyn gotten word of this?

Then it hit her. Her parents didn't know.

Primping her gelled hair, Mama V was playing it safe. Having it her way. If she had even breathed a word about Howard and her budding romance, her daughter and son-in-law would have checked him out immediately. With his career in finance, Dad would have gotten all the key information. Income. Credit score. Debt ratio.

Her mother clearly considered Mama V an invalid. "Be sure she's not overdoing it and takes all her medications."

What medications? Cabernet? Mama V winked at her over the lip of her wineglass.

Okay, so her grandmother didn't need her help, not the way she'd imagined anyway. Maybe Carolyn should consider this visit a different kind of duty. First, she'd vet Howard so she could explain him to her mother. Carolyn smoothed the linen napkin over her lap. Yep, that's exactly what she'd do.

"So, your grandmother tells me you're a teacher," Howard began after their order had been taken.

"Yes, high school English." She lifted her glass for a sip that became a gulp. The wine hit the back of her throat with a pleasing spray of oak.

Howard's eyes narrowed but his forehead stayed smooth. Botox? "In a town on a lake? Is that what I understand?"

"Lake Michigan." How could she explain the peacefulness of Gull Harbor? No wide lanes of traffic racing down *their* Lake Shore Drive. Just the peaceful shoreline. Soaring gulls. The lake breeze rustling through pine trees. In Gull Harbor an exciting Saturday night meant watching a DVD or shopping online for another pair of khaki pants. Yippy, skippy.

"Must be quiet there in the winter."

"You'd be surprised. Visitors come for the snow sports."

Alan came to her aid. "Snowmobiling, I suppose? Cross-country skiing?" His voice drifted off, his list depleted. But she appreciated his intervention.

"Yes, some of that. We get a lot of snow."

The waiter brought a bread basket, Howard placed a large hunk on his plate and a smaller one on Mama V's. "We have snow," he said. "But nothing like the Midwest. Ours is gone like that." And he snapped his fingers.

After the waiter served the soup, the table fell silent. Her eyes flagged. The warm room and the wine were making her groggy. Dipping her soup spoon into the creamy bisque, she longed to be in bed with a book.

When she fell asleep tonight, would her dream about Brody return? Carolyn's hand jiggled and soup splattered her blouse. "Oh, honestly."

Alan snatched his napkin from his lap, but she got there first. No way was Howard's son blotting her boobs. He seemed to realize it. With apologetic eyes, he returned his napkin to his lap while she worked on the stain.

"Oh, your pretty blouse. We'll just have to get you some new clothes," her grandmother chirped. The words struck her as criticism. She scrubbed harder at the stains. Mama V's flowing top looked as if it had come from Picasso's studio, all colorful swirls and dots. Purple pants matched the violets embedded in her heels. Recovering from a hip fracture and her grandmother was wearing heels, the plastic kind with flowers.

"Everything okay?" Alan murmured.

"Fine." She felt like a first grader with oatmeal on her shirt.

"They really know what they're doing in the kitchen. Four star restaurant." Howard leaned toward her with this bit of news.

For a few seconds they sat and sipped. Waiters moved with quiet authority between the tables and booths. The restaurant was full. These reservations had probably been made some time ago. She wished she'd been warned.

"What about your career plans?" Howard broke the silence. "Will you stay in Gulfport?"

"Gull Harbor," she supplied, pushing her half eaten soup aside.

"Right. Gull Harbor. Kind of quaint, isn't it? Will you stay there until you...well, make more permanent plans?"

"Howard?" Mama V put her spoon down.

"What? I'm just asking." He turned up the palms of both hands.

What were "permanent plans?" Carolyn had a feeling they involved a husband and children. "Right now, I have no plans to relocate. I love Gull Harbor." Even if she whipped out her phone and showed Howard shots of spectacular sunsets over the lake, it might not matter. Sleepy, little Gull Harbor wasn't for everyone.

"But the pool of eligible young people. Oh!" He cast a quick look at Mama V. Had she kicked him?

"How is that soup, Dad?" Alan broke in. Maybe he realized his father was about to point out that Carolyn was "getting on." When had thirty-two become middle age?

Time to turn the tables. "My grandmother tells me you have a store." Not a shop, but a store. Carolyn watched Howard draw himself up. She almost expected peacock feathers to unfurl.

"Yes, Haynes Jewelry." Howard poked his butter knife toward the window. The heavy gold ring on his right pinkie gleamed. "Just down the road."

"Alan makes some of the jewelry himself." Mama V fingered a necklace sporting a huge opal.

"Alan's a master designer." Howard smiled with satisfaction. "He studied in Europe. His designs have won awards."

"And here comes our dinner," Alan broke in. "Time to finish up that soup, Dad."

Howard's son was slowly endearing himself to Carolyn. His attempts to manage his father almost made her laugh.

As the waiter drew closer, the air filled with tantalizing smells. Carolyn was starving. For a few minutes, they concentrated on the food. She savored the silence and her salmon. It might be hard for Howard to put his foot in his mouth again when it was filled with prime beef.

"So you're a teacher," Alan said quietly while her grandmother was making eyes at Howard. "I'll bet the kids love you."

Thinking back to the Christmas gifts students had left on her desk, she smiled. "Maybe."

"I always wanted to be a teacher," Alan said, with a note of regret.

"Why didn't you? We always need more teachers."

Alan slid his eyes across the table. She didn't need a road map.

"A successful family business provides security." When Alan drew himself up like that, he looked just like his father. "Look, I think you're doing a real service by teaching. You grew up in Chicago?"

"Yes, but I didn't want to stay there." And she wasn't going any further with that. "Are you and your father Santa Fe natives?"

"Oh, no. Not many people here actually grew up in Santa Fe. But they're drawn here in droves. The art market is second only to New York. But some come because they feel the area has an aura. Something to do with Indian folklore and their mystical past."

Here he rolled his eyes. "I'm not really sure what that's all about."

"So where do you call home?"

"I grew up in Palm Springs. Berkley for school." He nodded at his father, still wrapped up in her grandmother. It was kind of cute. "Dad still keeps a place there."

Both father and son oozed culture and money. Well-heeled and well-dressed. Here she sat, her simple clothes wrinkled and stained. Her friend Diana would definitely not approve. She owned a boutique called Hippy Chick. The colorful skirts, embroidered tops and fanciful jewelry would fit in here. Her stylish grandmother would love them. Carolyn felt drab tonight, compared to her grandmother. Deflated, she devoted herself to her garlic mashed potatoes.

"You'll have to come back in opera season," Howard was saying. "Alan loves it. But perhaps you've been here during the summer?"

"Thought about it but never made it. I usually teach summer school and work in a local deli." That probably sounded as exciting as watching paint dry.

"You should consider it. I'd love to take you to the opera this summer." Alan had finished his meal. The waiter was clearing. "I hope this trip is one of many."

"Sounds nice, Alan." Keeping her expression noncommittal, Carolyn was relieved to see the waiter arrive with coffee. "Decaf please." The last thing she wanted was to be kept awake tonight. Her body felt exhausted but her mind wasn't.

Somehow, she got through coffee. The flourless chocolate cake restored her spirits and she mellowed out. But why did the warm, rich cake remind her of Brody? If only she could stop thinking about His Hotness. In her overactive imagination, he was a man who invited decadence.

"What are you smiling about, dear?" her grandmother asked.

"Oh, nothing."

Howard threw a meaningful glance at Alan, as if to say *good job*. But he had it so wrong.

"So tell me about your design work, Alan? Do you prefer working in gold or platinum?" If she kept asking questions, maybe they'd do the talking. By the time they called it a night, her eyelids felt heavy as stones. Always a gentleman, Alan helped her from the chair and handed her the plain quilted jacket. Then they were out in the crisp night air. "Look at that sky. Don't you just love it?" her grandmother asked, linking her arm through Carolyn's.

"It's always so spectacular." The indigo blue sky in New Mexico held a million stars.

"And now, I have a surprise for you!" Howard rubbed his hands together.

Carolyn turned, suddenly cautious. The expression on her grandmother's face indicated she knew what was coming.

"El Farol next door has flamenco dancers. The best in the region." Motioning to them, he was already walking up the road.

What? No way. She stood her ground. "Oh, thank you but I have to get some sleep." And she yawned so wide, Howard could probably see her tonsils before she covered her mouth with one hand. Hardly ladylike but she didn't care. By this time her grandmother looked stranded between them.

"Nonsense." Howard waved to Alan. "Tell Carolyn how much she's going to like this."

Geesh. This guy wouldn't give up. Why didn't her grandmother say something?

"Dad. Not tonight." Alan took her elbow and they started down the narrow walkway. She wanted to hug him. With a grumble, Howard fell in behind them, Mama V's arm linked with his. What a relief. Howard's heavy-handedness wasn't winning him any points, that's for sure. They passed a few visitors staring into shop windows.

"Sunday is a big day for you, I suppose?" She had no idea what to say to Alan. Her tank of polite conversation was running on low. "Tourists arriving and all that."

The sidewalk was uneven and her sandal turned. Alan tightened his hold to steady her. "Tourist traffic is a bit heavier on the weekend."

The sidewalk had become even, but he still held her elbow.

"Why don't you stop in tomorrow? I can show you around."

"I don't know what my grandmother has planned. She might want to be in her gallery on Sundays."

Alan chuckled, low and easy. "Well, I'm inviting you, not your grandmother. She's seen everything."

"Maybe" was all she could manage. If she hadn't run into Brody today, what would her reaction have been to Alan? He seemed nice enough. But she was beginning to think that "nice enough" wasn't what she wanted. "If I have time, I'll stop, okay?"

When they reached the casita, she thanked Howard, said a quick good night and ducked inside. Would her grandmother follow? Did she have a drawer at Howard's where she kept a few things? But her grandmother hustled in behind her. "Now wasn't that lovely?" She shrugged off a suede jacket. "What did you think of Alan?"

Leaning over, Carolyn kissed her grandmother's cheek. "He's a very nice man. I'm going to bed. See you tomorrow, Mama V."

"Sorry, sweetheart," Mama V whispered.

With a wave, Carolyn headed for the long, cool hallway. Exhaustion weighed each step. Once inside her bedroom, she slipped out of her clothes and into her sleep shirt. After quickly brushing her teeth, she settled under the comforter. Once on her side, she listened but heard nothing.

Chapter 4

The sun beat down as Carolyn yanked weeds from Mama V's yard the following morning. The back of her neck burned, and she dashed inside for one of her grandmother's hats. Soft morning sunlight filled the house. After a quick breakfast of croissants and coffee, Mama V had taken off for the gallery. To Carolyn's relief, she hadn't peppered her with questions. In fact, her grandmother had seemed preoccupied. Something was on her mind. Carolyn could see it in the tiny smile that teased her lips.

Had Howard brought that smile to her face? Maybe Carolyn was being too hard on the man. Maybe he wasn't as stuck up as he seemed. Thank goodness, Alan had intervened when Howard tried to pressure her into flamenco at El Farol. Thundering dancers had filled her dreams. Heart pounding, she'd jerked awake and listened for a man snoring across the hall. Nothing.

Stop it right there, missy. Was she her grandmother's keeper?

Confusion muddled her mind. Jamming her grandmother's pink hat on her head, she went back outside to do battle with a few scrawny weeds. But as she yanked on worn gardening gloves, her head still spun. Dinner had been fine. A week ago she would never have guessed she'd be sitting in that elegant restaurant with an eligible man paying attention.

But it was Brody on her mind, not Alan Haynes. The former student who could never tell a semicolon from a colon, not that she cared a whole lot. In fact, Carolyn chuckled when she thought of the small things that had seemed important back then.

She went back to tugging the stubborn weeds when a vehicle slowed and stopped outside. That engine sure sounded familiar.

Jumping up, she peeked over the adobe wall. Good grief. Brody Wolf leapt from his SUV in low-slung jeans and a pale blue V-neck under his leather jacket. So. Darn. Hot. Head down, he walked toward her, rocking each step with confidence.

Her faded sweatshirt felt ridiculously heavy and so did her jeans. Stripping off the gardening gloves, she tossed them into the weeding tub along with the trowel. Smiling at her over the blue gate, he tipped his hat. "Morning, Miss Knight."

"Morning, Brody." Wasn't this how they'd greeted each other in English class? Only back then he'd been skidding in late. Now the gate squeaked open.

Her eyes swept from his dusty hand-tooled boots to the broad shoulders. "What's up?"

"Nothing much. Just checking up on you." His Hotness peered at her from under the brim of that hat.

Crickets were singing *His Hotness, His Hotness, His Hotness.*

"What are you pulling out?" He glanced at the gardening basket.

"Weeds."

His thick brows vaulted. "Ma'am, in Santa Fe, we welcome anything that's green."

"Really?" Remorse deflated her. She stared at the ground around her. "My grandmother never mentioned that. Guess I should have known."

Snatching a sprig of something from the basket. Brody let it dangle from his fingers. "We don't get that much rain in these parts. If anything green splits through that hard-packed earth, we welcome it."

"Oh, my gosh. I never thought of it like that."

"Look, don't worry about it. I'm only teasing." Brody's full lips curved into an easy smile. "Thought I'd stop by. See how you're settling in."

She played with the tip of her braid. "Fine. I'm just helping out."

"So you came all this way to tidy up your grandmother's yard?"

She ran her hands down the heavy jeans. "When you say it like that, it sounds silly."

"We don't have yards here like in the Midwest. Lawns don't flourish. In Santa Fe plants hang on for dear life." He looked pointedly at the limp victim in his hand. Then he laid it in the basket with silent respect. She felt terrible, as if she'd been given a scolding. From Brody. Now wasn't that a hoot?

"Gee, you sound like a teacher." Their eyes met and, darn it, she giggled. Teeth flashing in the sunlight, Brody let loose a raucous roar that made her toes curl. He'd always had a hearty laugh. For a second, they were back in Gull Harbor, chuckling over the fact that Jay Gatsby should have bought a boat to reach Daisy's dock instead of staring at that green light every night.

Brody always took the direct approach.

"You up for an adventure?" He hitched a thumb toward his SUV.

"Sure. Why not?" Her grandmother would be gone for a while. "Give me a minute, okay?"

Brody checked his watch. "One. Maybe two." And he laughed again. His boots rang on the shallow steps as he followed her onto the back porch. While she pushed open the screen door, he folded his tall frame onto a bench.

Dashing back to the guest room, she peeled off the sweatshirt along the way. What should she wear? At first, she grabbed a moss green turtleneck. Then she switched to white. Yes, a fresh white turtleneck with soft, well worn jeans. Like Brody's. Her wardrobe was in pathetic shape. All khaki and jeans, with very little color.

Last night women, including her grandmother, had bloomed around her like exotic desert plants. Later, she'd put out an SOS to Diana.

Taking a moment in front of the bathroom mirror, she brushed out her hair before weaving it into a thick braid. She was putting on lipstick using her grandmother's magnifying mirror when she noticed it.

Wrinkles fanned from her mouth and eyes. This darn dry air. Avoiding the guest drawer, she pulled open her grandmother's makeup drawer. Okay, she felt weird about it but she needed help. Mama V bought skin creams as freely as peanut butter. As her fingers closed around the pale aqua jar, she noticed a soft pink plastic shape tucked in the back. She froze.

Had this drawer become a secret stash of toys? The intimate kind? Carolyn stood there, mystified. For years her grandmother had been a role model of matronly security. Things had changed and uneasiness crept over her. Who was this woman?

On with it, girl. After swirling a layer of cream over her skin, she screwed the lid on tight, popped the jar back in the drawer and slid it shut.

That damn green toothbrush. It was all his fault.

Grabbing her jean jacket, she was out the back door.

Rising slowly, Brody took her in. "Nice."

"Thank you." As she swept past him, she patted her braid self-consciously.

The door of the SUV squeaked when Brody swung it open. "Been meaning to fix that," he murmured.

"So you're the type that can fix things?" She slid onto a warm seat and buckled up.

"Cars are easy. Other stuff? Not so much."

Join the crowd. When she first started teaching, she thought she could fix anything. Anyone. Not anymore.

Watching Brody circle the front of the vehicle, she wondered where they were going. Her Santa Fe map must be back in her suitcase. Carolyn liked to chart her course. His Hotness slid in beside her. Student or date? Uncertainty prickled across her chest.

Then he smiled. "Hungry?" Brody punched a button with his thumb, and the engine roared to life.

What the heck. He was uncharted territory and she was feeling reckless. "I had a croissant for breakfast."

His Hotness snorted. "Okay, you're starving. I've got just what you need."

Oh, really? Apparently, her body agreed. Parts of her tightened and swelled.

Moments later, she was hanging on as he gunned it up Canyon Road. Dust rose and pebbles scattered. It was almost eleven, time for the shops and galleries to be opening. Right now, the street was empty. Too late, she wished she'd left a note for her grandmother. But she wouldn't be gone long.

When they passed Geronimo's, last night felt like a week ago. Howard and Alan? Sorting out her grandmother's personal relationships wasn't why she'd come, and she wouldn't overthink this. Just as she would not overanalyze this breakfast with Brody

At the top of the hill, Brody turned left and they headed back down to the square. He drove the way he'd played football and basketball. Muscling around parked cars, he hardly paused for stop signs.

"Aren't you afraid you'll get a ticket?" she teased after another rolling stop.

"Naw. All these guys are my friends. They know I'm careful."

"Sure. Not the Brody I knew."

He got really quiet, gearing down with smooth precision at the next stop sign. "But I'm not. Not anymore."

"I didn't mean anything, Brody. Sorry," she whispered. His jaw clenched. Had he heard her?

Before long, he took a side street and parked. "Here we are."

Getting out, she looked around. They were near the plaza, but she really wanted her map. "Where are we going?"

"Where the locals eat. Come on." With his long-legged stride, he led the way to a diner on the square. She matched him step for step, head craning every which way. Brody yanked open the glass door and she stepped inside. Bustling with activity, the place smelled like every good meal she'd ever had. Heavy white crockery thunked onto a long stainless steel countertop. Pies piled high with whipped cream crowded a glass case. With a painted tin ceiling, red booths and small wooden tables, the diner felt lifted from another time. When they were led to a booth, Brody insisted she take the side facing the street. "For the full effect."

"Thank you." Settling back, she slipped off her jacket.

"All I need to look at is you," he said.

"Sure. Right." Brody always joked around.

That was a joke, right?

Tossing his hat on the seat next to him, His Hotness combed a hand through his dark hair. The thick mass flopped every which way. When he caught her staring, his brilliant blue eyes twinkled. "See anything you like?"

Her cheeks heating up, she reached for a menu. "Haven't had a chance to look over the menu."

"Oh, right. The menu." With a wicked smile, he snapped his open.

Part of her wished he'd settle down. Stop whatever was going on. But maybe the kidding and teasing double meanings were all in her head. Had she forgotten how to be playful?

"What looks good?" he asked after about ten seconds.

"They have oatmeal. With brown sugar."

"Oatmeal!" Brody glanced around as if she'd said a dirty word. "You don't come to Santa Fe to eat pabulum."

"What's wrong? I eat oatmeal every day."

"Exactly my point. Don't eat from the bottom of the barrel when you can climb the highest mountain and have your fill."

She giggled. "Sorry, Brody. There are so many mixed metaphors in that. I can't even begin to start."

The bristly chin came up. "Then don't."

The waiter had arrived. "Hey, Brody."

"Hi, Manuel. A platter of chile rellenos for me."

The waiter scribbled on his green pad. "Coffee black, as usual?"

"You got it."

Manuel's attention swung to her.

Whatever Brody was having? She wanted it. "Same for me."

"Cream in your coffee?" The eyebrows peaked.

"Yes, sure. No." Seeing Brody's amused smile, she wanted to match him.

"You got it." The waiter left. "Coffee, black."

His Hotness still wore that grin. How often had she caught that smile in the back row of room 207? He'd be sprawled in his seat, the third or fourth she'd given him. Of course, he wasn't paying attention. Then he'd turn like a strobe light and zap her with that smile. Carolyn's lecture notes went flying.

She played with her turtleneck. "You come here often?"

He snorted and her face heated. "You trying to pick me up, teacher lady?"

"Not at all. Just kidding around. Being...playful." *Right. Sure. Like I know how.*

But his eyes softened. "Three or four times a week."

"With friends, I suppose?" Was she being too nosy?

Stretching his arms along the back of the booth, he said, "Sometimes. But not three or four times a week."

What did she care anyway? Flipping her braid over one shoulder, she played with the tip.

"You used to wear your hair down." He seemed to be unbraiding her hair with his eyes.

She thought back. "That was so long ago."

"Yeah, guess it was. We all change."

Well, he sure had. "Brody, are you getting all philosophical on me?"

He grinned. "Maybe. But what happened to your hair? How come it's braided so tight?" The grin morphed into frank disapproval.

She bristled. "Saves me time."

Manuel set down two coffee mugs, nudging a small pitcher of cream her way.

Brody blew on his coffee and sipped. "Saves you time for what? Lesson plans?"

"Maybe." Okay, it would be nice if she could ignore the dark bristles around his wet lips. Instead, she was mesmerized. Cupping the warm mug kept her from reaching out to cradle his square, stubbled chin. This was absolutely insane. The rich, warm steam curling into her nostrils must be frying her brain. If this kept up, she could burn her tongue.

His Hotness took another sip. Those wet lips pursed with satisfaction.

Carolyn's tongue tingled. Heck, she could burn more than that with Brody if she weren't careful.

"Come on." He threw her a crooked smile. "What could be more important to a woman than her hair?"

"A lot of things."

"Like...?"

Forgetting, she took a sip of coffee. Tears filled her eyes. Her mouth throbbed.

Brody reached out. "Hey, you okay?"

Glancing down at their hands, she nodded. "Your mouth must be made of steel."

"Want to check?"

Oh lordy. She really, really did. His hand felt good. He flicked a thumb across the inside of her index finger. *Whoa*. So she was sensitive there? Giving her hand a final squeeze, he pulled back and waved to Manuel. "Ice water, please?"

Yes, Manuel. Buckets of it. Carolyn hadn't done a lot of hand holding lately. Flexing her empty fingers, she suddenly missed holding a guy's hand. A lot.

Manuel brought the ice water. She took a huge gulp. "So...." Brody seemed to consider his next words carefully.

Why did she feel so off center with him? Sure, she'd met former students for lunch in the past, but they'd all been girls. They filled her in about their boyfriends. As time passed, the news shifted to husbands, followed by children. Like a conveyor belt, those reunion lunches spun through her mind—life passing her by.

"So you've stayed in Gull Harbor all this time?"

She had to focus. "All what time?"

"Since I graduated." He gave the year.

Her first year of teaching. Back then, her long blonde hair had gotten to be a pain. She could hardly see her notes on the lectern.

"Yep, been in Gull Harbor all that time." Her cheerfulness sounded as fake as diet pop. "I love my work. The kids and...everything." Carolyn considered teaching her calling, not just a job. She'd wanted to make her own way in the world. Pursue a meaningful career of her choosing.

"How about you?" she asked. "Why Santa Fe?"

The smiling eyes clouded. "I had family here."

The food arrived and conversation stopped. Brody doused his plate with hot sauce. "Man, you must like things hot."

Bottle in hand, he looked up. "Yes, I do."

Their eyes locked. She stopped breathing.

Sinking her fork into whatever it was she'd ordered, Carolyn swept it into her mouth. Flavors exploded, rich and pleasing. Tomato sauce, melted cheese and who-knew-what-else mated in her mouth. "Oh, my lord," she managed around a mouthful. "This *so* beats oatmeal."

His eyes crinkled when he smiled. "You like it?"

"Let me check." Another forkful. "Yep, I more than like it."

Chewing and content, they stared happily at each other. What was happening here? Carolyn swallowed hard, dropped her eyes and poured cream into her coffee. Time to get back on track. See this breakfast like a debriefing, even though it sure felt like something else. Something *more*. "So tell me, do you ever see Randy Spears? You two were good friends, as I recall."

Brody launched into a recap. Carolyn nodded, as if she had an interest in every football and basketball player in his graduating class. She loved the way Brody rested his chin on a propped up hand when he became thoughtful. A woman could tell so much about a man from his eyes and his hands. His eyes were trouble. His hands? She shivered.

"So you remember all those guys?" The question brought her wandering mind to a skidding halt.

She licked the last string of melted cheese from her lips. His eyes followed the swipe of her tongue. "Yes, yes, I do." But frankly, none like him. He'd been such a challenge, always asking to use the restroom. The one request she couldn't deny. The other kids would chuckle, listening to his untied shoelaces slap the tiles on his way down the hall. Or he'd raise a hand, asking her to turn down the heat or turn up the air conditioning, depending on the season. He knew classrooms didn't have individual thermostats.

Brody Wolf required a lot of attention back in the days when she wore mini skirts and boots.

"Did you really have to use the restroom so often?"

His lips tipped at the corners. "Nope. Just liked to see you get all flustered. You never noticed that Randy was doing a countdown after class started?"

"What?" She yelped so loud people turned. "You mean when

you were supposed to be writing in your journals?"

"We got a kick out of it." His jaw shifted. "Usually you let me leave within the first five minutes."

"How amazing." She played with her braid.

"The guys would be jealous as all get out to see us sitting here."

"Oh, I doubt it. Just a teacher catching up with a student. Not much to remember." She pushed her empty plate closer to the edge of the table so Manuel would see it.

"Uh, huh. Want to bet?" With a sly dip of his head, he chortled. "The way you'd push your hair back behind your ears? It would catch on those long dangly earrings you liked to wear. You'd get so mad. It was kind of cute."

"Oh, no." She groaned. "Those chandelier earrings were so inappropriate for class."

"I liked them. But then, I like 'inappropriate.' "

She decided to ignore the flutter in her stomach. "How do you remember all this?" She fingered her silver hoop, the practical type of earring she wore now.

"You're easy to remember."

The words sent her into free fall. And she hated heights. With relief, she watched him pick up his fork again.

When they'd finished, the waiter appeared. "Dessert?"

Brody arched a brow. "Banana cream pie?"

"Right, banana cream." Carolyn shifted her gaze to the glass case.

"One piece or two?" Manuel asked.

"The pieces are large," Brody told her. "As big as Moby Dick."

"Wow. Well?"

"We'll share," Brody told Manuel before turning back to her. "The Cliff Notes for that book were huge."

"So was the book." She sighed. "Might have been a bit ambitious for high school."

"Call me Israel," Brody said, with such seriousness that she had to laugh.

"It was *Ishmael*, not Israel."

But he wasn't laughing. "I know, Carolyn."

"Oh, well." Feeling foolish and off balance again, she sat there. Then it hit her. He'd called her Carolyn easily, not to make a point. Shaped her name with those lips that sent an unwanted chill rippling through her. Spoke to her as an equal. She was relieved when Manuel arrived with the pie, along with two forks.

Throwing moderation to the winds, she plowed into a five-inch-high chunk just so she wouldn't say anything stupid for a while. The pie kept them busy and became a battle of the forks. Brody was laughing. "You're so skinny. I never would have figured you for a pie eater."

"Well, you figured wrong." She captured the last bite. "There's a lot about me you don't know."

He cocked his head, wearing that maddening grin. "Can't wait to hear it."

That chill again. They must have turned up the air conditioning.

Their meal finished, they wandered out onto the plaza. Benches studded the crisscrossed paths. Vendors had set up food trucks. The scent curled over the square, while a hobo band of musicians played in front of a small band shell.

Back in Michigan, ice floes were still melting from the shoreline. Spring flowers hadn't even thought of blooming except for a brash crocus or two. Here the air softly teased tendrils from her tight braid. Music floated on the early afternoon air. "Is that Beethoven?"

"Does that surprise you?" He turned but those aviator sunglasses hid his eyes.

"Yes, I guess. Don't know why." She kept walking.

"Looks can be deceiving. Take you, for instance. Now, I know you as the attractive, sexy school teacher."

Carolyn sucked in a breath. She wanted to be that woman.

"Who had all the guys drooling in high school."

"No." Exhaling, she shook her head vehemently. "Not true."

"You don't seem to realize that. Amazing." Brody raised his brows and shrugged. Then he led her to the left. Native Americans displayed jewelry in the shade of the loggia that ran along Palace of the Governors. Stunning bracelets, earrings and key fobs were spread out on blankets, watchful artists sitting against the wall.

Brody picked up the conversation. "A lot of guys went off to college in search of a girl with blonde hair who reminded them of Miss Knight."

"They did not." Was that crazy or what? But she liked the idea. "Impossible."

"They sure did." He pulled the words out slowly. Was he talking about himself? "Not one could even come close."

"That can't be true," she murmured, more to herself than to

him.

"Cross my heart." And he made that sign with his fingers on his jacket.

But it was her heart that galloped as they leaned closer to the silver designs winking in the sun. She could feel his breath on her cheek. Smell the unmistakable scent she was beginning to recognize.

Moving slowly down the row, Brody nodded to the artists, greeting some by name. The jewelry was so darn beautiful, mostly silver with turquoise or abalone shell. But one pair of earrings stood out. Shaped like a feather, they were long and dangly, kind of like the ones she'd worn years ago but much more beautiful.

Breaking away, she squatted. Above her, Brody asked the craftsmen questions. Words like "sterling" and "genuine turquoise" floated above her head while she tried to stay grounded. Then she straightened and he turned with a mysterious smile.

"See anything you like?"

"The feathers are my favorites."

Too late. Before she could stop him, Brody had handed the glistening pair to the artist. The man's weathered face creased into a smile. He scooped them up. The purchase was made so quickly and she felt uneasy. "I can't accept these," she breathed when Brody handed her the bag. Her fingers closed over it, too precious to refuse.

"Of course you can." Taking her elbow, he maneuvered her across the street. She tucked the bag into her tote. Somehow, she'd make this up to him later.

Later? Would there be a later with Brody?

Cutting across a corner of the square, they window-shopped. If only her friend Diana could see this. Behind the glass, colors exploded. Mama V must shop here. Everything was so different from Michigan or Chicago, from embroidered blouses to fringed suede jackets. Together they wandered from window to window, passing hats like Brody's, belts with shiny buckles, even long coats with fur collars. "Must get cold here in the winter."

"We're in the mountains, and we do get snow," he said. "On Christmas Eve, Canyon Road will be all lit up with those small bags."

"Luminaries?" she murmured.

"You've seen them?"

"No, but my grandmother told me about them. I came right after Christmas this year, when she, you know..."

"Had her accident," he prompted.

But she didn't want to talk about it. Things still weren't clear in her head. How had her grandmother gone from the patient she'd helped through a health crisis to the ecstatic woman, head over heels in love?

Whoa. Was that possible? Her grandmother was in love?

That brought a whole new twist to this visit.

~.~

Brody watched emotions play across Carolyn Knight's face as if it were a movie screen. Did she ever have a thought that didn't show on her face? He'd always liked that about her. Back in high school, he enjoyed reading her expressions more than the Cliff Notes stuffed in his locker.

Pulling away from the store window, she said, "I should get back."

"We're parked around the next corner." He wasn't ready to take her home and didn't really know why. Why had he driven past her grandmother's house this morning? If she hadn't been outside, would he have gone on? Left Carolyn Knight in his past?

Justine would be furious if one of her friends saw him in the plaza with another woman. Wasn't hard to picture his current girlfriend going ballistic. And she didn't deserve that. Was Justine his girlfriend? She'd known from the start that it wasn't serious. Said as much.

His casual dating pattern was getting old. Hell, he was getting old. But no one had given him reason to stay. The women were more friends than lovers. He'd started to lose hope. Wondered why people ever got married in the first place.

Carolyn was quiet on the way home. Saturday and damn, he had a date tonight. For a second, he thought of breaking it. But Justine would have his head...or something else more personal and painful. Santa Fe was a small town. Indecision buzzed in his cluttered mind.

Heading back up Canyon Road, he took his time. His gut churned while he wondered how to handle this. Because right now, his head was full of Carolyn Knight, like an old obsession come to roost. Was that another mixed metaphor? Smiling, he couldn't believe what she had him thinking about.

Carolyn turned. "What? Did you forget where my grandmother

lives?" she asked sweetly, pointing. "It's right up ahead. Third gallery on the right. Then turn down the alley."

"Yeah. I see it." As if he were that clueless.

A sweet navy blue Jaguar sat in front of her grandmother's house. The sun bounced off its shiny hood, like it had just been washed. Who the hell washed their car in Santa Fe? Brody parked behind it. The jaguar had a vanity plate. "Jewels?"

A frown wrinkled Carolyn's forehead when he opened her door. She slid out, one long leg after the other. Her eyes were on the man sitting on her porch. "Hi, Carolyn." The guy waved.

Brody clenched his jaw so tight, his molars hurt. Getting to his feet, the visitor looked at Carolyn with puppy dog eyes. He knew that look. Felt it deep in his gut, times ten.

"Hi, Alan," Carolyn said as they walked up onto the porch.

Navy blue blazer and neatly pressed gray slacks. Gold cufflinks and a designer tie. *Well hello, Dapper Dan.*

"Do you two know each other?" Carolyn's eyes circled between them.

"Brody Wolf." He held out one hand.

"Alan Haynes. Nice to meet you." But he sure didn't look thrilled. Alan Hayes had one of those hands that was always damp.

"Brody's my student," Carolyn threw the words up like a shield. Brody looked at her. *Really?* "We ran into each other at the airport."

Oh, great. Had he been labeled and dismissed? Brody wasn't liking this at all. Alan traded his frown for a smug smile. *Oh, well, that explains everything.*

No, Alan. No, it does not. Brody jiggled his keys.

Carolyn turned to him. "Alan is..."—*wait for it*—"...a friend of my grandmother's."

This just got better and better. Carolyn's "friend" didn't like his category either. The English teacher had slotted them each into a box.

Alan's attention turned to Carolyn. "I thought you were going to visit the shop this afternoon." The words held faint accusation. Brody almost roared.

"Oh, I'm sorry." She pressed a hand to her lips. The lips Brody was becoming obsessed with. Soft and sweet. That's how they'd feel. Kissable. His body began to react, like Pavlov's dog.

Down, boy. Think of snow-capped mountains.

"I forgot," Carolyn said.

Alan checked his watch. "Well, there's still time. Even if Dad's closed the store, I could show you around."

Dad? The flash of what sure as hell felt like jealousy whipped through Brody.

"Oh, sure. Right. If you'll just give me a minute?" Hand on the front door, she turned to him, a question in her eyes.

Carolyn looked tired, but she'd give this guy the afternoon? She'd been like that in high school. Sometimes Brody would drop in after the last bell with some lame excuse, like he wanted to check on the homework assignment. Right. Like that would ever happen. But if he wasn't the first guy in the door, he didn't bother. They would be lined up, offering to fix a window or a squeaky chair. Crazy stuff. Looking tired after the day of classes, she never saw through them. Sweet Miss Knight.

She was sweet all right.

"Look, I've got to run." He tipped his hat. "See you later, Carolyn."

Her intake of breath at hearing her first name in front of her friend made Brody smile. Alan's face froze.

Miss Knight, my ass. No more of that. He hummed all the way to the car.

Chapter 5

Carolyn strained to listen, covers pulled up to her chin. No manly snores coming from across the hall. Okay, good. She listened harder. No quiet conversation in the kitchen either. Just the comforting smell of toast. Falling back on the pillow, she wriggled deeper into the warm bed. Outside her window a mourning dove cooed, answered by her mate. Snug in her grandmother's casita, she relished the smells and sounds. Even though Mama V may have lured her here under false pretenses, Carolyn was so happy to be in Santa Fe.

Brody. How nice to see a student again.

But her tingling breasts and the nervous swirl of her stomach told her he might be more than that. *Was this foreshadowing?*

Carolyn often thought of life in the literary terms she used in class. But if this was foreshadowing, what was still to come?

Oh, lordy. This was just plain stupid.

His Hotness? He probably was just being nice to his "favorite teacher," if she were to believe that. Had she imagined that dancing light in his eyes? The casual brush of his body against hers as they walked yesterday? She'd tried on the earrings the minute she got in the house after touring Haynes Jewelry. The simple silver feathers were so much more attractive than all that garish gold in Howard's shop.

Although Alan wanted to take her out for dinner last night, she'd pleaded off. Mama V had planned some girl time. They'd driven to a casual restaurant with a cowgirl theme for burgers. After gossiping and giggling with her grandmother, Carolyn had gone to bed early. Had she dreamt that she heard Howard's voice in the living room?

Restless, she threw back the quilt. Her grandmother went easy on the heat. When Carolyn pressed her bare feet squarely onto the pine floor, the cold woke her up fast. Grabbing her robe, she scurried out the door and into the bathroom.

Five minutes later, she was seated at the kitchen table with a mug of coffee and an English muffin. Her grandmother was fussing over her. She loved it. Carolyn pulled one bare foot up under her and took a sip of coffee.

"So what did you think of Howard's shop?" Mama V's eyes burned with curiosity.

"It's lovely."

"Isn't it, though?" Getting up, her grandmother rummaged around in the refrigerator, her lilac and pink caftan billowing around her.

"All that purple velvet," Carolyn said. Lengths of luscious purple velvet was draped in the cases, setting off gleaming gold, sparkling diamonds and other precious stones. "Looks like Howard knows what he's doing. Well, and Alan of course." But clearly, his father ran that show.

"Yes, he does. The color of royalty. Perfect backdrop, right?"

The words so obviously came from Howard that Carolyn smiled. "I guess so but I like silver. It's so simple."

"What's that, sweetheart?" Returning with a jar of marmalade, Mama V sat down. "You're getting a pimple?"

Horrified, Carolyn ran a hand over her face. "Am I?"

"Oh, no. Not at all." Looking flustered, Mama V struggled with the top on the jar. Taking it, Carolyn quickly twisted it open.

Sighing with satisfaction, she spread a thick layer of marmalade over the toasted surface. "Have I only been here a day? Seems like I've been so busy."

Mama V chuckled. "Oh, my. Two men. Every girl should be so lucky."

Carolyn nearly choked on her muffin. "Don't get any ideas. Alan's a new acquaintance. And Brody's just one of my students."

"You sure that's all, honey?" her grandmother murmured as she nibbled.

"Of course. *Former* student."

"And Alan's just an acquaintance? What do you think of him?"

Did Mama V have hopes about Howard's son? She hated to disappoint her. "I just met him."

"He seems like such a catch. Good-looking. Settled and all that."

"Maybe. Alan acts older, though. Like Howard's younger brother, not his son. Hey, are you matchmaking for me?" She should be appreciative. How long since her last date?

Her grandmother's lips pursed. "I thought you two might have something in common, that's all."

What? Like we're both single? That didn't seem like enough to ensure compatibility. "We'll see. He's taking me on a tour of Santa Fe today."

"Wonderful." Mama V clasped her hands together.

"You don't mind, do you? I feel terrible coming all this way—"

"To push me around in a wheelchair," her grandmother said with a mischievous grin.

"Yes. But it's only a sightseeing tour, Mama V. That's all." Carolyn wished she felt more excited.

"You never know." Her grandmother's thinly-drawn eyebrows arched.

"I did come here to take care of you." That sounded so ridiculous now.

"Oh, don't be silly." Mama V waved Carolyn's concerns away. "I'm perfectly fine. Besides, you and I had a good time together last night. I want you to have fun while you're here."

"Yes, I can see that."

Was this the time to ask questions? She could never count on being alone with her grandmother. "So what's going on between you and Howard?" *Enquiring minds want to know.* Her mother might be calling soon.

Mama V took her time answering. "We enjoy each other's company. Howard's a recent widower and…"

"And?" Was there anything more?

But her grandmother leapt up, nearly tripping on that caftan as she took her plate to the sink. "How about that Brody?" she tossed over her shoulder.

Obviously, Mama V didn't want to discuss Howard. "What do you mean?"

"Well, he certainly is *something*."

"Right. Something." *His Hotness.*

"You make quite a couple."

Pffft. "He's much younger."

"Not that much. You couldn't even tell. Besides, does it matter at *this* time of life?"

"What do you think?" Carolyn's hair was caught up in a claw clip and she played with an escaped strand tickling her neck.

"I think a younger man is…might be, that is…fun."

"Maybe. I don't know." But they'd had a good time together yesterday. At least, she thought he'd had fun. Time to move along. "Think I'll shower and get dressed. Alan is picking me up around eleven for the tour."

"Oh, goody." Mama V clapped her hands with glee. "I'll be waiting in the gallery to see how it goes. Be sure to come straight over."

~.~

Sitting next to Alan on the tour bus later that morning, Carolyn would have preferred the back row. Back there, she could count on a breeze. But Alan had chosen seats in the center. "You probably don't want your hair blown all over," he'd said with a quiet smile.

"That's so thoughtful." So she slid onto the bench seat, leaving a respectful space between their thighs. The open-air bus with a canopy over the center took them through downtown. The shop windows mocked her plain jeans and jacket. Really, she had to call Diana about some wardrobe reinforcements. Sure, this was a short trip, but she was beginning to feel plain and boring.

Alan's chinos bore a fresh press, and he was wearing that navy jacket again. Very preppy and proper. That was Alan. Now Brody? He made jeans come alive. She touched the earrings and smiled.

On the way up Canyon Road, the bus driver explained that Santa Fe had a busy art market, second only to New York. She could almost see Alan's chest expand when they reached Haynes Jewelry. She totally understood, feeling the same pride as they passed Mama V's gallery. That turquoise sign out front with *Vera's* scrolled across it looked so professional. Then the bus continued on into the surrounding area, and the houses thinned out.

"Such beautiful countryside," Alan said, smoothing a thin plait of his brown hair. "So different from California."

"Is that why you moved here?" When she noticed his manicured nails, she didn't get the same buzz she felt looking at Brody's hands.

"My father needed the help. Of course, the expectation is that I'll take over the business eventually. Why not, right?" He glanced over, as if expecting an approving nod.

Jewelry. A shop. Standing around all day. "Nothing else interested you? You mentioned teaching."

"Why bother? With our family business, my future is secure." His eyes seemed to gauge her response.

"I guess so." Carolyn's father worked in finance. She'd never considered following in his footsteps.

"I mean, I have tremendous stability." He tossed the words out like a hook. "Haynes Jewelry is very successful. We have a store in Palm Springs too."

We. Yep, he was definitely trolling. "Sounds glamorous. I've read about Palm Springs. Pretty exclusive, isn't it?"

"Yes, all the right people live there."

The right people. Alan Haynes would probably be impressed by her parents' condo overlooking Lake Michigan.

The bus had reached the top of what was known as Museum Hill.

Staring over the parking lot, she lifted her gaze to the adobe structures outlined against the sky. "These museums make me kind of sad." Using his microphone, the tour driver parroted an official explanation. The four structures held world-class collections of art and artifacts. She'd never had time for a visit.

"Sad?" Alan turned with a quizzical look. "Why is that?"

"We stole their land."

"We did?" The idea seemed foreign to him.

"Weren't the Indians here first? It seems that way to me. Have you ever been to the pueblos nearby?" Now *that* interested her.

Alan shook his head. "No, we don't carry pottery."

"Oh, not for shopping, although I suppose they sell things. I meant to learn about their culture."

"Maybe we should do that sometime." But he looked clueless, so the idea of visiting a pueblo with Alan seemed pointless.

The bus turned around in the lower parking lot, and they left the museums behind. The day was sunny and the view, fabulous.

But something was missing. Yesterday, she'd felt so alive walking around the square with Brody. Today the rhythm of the bus almost lulled her to sleep.

After the tour, they wandered down to the square for some lemonade. Carrying it to a bench, Carolyn and Alan made polite conversation. In her head, she wrote his character sketch, a project she usually gave her writing students. "Think of key personality components," she'd tell them. For Alan, words like *proper* and *cautious* came to mind. Obviously, he admired his father. Respected him and valued following in his steps. Nothing beyond that, she suspected.

"Everything okay?" Alan asked as they sat there in the sun. The musicians weren't here today. The plaza didn't feel folksy and intriguing. Their conversation drifted off, like a dangling participle.

"Yes. Fine. I think I still have jet lag." That seemed to satisfy him. With obvious reluctance, Alan drove her home in his Jaguar. Poor guy. He'd done everything right. As they sat in the cobblestone alley, he suggested dinner but she begged off. "My grandmother and I have plans."

Fingers tapping the steering wheel, he looked pensive. She leapt from the car before he could suggest another group dinner with his father. "Thanks for a great day, Alan." She was through the blue gate in a second, turning back in time to see his helpless alarm.

"Okay if I call you?" The words floated on the breeze and she waved, as if she hadn't heard them.

That night she ate dinner with her grandmother at Cafe Pasqual's. She loved their roasted tomato coconut soup and the colorful Mexican decorations that crisscrossed overhead. The restaurant always felt festive. Unlike the stilted conversation with Alan, Carolyn and her grandmother chattered effortlessly across the small table.

"What else would you like to do while you're here?" her grandmother asked.

"Oh, I don't know. I don't think ahead."

"Right. You thought you'd be helping your old granny." This was becoming their private joke. "Sweetheart, can't you consider this a vacation? Do what you like. Go where life leads you." When Mama V squeezed Carolyn's hand, they were back in Petersen's Ice Cream Parlor in River Forest, enjoying hot fudge sundaes.

Carolyn settled back in her chair. "Okay, I'll get into vacation mode. But now that you have Howard in your life, I don't want to interfere with any plans."

"Interfere? Oh, for heaven's sake." Her grandmother shook her head as if this were ridiculous. *Right.*

A girl didn't grill her grandmother. The very idea was crazy. But then so was the fact that her seventy-something grandmother was dating. If her mother were here, she'd be asking decisive questions that quickly sized up the situation.

Thank goodness, her mother wasn't here.

Later that night Carolyn called Diana, relieved when her friend picked up after two rings.

"Hey, how's the trip? Your grandmother doing okay?"

"I'd say so. As in, she doesn't really need a nurse." And she described the situation, even mentioning Howard and his store.

"Do you like the son? He took you sightseeing?"

"I didn't come here for a man." Should she feel guilty that she hadn't mentioned Brody? Here she paused. Sucked in a breath. She was seated on the front porch, the very bench where Brody had sat, still warm from the sun. "I need help with my wardrobe."

"Ah, huh. Now we're getting somewhere."

She could picture Diana relaxing on the sofa in her small yellow bungalow in Gull Harbor. Together they decided what Carolyn needed, Diana jotting things down. "So, a longer skirt? And you look good in lilac or green. Some tops. Maybe some more slacks."

"Here, I'll give you my credit card number."

"Oh, we can settle up later."

"You have to let me pay for this." She dug in her heels.

"Carolyn, after everything you did for me." There was a pregnant pause.

"Anybody would do that."

"No, they wouldn't."

Last fall her friend had suffered a terrible accident involving a burn. For a while, Diana had needed help washing her hair and a lot of other personal things. Their book group had all pitched in, but Carolyn spent more time with Diana than the others. They were developing a special friendship.

"What fun I'm going to have," Diana said, as they wrapped up. "I'll overnight the clothes."

"No need to hurry. That's extra postage."

Diana snorted. "You kidding me? I know a girl in need when I hear one."

Ending the call, Carolyn stared up at the sky through the aspens. She did a lot of thinking that night. Maybe her grandmother was right. What were a few years? She wasn't *that* much older than Brody.

But she was getting way ahead of herself.

Chapter 6

"I'll get it." Mama V set down her coffee when the phone rang the following morning. The night before, Carolyn overheard Mama V talking to "her beau," as she called Howard, with a chirpy, flirtatious voice. They were discussing some pretty personal stuff. Why did her grandmother talk so loud? The two kept in constant contact.

Carolyn pushed the blueberries around in her oatmeal. Maybe she'd add some brown sugar. Live it up. Her grandmother moved to the wall phone with a hitch in her step. She would never complain.

"Hello? This is Vera." *Yep, chirpy and flirtatious.* Then her expression changed.

"It's for you, dear." Mama V cupped a hand over the receiver.

Inwardly, Carolyn groaned. She hated to hurt Alan's feelings. Yesterday had been nice. But she should be spending time with Mama V on this vacation. At least, that would be her excuse.

Handing her the phone, her grandmother mouthed, "It's a man."

Right. Okay. Taking the phone, Carolyn steeled herself.

"Are you up for a ride in the country?"

She twisted a finger through the old windup coil. "Maybe. Who is this?" Like she didn't know.

Brody's chuckle stirred something deep. *Really* deep. "Forgotten me already, Miss Knight?"

Sure. Like that could happen. "So we're back on last name basis, Mr. Wolf?"

"Only if you want to be."

Her grandmother pretended to read the paper. It was upside down. Wandering over to the window, Carolyn watched finches flitting around the birdfeeder with feverish excitement.

"I think my grandmother and I were going to—"

"Don't worry about me," her grandmother sang out. "Howard and I have plans, if that's all right."

That sealed it. "What time?"

"Eleven?"

"Casual dress?" She couldn't wait for Diana's care package.

"Santa Fe is always casual. See you soon."

She almost dropped the phone. Flipping the paper right side up, her grandmother grinned at her.

When Brody pulled up promptly at eleven, Carolyn was outside on the bench, staring at her dirty tennis shoes. Santa Fe was definitely a boot town. Why hadn't she brought more clothes? But she didn't want *her* clothes. She wanted *Diana's* clothes. The morning air felt cool and her white turtleneck would keep her warm under the jean jacket. She hadn't braided her hair. The silver earrings from Brody glittered in her ears. She'd probably be untangling them all day.

"Hello, Brody." Her grandmother came to the screen door, looking smart in a hot pink top and pants. Carolyn was still getting used to the violet eye shadow. "You two be good now." Then Mama V squeezed her shoulders together, like she'd said something really racy.

"You can count on it." Brody smiled from under the brim of that Stetson. Carolyn almost tripped. Maybe she didn't want to be good with Brody.

With a final wave, Mama V closed the front door and Brody and Carolyn walked to the SUV. "Never mind my grandmother."

God, he was devilishly handsome.

"I like her. It's easy to see where you get your looks. Although, I haven't met your mother."

"Mom's very attractive. In a preppy and pearls way." Carolyn had to give her that. "I'm the plain one in the middle."

Opening the passenger door, he gave her a puzzled smile. "Plain? Hardly."

The boy must be blind. But that sure sounded good.

But Brody had always tossed compliments around like confetti. The girls who staked out his locker could count on that. "Looking hot today, Ashley." "Hey Greta, nice hair." They loved it. All of them.

~.~

Brody gunned it. Seeing Carolyn wearing his earrings unleashed something warm and wicked inside. "How about a trip through the hills? Want to see a house I'm working on?"

"I'd love that." She shot him a shy smile.

Those smiles had been his undoing. Sure, she'd been a great teacher but she had a shy side too. Brody felt ashamed thinking back to the times he'd pushed her to the max. The uncertainty in her smile sometimes made him feel guilty. If Randy got crazy in her class, Brody would glower at him. She was a new teacher. Brody wanted her to stay.

But that was back then. Right now, he had to deal with today. Justine had been furious when he didn't spend the night Saturday. First, she'd pouted. Then she'd looked like she might scratch his eyes out. He'd stumbled out into the cool night, feeling as if he'd escaped. When it came to women, he pretty much went with the flow.

This thing with Carolyn felt different, and Brody didn't want to over analyze it. But he had to make some decisions.

Dressed in denim with those little tennies on, she looked so cute and cuddly sitting next to him. And then there were her earrings. His earrings. But he better keep his eyes on the road.

"This land is so…different," Carolyn said when they reached the outskirts of town.

"It's not the city, that's for sure. That's why I love it." Popping open the sunroof, he let the wind ease his worries. Side-glances could get him into trouble.

"The land's like you, Brody."

"What? Flat and brown? Thanks a lot." He loved to tease her.

"No. Wild. Look around." She fluttered a graceful hand.

"What makes you think I'm wild?" Too wild for her?

Her laugh bubbled, soft but certain. "Because I had you in

school."

I had you. His lap burned. Didn't he just wish. Then shame swamped him. After all, this was Miss Knight. A woman any guy in school would protect and defend. And he had been an idiot in high school. *Get it together.* Tumbleweeds rolled across the landscape.

"Always in movement. That was you," she continued. "On the basketball court. Or football field. Running. Charging."

High school seemed so long ago. "Goofing off was more like it. Randy, Frankie and me. We had some good times." He hadn't talked to them in years. They didn't understand his life now.

"You were all crazy but not in a bad way. After all, you boys were all so young."

That didn't sit right. "Not our best years, I'm afraid."

"Weren't they?" A wistful smile tweaked her lips. "I thought high school was fun for students. That's why I enjoy teaching that age group."

"Oh, we had fun all right." And some of it was downright embarrassing. He was glad to put that all behind him.

"And it's a time of huge changes. Big decisions before you."

"Yeah, but we didn't know that. Not really." Her eyes studied him while he struggled. He felt almost naked under her frank gaze. She'd been the kind of teacher who saw everything. No way could you text in her class, or she'd take your cell for the day. Miss Knight's lower desk drawer? Full of phones. The girls hated it. "Maybe that's high school. Stupid pranks. Drove my mother crazy, all those calls from the principal."

"Shaving cream all over the cars and school windows the final days of school." When Carolyn threw her head back to laugh, he wished she wasn't wearing that turtleneck. She had a long neck. A kissable neck with soft skin. At least, he thought it would be soft.

What had they been talking about? High school graduation pranks. "I'd kill any kid who did that to one of my cars now. We were young and stupid."

When she shook her head, the earrings caught the sun. "The seniors still do it. Doesn't matter what punishment Mr. Rousey doles out."

"Glad to hear the tradition's still alive."

"You bet." She didn't seem to mind.

"You were always on our side. I do remember that part."

"It was all mindless fun back then. Call it growing pains. What a mess you had to clean up if you wanted to graduate." When her head dipped to one side, an earring caught in her hair. She played with it, running her fingers down the shaft of the silver feather.

His throat swelled. Brody cleared it, turning his attention back to the winding road. They started to climb.

"Didn't you think high school was fun?" She was staring at him like she had in class when he didn't have an answer.

"W-what?" He'd completely lost it. Thinking about her hair, her lips.

For a second, she sat still. "Nothing. You'd better just drive."

Right. Because I can't chew gum and lust over you at the same time. Disgusted with himself, he revved the engine and they rocketed up into the hills.

With a gasp, she gripped the door handle.

"It's so beautiful out here." He was glad he'd gotten this SUV with the wide windshield.

"It's not the beach, that's for sure" She'd turned pale.

"No, but beautiful in its own way."

The road got steeper. The hairpin turns gave him a charge.

But next to him, she'd grabbed the dashboard with her left hand.

"Hey. What's wrong?" He eased up on the accelerator.

"Nothing. I'm ah...." Her eyes were round and panicked. "I'm not good with heights."

He tapped the brakes. "Want to go back down?"

Her chin came up. "Absolutely not."

Chapter 7

Carolyn felt like such a wimp. Snatching her hands back, she knotted them in her lap. "Don't mind me. I'd hoped to grow out of it someday."

"What? Fear of heights?"

Nodding, she didn't miss the surprise in his voice. High places probably never frightened guys.

"Some things we never grow out of," he said.

Was there an echo of hurt in that comment? Curious, she swiveled to face him. "Tell me one thing you've never grown out of."

When he flashed that beautiful smile, it hit her. That tooth. "You don't have that chip in your front tooth anymore."

Brody turned a deep scarlet. "Had it fixed."

"Aw, I thought it was kind of, you know, rough and athletic."

"Are you kidding me?" He drew that square chin back. "Unfortunately, I didn't get it on the basketball court. I fell against the coffee table chasing my brother. I was ten and Braydon was nine. It looked terrible."

"Never seemed to bother the girls. You were on Homecoming court, weren't you?"

Brody snorted. "Big deal. Homecoming court. I never smiled for any pictures."

He downshifted. They kept climbing. Looking out the window was dangerous, so she studied her earth-dusted shoes. That usually worked. That and deep breathing kept her grounded. She tried not to make too much noise.

"So, you've had this all your life?"

"Pretty much. I don't know why."

"That must have sucked."

Carolyn laughed. "It does."

"Did your folks try to help you with it?"

"They did but not in a helpful way." Nothing good about that memory. "My mother always took a very direct approach."

"Sorry. Didn't mean to bring up something so personal."

She hated whiners. "Time to get over bad memories, just like it's time to get over my fear of heights."

"Wow. Sounds like this really was an issue."

Might as well wade right into it. "My parents decided to take me to Great America, that amusement park just north of Chicago. I should have suspected something fishy. They never had time for that type of thing. Outings were covered by field trips at my private school. The day was more a lesson than a fun trip, if you get my drift."

But the frown told her Brody didn't understand. "So, it wasn't fun? I heard Great America was a blast."

"While my dad was finding a place to park, I saw this ride with three huge arms. Each arm held three spinning cages. They swirled high in the air, and I could hear screams through the closed windows. My parents almost couldn't get me out of the car."

"How old were you?"

They kept climbing. "Seven or so. Maybe second grade." The air up in these mountains felt hot and dry, harder to breathe.

"Hey, if you don't want to talk about this, you don't have to."

The mountains were so beautiful. Why couldn't she just enjoy them? But she wanted to finish this and pushed on. "No, really. I'm fine. Anyway, we got inside the park. My dad wasn't happy to be there. I heard my mom insist that my doctor had suggested it as therapy. After all, we lived in a high-rise, and I wouldn't look out the windows."

"An amusement park was therapy?" Brody's face had blanked.

"Yep. My mother headed straight for that ride. We had to wait in line for about half an hour. Longest thirty minutes of my life, listening to all that hollering. My mother kept telling me that it would be good for me."

"That's terrible." Brody had pulled up in front of a fabulous home. Saws sliced the morning air, punctuated by hammering.

"Oh, the kids all came out smiling. My mother pointed that out. But for me it was totally terrifying. After one swirl or so, I threw up. My parents got into a huge fight." Nothing like getting down and dirty with a guy.

"Man, it doesn't get much worse than that." Brody's tan had paled.

"So no roller coasters for me," she quipped.

He threw her a reassuring smile. "We don't have that stuff out here. You have to go to California."

Her mother had cried quietly as she cleaned Carolyn up in the ladies' room. She wasn't going to mention that to Brody. "I'm so sorry, sweetheart. I really thought it would help." She'd ended up patting her mother on the back, trying to comfort her. When they came out, they found her dad chatting up one of the pretty young workers. Nothing unusual there. On the ride home, her parents didn't say anything. Her grandmother had been furious when Carolyn told her about it.

"I'm sorry you had to go through that." Brody had gotten so serious. She was ruining the day. They both got out of the SUV.

Why the heck was she sharing this? So they were up in the mountains. She just wouldn't look down. "What a beautiful house. This is your project?"

"One of them. Yes." Out in front, two men were sawing lengths of wood. They smiled at her with curiosity. "Jose. Everett."

Nodding to the guys, Brody held the massive front door open. "Now watch your step."

When he took her elbow, sparks sizzled through her. Made her a little weak at the knees. Inside, two men were putting up what looked like molding.

"Morning, Paco. Wayne. I'm just giving a friend a tour."

A friend, huh?

Carolyn stepped carefully over the cord leading to a table saw. Sawdust floated in the air, smelling as clean and fresh as the blue shirt Brody wore slightly open under his leather jacket. Like most of the guys, Brody had dressed in over-sized T-shirts in high school. This was a much better look.

This was a much better body.

Now be good.

Looking around, Brody said, "Don't mind the stares. These guys aren't used to visitors."

"I don't want to bother them." The rooms were large. Beautiful beams patterned the vaulted ceilings. "Such a big place."

"We're not bothering anyone. I stop in all the time to check on things."

"How many projects do you have going at one time?" A sense of authority clung to him. This was a new look for him, at least to her.

He rolled his eyes to the ceiling. "Hmm. Just started on the fourth."

Did he ever bring a woman here? The surprised looks on their faces answered that question.

 Holding out a hand, he edged over to a huge window. He was taking baby steps. "You okay with this?"

"Sure." Her hand felt safe in his. She stepped closer. Below them, the hills rolled and her stomach pitched with them. "The drive didn't seem that steep. But it is gorgeous."

"Pretty awesome." He tightened his hold. "Let me know if you get uncomfortable."

She looked over. "I can see why you wanted to return here."

How beautiful it would be to wake up to this every morning. Lots near Canyon Road were small, precious and crowded together. It wasn't easy to get a view of the mountains from the casita.

Dizziness caught her and the mountains tilted. Dropping his hand, she jerked and turned. Bad move. Pain shot through her foot and she yelped. He caught her just as she reached for a table nearby.

"What is it?" Scooping her up, Brody sat her on the table. His face was set with worry.

She felt like a clod. "I stepped on something. I'm so sorry."

"*You're* sorry?" He tossed his hat on the table. The pain in her foot wouldn't stop.

"I'm the one who should be sorry. They're supposed to clean up at the end of the day." He shoved a hand through his hair. "Which foot?"

She pointed. He took her left foot and gently turned it. A nail had punctured the sole of her shoe. *Well, that's gross.* Head spinning, she grabbed his arm.

"I'm going to have to take that out, Carolyn. Unless you want to go to an ER."

"I've had a tetanus shot. Take it out. Please."

"Be right back." He stormed out to his car and along the way had a few words with his men. The air fell silent and they disappeared.

"Break time for the guys," he said, returning with a red plastic kit. Sure. He just didn't want them to hear her scream. The pliers he took out looked huge. Thank goodness, the nail hadn't gone in any farther. There was enough of a head to grab. Feeling woozy, she closed her eyes.

Brody tipped her chin up. "Hey, you okay?"

"Fine," she said, blinking. Staring into the inky depths of his eyes only made her feel more off kilter. "Go ahead. Let's g-get it done." First the height, now this. Maybe she really was a wimp.

His jaw clenched.

Oh so slowly, he removed the nail. She sucked the pain in through her teeth and held on tight. *I'm a total baby.* The whimper was a surprise. The nail came out.

"I'm going to take your shoe off now." He started to unlace the ties.

"And the sock." Leaning back on her elbows, she watched. This felt so wrong to be turned on right now. But the look on his face touched her. Running a hand over the bottom of her foot he frowned. "You're doing great."

She wanted to say *do that again, please.* "Right."

Poor guy looked like he might pass out. Pouring alcohol onto a cotton ball, he swabbed her foot. It tickled. "I'm so sorry about this, Carolyn."

"You'll have to pay up," she told him as he bandaged her foot.

He threw her a slanted look. "How much is a nailed foot worth?"

"Lunch at the diner?"

"You got it, Teach. I mean, Carolyn…Miss Knight."

"Carolyn," she purred, loving the blush that burnished his features.

Almost made the whole thing worthwhile.

~.~

Brody stood on Justine's porch, hands in his pockets. He'd never felt this bad on a woman's porch before. But this was the right thing to do. His gut told him that. Guess there was a first time for everything, and this was the first time he'd been the one to end it. Usually women felt him pulling away. Tired of his "ambivalence," as one woman called it, they cut the strings. Not this time and he hated it. A light glowed overhead.

The door flew open just as he rang the doorbell.

"So. Here you are." Justine's dark eyes flashed. That had been one of the things that had attracted him. He had a thing for dark eyes. Well, he *used* to anyway. Carolyn had soft brown eyes that were more like warm caramel than M&Ms.

When had he studied a woman's eyes like this?

"Yep. Here I am." No teasing note in his voice tonight and she heard it.

Opening the door wider, she didn't even crack a smile. "Come on in then."

Her cozy living room was full of bright colors, bordering on neon. Definitely a chick's place. That was Justine. Ultra feminine, but more Tina Turner than Carrie Underwood.

"How about a beer?" She turned, already on her way into the kitchen.

"No thanks."

She arched a brow.

"Can we talk?"

Disappointment flickered across her face and was gone. Standing stiff at the edge of her sofa, he wanted to kick himself.

"Justine, I really like you."

Her nostrils flared. "Why do I feel a kiss-off is coming here?"

He swallowed. With one hand, she shoved him down onto the sofa. Then she took the rocker across from him. Looking totally hot in skintight jeans and a casual denim shirt, she wore tons of beads around her neck. That was Justine. She clattered when she walked. There was nothing subtle about her, and he'd always liked that.

"So who is she?"

He tensed. "Aren't you jumping to conclusions?"

She tilted her head. "Brody, we both knew this day would come. You're restless."

On with it. "You're wonderful, Justine. Terrific. Gorgeous and really good in…"

She held one hand up flat. "Stop right there."

Crap. He didn't blame her. "I'm not the one for you."

There it was again, that disappointment. Like she was his mother and he'd let her down. Dropping her gaze, she swept a length of coal dark hair behind her shoulder. "I know that. But you were fun. I-I enjoyed my time with you."

She was being nice about it. That only made him feel worse. "Look, I'd feel a hell of a lot better about this if you'd scratch my eyes out and call me every name in the book."

"Maybe I will." The laugh was so Justine, like a sister who'd called him on his shit. "Hold that thought."

"I wish you had fooled around on me or gave me the finger once or twice."

"Look, don't feel bad okay?" Resting elbows on her knees, she leaned forward. She had to realize she was granting him full view of her assets. Brody became wary.

Planting his hands on his knees, he braced himself for anything she might toss his way. "I really like you. We had some great times together." In his heart, he always hoped. Maybe a woman would turn out to be something magical.

But back then he didn't know what magic was. How it could feel, at the touch of a foot.

"You already said that," Justine said, her voice brittle. "I always knew we weren't headed down the aisle together."

"Okay then. So we're good?" He stood up.

She hitched a shoulder. "Of course we are. I want you to be happy."

"There's a great guy out there for you." The words sounded so lame.

Her smile stretched tight, bold and bright in that cherry red lipstick. "Yes, there is and I will find him. Hey, if you found yours, I can find mine, right?"

Feeling his chest expand, he felt better. Absolved. "You're too good for me."

"Probably. But I think this woman must be better. Because you have changed." She followed him to the door.

"I have?" He didn't see this coming.

"Yes, you have. You are softer, somehow. Thoughtful. Call it weird but I saw that Saturday night and wondered."

"I'm sorry. I didn't plan this." When she wrapped her arms

around his waist, he kissed her forehead and then gently pushed back.

"Now hit the road." Her eyes flashed. Sometimes Justine could blow hot and cold. Her mood changes had always caught him by surprise.

When he got into the SUV, he felt almost giddy with relief. Was something happening that he didn't even realize? Whatever it was, it had sharpened his focus and brightened his life. Whenever he got charged up, Brody drove into the mountains. Roared around the back roads until the red arrow told him he was running out of gas. This was almost as good as running. Or great sex.

But with Carolyn, if they ever got that far, it wouldn't be just sex. And that settled him down fast.

One thing still bothered him, though, as he pulled into his garage.

Carolyn wasn't taking him seriously. She still treated him like a boy.

The boy she used to know.

That had to change.

Chapter 8

Mama V helped Carolyn wrestle the large box through the front door. Diana had come through. Sure felt like Christmas and just in time.

"My goodness, have you been shopping online?" Mama V loved the unexpected.

"Not exactly. This is from my friend Diana. Do we have a pair of scissors?"

"Of course. I'll get it."

Carolyn's foot throbbed and her head spun. She collapsed on the edge of the sofa. It wasn't the Santa Fe air making her dizzy. Nope, she couldn't stop thinking about Brody's hand on her bare foot. His warm breath on her cheek. The smell of his mint lozenge after they finished their burritos.

But he hadn't kissed her yet. Hadn't even tried. Her disappointment confused her. But he'd asked her to go with him to El Farol tomorrow night. And now she'd be decked out in whatever was in this box from Diana. She trusted her friend completely.

A kitchen drawer slid open and shut. Mama V bustled back in waving a pair of scissors.

"You'll love Diana." Carolyn sank the scissors blade into the cardboard. "Her shop is kind of campy but cool. I haven't shopped there much. Well, until now."

Her grandmother clapped her hands. "I like her already."

"Next time you visit I'll take you to Hippy Chick so you can meet her." Chuckling, Carolyn pulled up the flaps. Brilliant colors met her eyes. Reaching in, she felt soft fabric. No more turtlenecks and jeans. She gently tugged out a turquoise top.

"Oh my. So colorful." Mama V was fascinated.

The bright fabric flowed over Carolyn's fingers, soft except for the delicate rows of aqua, yellow and turquoise beads around the neckline. Whipping off her turtleneck, Carolyn pulled the new top over her head. Her grandmother sat back, her eyes sparkling with appreciation. In the hallway was a full-length mirror. Carolyn stumbled toward it while her grandmother hovered.

"Are you sure you don't want to see my doctor for that foot?"

"Oh, no. What a waste of time." Who was this woman in the mirror? Carolyn ran a hand over the gauzy fabric.

"Maybe you need some jewelry." Her grandmother started for her bedroom.

"I don't think so. The beading takes care of that. Do you think this is too big for me?" She pulled at the wide neck.

Tapping her lip in concentration, her grandmother drew closer. "A girl came into the gallery last week wearing something like this. She called it chilly shoulders or cold shoulders. Maybe it just needs an adjustment." With that, her grandmother smoothed the top down and cool air breezed over her shoulders.

"Wow." Carolyn shivered. "How will I hold it up?"

"Don't they still sell strapless bras?" Nearly toppling into the box, her grandmother hooked something flesh-colored and waved it in the air. "See? Strapless!"

Way to go, Diana. "That girl thinks of everything." Turning to the mirror, Carolyn swept her hair up and turned. "What do you think? Oh…is it okay if I go out with Brody tomorrow night?"

"Well, of course. You don't have to ask me, sweetheart."

"You won't feel abandoned?"

Mama V puffed out an exasperated sigh. "Nonsense. Of course not. I have a date with Howard tomorrow anyway." She wandered into the kitchen to return the scissors.

"Isn't this too much skin?" This off the shoulder thing wasn't her.

At least, it wasn't the *old* her.

"Oh, no. Did you hurt your shin too?" her grandmother called from the kitchen.

"*Skin.* I said skin." Carolyn was beginning to wonder if Mama V had a hearing problem.

Returning to the living room, her grandmother joined her in pulling out the treasures. She spread a pair of well-worn jeans out on the sofa and frowned. "My goodness, she sent you ripped clothing. Goodwill wouldn't even take these."

Carolyn checked the label. "Oh, yes they would. This torn look is the rage now. And it's expensive." Pulling out her treasures, she carted an armful back to the bedroom, her grandmother right behind her.

Dumping the pile onto the bed, she studied herself in the mirror over the dresser. "If only I were a natural blonde," she said. "I didn't have time to have Phoebe do my hair before I left."

"What's on your schedule tomorrow?"

Turning Carolyn grinned. "I like the way you think."

Since her grandmother didn't have plans that evening, the two of them went over to Mucho Gusto, a quiet family-run place where locals ate. Because of Carolyn's throbbing foot, Mama V drove them there in her trusty Ford Focus. But her driving made Carolyn nervous. "These streets sure are narrow," she said as her grandmother nearly sideswiped a Volkswagen.

"You're telling me." Mama V peered over the steering wheel.

Although she'd been tempted to wear one of the outfits Diana had sent her, Carolyn hesitated. She wanted her hair to be right before she tried out her new look. Besides, the restaurant was casual.

Heads together, they giggled over their margaritas. Her grandmother had made a call to a hairstylist in town. "Sonrisa will know just what to do," her grandmother assured her with a wink. The evening passed quickly. The only subjects they didn't touch on were Howard and Brody. She felt as if they'd called a truce when it came to men.

Later that night after her grandmother had gone to bed, Carolyn gave Diana a call. "Are you still awake?"

"Yep, you bet. You're two hours behind us, remember?" Diana laughed.

"Your box arrived. I think you're trying to make a new woman out of me."

"Never too late for a do-over. Oprah would approve."

Was that what she needed? A do-over on her life?

"Still there, Carolyn?"

"Yes, I am. So you think I'm a hopeless case?"

"Of course not. You could make more of your strong points."

"When I get back, I'll hand myself over to Phoebe." Lounging back on the soft pillows, Carolyn frowned. "Oh, Diana, I'm not beautiful like you."

Her friend sputtered. "What are you talking about?"

"I'm talking about a nose that's too long...

"Very patrician and regal."

"Eyes that are too small."

"The warmest brown ever. Your students drool over you. At least that's what I overheard some of the girls say in the shop one day."

"No way."

"I kid you not. 'If only I could look like Miss Knight.' I've heard that more than once."

Was that the truth? In college, she'd been attractive. At least that's what her friends and Jeff had told her. Striking. "I just don't know what happened after graduation."

"Hey, girlfriend. Life happens." The finality and forgiveness in Diana's voice soothed her. "So what outfit did you like the best?"

"Is it cold shoulders or chilly shoulders? My grandmother is educating me."

"Either one. And yes, men love that look. I tried one top out on

Will."

"The more skin the better?"

"Something like that."

For the next few minutes, they giggled together. Although she was embarrassed to admit it, she needed the tips her friend gave her. Always too busy grading papers, she rarely had time to read magazines, and Gull Harbor could be kind of sheltered. "Between you and my grandmother I'm learning a lot. She was so proud when she found the strapless bra."

"Or you could go braless," Diana teased.

"Ah, I don't think so." And they were off on another laughing spree.

"So tell me about him," Diana asked.

"Who? My grandmother's boyfriend or his son Alan?"

"The way you say those names, I know it's not either one. You're holding out." Diana's voice had become more insistent with each word. Carolyn got up to close the door. Even the pain in her foot reminded her of him. Go figure. How twisted was this?

Time to confess. Diana didn't just fall off a turnip truck. "His name's Brody."

"Brody." Diana repeated the name like whispered confession. Did Carolyn really sound like that?

"He was my student years ago." The words created that flurry of uncertainty in her stomach. "Of course, he never would have attracted me back then, not in that way. All the girls loved him, though. Hung out at his locker. Cheered him at the games."

"Ah, huh. Really a bad boy?"

Smiling, Carolyn sank back onto the bed. "Brody was a teenager and he was popular. Brooding one moment and class clown the next."

"But now?"

"Now?" What were they now? "I really don't know. Besides, he's younger, of course."

"Sounds good to me. Does he make you feel old?"

"No, but it just feels strange. This change in roles, I mean." She kept waiting for the old Brody to surface. The boy in a torn T-shirt, ambling down the hallway with the bathroom pass he really didn't need.

"Listen, lady, I think you're *making* yourself feel old. A younger man? Perfect." Diana sounded more than delighted. "Nothing wrong with being a cougar."

Carolyn had to turn that term over in her mind. "Is Will younger than you are?" Diana's fiancé Will Applegate was both sweet and hot.

"We've never talked about age. Not that it would matter. Think of all the women you know who married younger men. It's like a good insurance policy, Carolyn. Heck, we live longer. Who wants to be left alone?"

"Yeah, maybe you're right." Thinking of her grandmother and grandfather, Carolyn agreed. But how did Brody feel about the age difference?

An uneasiness settled over her. Was he interested, really interested in her? Or would she just be another conquest?

After they hung up, Carolyn got into bed. Getting to sleep took a long time.

The next day, her grandmother hustled her off to her hairdresser. Facing Carolyn in the mirror, Sonrisa was pretty and a fast talker. She ran her hands through Carolyn's hair and turned her chin this way and that, making suggestions. Before she knew it, her hair was tucked into a glittering mass of foil. The chemical smell in the air wasn't as bad as she remembered. Sitting in one of the black vinyl chairs waiting for the color to set, she leafed through magazines. Summer fashions brightened the pages and she smiled. Diana was right on target when it came to style. And the blondes in the pictures sure popped off the pages.

Why had she ever let her hair go brown? When her mother asked her that question a few years back, Carolyn had been upset. Now she wondered. It's not as if she made a decision. Maybe she'd just gotten too busy with school work.

When she left Sonrisa's Salon that afternoon, she felt fabulous. The difference had an immediate effect. In the space of one block, two men turned to stare. Passing a shop window, she caught a glimpse of herself. Her blonde hair hung straight and shiny past her shoulders. Amazing.

When she first began teaching, she'd been flattered to be assigned junior and senior classes, especially the honors class. Soon they would graduate and face new challenges. Her responsibility was to prepare them. Carolyn worked her students hard. They had to turn in a composition each week, which meant she had to grade them. That kept her really busy.

As the years passed, her dedication grew. She attended national conferences and served on the school's curriculum committee. Had she let her work consume her? Gull Harbor was a pretty little town but it was small. Not a lot of single men, although Kate Kennedy and her sister Mercedes had found Cole and Finn there. Diana was engaged to Will. And for all three of her friends, the matches had been made against all odds.

But that hadn't happened for Carolyn. Not in Gull Harbor.

Shaking out her hair, she set off for Canyon Road and her grandmother's gallery. The pain in her foot had eased. But she hadn't gone far when a window display of boots caught her eye. Although her foot injury presented a challenge, she came out twenty minutes later swinging a purple bag. When she passed Haynes Jewelry, she crouched and sped past. Was that Alan behind the counter? When he didn't look up, she felt relieved. Maybe he wouldn't even recognize her.

But her grandmother sure did.

Mama V was working on her laptop in the back office of the gallery when Carolyn walked in. She struggled to her feet. In unguarded moments, she revealed an awkwardness that tugged on Carolyn's heart. "Oh, my word. You look fantastic, sweetheart. With this look, you could be a college girl again."

Was that a backhanded compliment? Still, it felt good. "So I'm getting back to being myself?" She perched on the corner of Mama V's desk.

"Yes, I think so."

Laughing together, they talked for a while. Mama V showed her some recently showcased works. Her assistant Wendy was there, watching the front of the store. Carolyn had always liked her and was grateful her grandmother had some trustworthy help. After a while she said goodbye and walked back to the casita.

What to wear that night? Her closet now presented some exciting options. She decided against the jeans. Not tonight. Maybe later. Then she laughed. There might not be a later with Brody. All kinds of obstacles clouded her mind. After all, she was leaving Sunday. But she pushed that out of her head.

Finally, she decided on a long skirt that moved like a waterfall of aqua and purple. A woven purple top could handle the cool night air, and the glittery beads set it off perfectly. Diana had also sent a thick bracelet set with red and turquoise beads. When she tried on the outfit, the new boots looked perfect, the aqua tips peeking out from under the skirt.

Her hair was where she really went crazy. Piling handfuls on top of her head, she secured the mass with a claw clip. Then she teased out some tendrils. The effect looked casual, but sexy, like in the magazines.

Heart pounding, she found her way to the kitchen. The long skirt felt strange around her ankles. And the air on her neck? Different and maybe not her. While she was getting dressed, her grandmother had come home and was tidying up. Carolyn found her arranging the magazines in a neat row on the coffee table. Looking up, she smiled.

"Maybe I should change. Mama V, this just isn't me."

"For goodness sakes, it sure is." Her grandmother took her shoulders. "You look perfect, sweetheart. Don't change. And those boots? They're perfect too." A cloud of perfume enveloped her when her grandmother kissed her forehead.

Taking her hands, Carolyn squeezed them gently. "And look at you!" Mama V's tunic and capri pants were a brilliant petunia pink.

What a change. Her grandmother had become a new woman since her fall last Christmas. Carolyn's throat swelled. Why hadn't she noticed this attitude shift when they talked on the phone? She'd been so busy with her term papers and student exams. Her determination to broaden her life grew.

Running a hand up through her pert hair-do, Mama V blushed. Just then the doorbell rang. Excitement quivered through Carolyn. "Oh, let me," her grandmother stepped to the door.

"Well, hello there!" Backing up to allow Brody to enter, Mama V threw a coquettish glance over one shoulder as if to say *isn't she gorgeous.*

Carolyn held her breath. Brody walked in, the usual white shirt completed with a bolo tie. A western silver buckle added style to his jeans. His broad shoulders strained in a corduroy jacket that added a rugged touch to the square jaw that dropped open.

"Well, now. I don't know what to say."

She fidgeted in her boots. *Say something.* Okay, she looked ridiculous. Maybe she'd become a Santa Fe parody. While his mouth opened and closed, her heart shrank.

"You look beautiful," he finally said, his voice thick.

"Really?" The look in his eyes about stopped her heart.

He nodded. "Oh, yeah."

Mama V looked downright gleeful.

When Brody's glance swept her hair, Carolyn felt every root tingle. Then he smiled. "Looks like Miss Knight's back in town."

Her shoulders relaxed. The three of them laughed. Everything was fine.

"Okay if I join you?" Howard appeared at the open door. His white hair waved back from his forehead and his face shone. The way he stepped inside? He was used to walking through that door. Maybe he even had a key. Carolyn struggled to put a lid on her misgivings. But although Brody had made a big deal out of Carolyn's new look, Howard only had eyes for Mama V. "Vera, you look lovely tonight."

"Thank you, Howard."

The look they gave each other would have melted one of the candles on the wall. What would she ever tell her mother?

When Howard pivoted to Brody, his expression changed.

"Brody Wolf." Brody's hand went out, and Howard slowly shook it.

"Oh, Brody's just a..." she began.

"An old friend," her grandmother supplied, with a warning glance in Carolyn's direction.

"I see." Howard's eyes narrowed, as if he was wondering where his son had missed the mark. That wasn't the point at all. "So you two are off to paint the town?"

"Something like that," Brody said quietly.

"Well, we're going to… What was that restaurant again, Howard?" Mama V's hands fluttered in the air.

"Galisteo Bistro. Where are you two headed?" The question

was directed to Brody, as if men handled all the decisions. Yep, he could be annoying.

Turning, Carolyn swept her shawl from the back of the sofa. Time to leave.

"We're heading up to El Farol," Brody said, draping the soft black shawl over her shoulders. "Check out the flamenco."

"Oh, I know it well." Howard's eyes snapped, maybe because she'd turned down El Farol the night she arrived. But she'd been so tired.

Hurrying to the closet, Mama V grabbed a dove gray leather jacket. It slipped from the hanger, and Howard stooped to retrieve it. Her grandmother looked flustered.

"Ready?" Brody arched his brows.

Oh, boy. Was she ever.

Chapter 9

A million stars pierced the sky overhead when Brody and Carolyn stepped into the cool night air. At the gate, he hesitated. "What do you think? Drive or walk?"

"Walk." And she struck out.

"Hey, wait a minute." He took her arm gently. "How's that foot?"

His concern touched her but she wanted to stretch her legs. "We're not that far from the restaurant, and it's so nice out tonight."

"Fine with me." But he didn't move. Just stood there while moonlight sculpted his unbearably handsome features. For a second she thought he'd kiss her.

Then he shook himself and fell into step beside her. Blue shadows lengthened over Canyon Road, a relief from the daytime glare. Her new boots crunched on the narrow walkway dusted with reddish soil. Any breeze left a calling card.

"So what do you think of your grandmother's boyfriend?" Brody asked, hands stuffed in his jeans.

"Howard's not my favorite person."

His laughter split the night air. "No kidding. You hide it so well."

Heat stoked in her cheeks. "That obvious, huh?"

"The temperature went up in the room the minute he got there. What's the problem?"

She had to think a minute. "Howard kind of bosses my grandmother around, and she lets him."

"Hey, now." He touched her elbow. "Looks like he cares about her. And I'd say the feeling is mutual. Doesn't that count for something?"

One touch. That's all it took and her whole body ignited. She breathed in to cool the heat. "Howard does fuss over her. She's so different from last Christmas. Happier."

"So shoot him, right?" Brody didn't even try to hide his smile.

She came to a halt so fast, her left foot felt it. "You're noticing things I'm not seeing."

"You think?" Yep, he was still grinning. "Okay, I'm looking at it from a guy's point of view. How serious are they?"

"I don't know." *But I better have answers for my mother.* "That's not really a question a granddaughter asks."

"Why not?" The walkway narrowed as it did in spots, and he fell in behind her.

"Because it would be rude."

"Maybe she'd be flattered. Your grandmother might take it as a sign of your love and interest."

"What?" Carolyn wheeled around so quickly, she found herself in his arms. "When did you become so perceptive?"

"I had a good teacher." Smiling, he looped his arms around her waist.

"Just *one* good teacher?"

"For me, there was only one. She was my favorite." When he tipped up her chin, she felt it coming. The kiss. How she wanted it. The crush of his mouth on hers, the tease of his tongue.

But nothing. A car roared past. Brody backed off but his arms stayed put. "You've changed over the years. Can't your grandmother change too?"

How did Brody get so wise? Sometimes she wanted things to stay the same, especially people in her life. But maybe change was a good thing. Her former student was opening new worlds for her.

 Glancing up, she fell head first into his deep blue eyes. "You're sure not the same," she murmured.

His lips twisted. "You mean now I'm seeing things I never noticed back when I was a moron?"

She jerked back. "I'd never call one of my students a moron. You were a teenager, okay? No different than any other guy at eighteen." Not totally true. He'd been way more goofy and charming.

"Feels like I've been put in my place, Miss Knight."

His arms dropped and he took her hand. So, he didn't like being reminded of the past? Moving up the road, she could hardly bear the disappointment. Forget dinner. She was hungry for his kiss. Thank goodness they'd reached the restaurant. Holding her new skirt up so she didn't trip, she mounted the wooden stairs to a broad porch. In nice weather, people ate outside, but not tonight. A chilly wind swept down the nearly empty street.

But warmth waited inside. El Farol had a cozy feeling of smaller rooms, round tables and a bar that stretched off to the left. The noise level in the front room was high. This was definitely a gathering place. "Hey Brody." The receptionist greeted him, her eyes widening when she saw Carolyn behind him. What was that about?

"Right this way." All business now, the girl led them through a dining room to the back. A few people nodded or lifted a hand to Brody. She wondered how often he came here.

They ended up in a large rectangular room with a stage. Long tables accommodated groups, but they were seated in a cozy corner. Tiny white lights were strung from the rafters, adding a festive air to the dimly-lit room.

"This okay?" He turned.

"Perfect."

Brody pulled out her chair, his hands sliding over her shoulders when she slipped off the shawl. Then he took the seat across from Carolyn.

"Have you ever been here?" he asked, handing her a heavy leather-backed menu.

"A couple times. Usually my grandmother and I sit in the other room. During the day, I prefer the teahouse at the top of the hill."

"Right. It's outside. One of my favorite places too."

When they smiled at each other, she felt almost giddy. Focusing on the menu wasn't easy. After ordering drinks, they studied the list of tapas. Chorizo and ham, artichokes and avocados. By the time they'd decided, her mouth was watering. When the margaritas arrived, they gave their order.

"Warm in here." Brody slid off his jacket. "Didn't you say you'd grown up in Chicago? Halsted Avenue has some great tapas bars."

"Right. Did you go there a lot?" Chicago was a two-hour drive from Gull Harbor, but Brody hadn't been of legal drinking age back then.

His cautious expression took her back to when he was a student who didn't know the right answer. Brody was a master at faking it. "Okay, I'll come clean," he finally said with a shrug. "Sometimes I'd drive into Chicago with the guys. My mother would have killed me. We all had fake IDs."

"So, drinking was involved and you'd drive back?" The question came automatically.

Without blinking, Brody leveled a look at her. "My mother wouldn't have been happy. But you're not my mother."

"Didn't say I was." Playing with her cocktail napkin, she twisted it into a tight roll.

"Back then, a lot of my decisions weren't wise." His eyes lightened when he smiled. "You, on the other hand, were kind of innocent."

"Innocent?" She took a sip of the frigid drink. "I was twenty-two and an adult."

"Yeah, you were but..." Brody let the words drift off, as if he didn't want to hurt her feelings.

She licked her lips. "I don't know. Tell me." He wasn't getting off this easy.

"Oh, Miss Knight," he said with a slow shake of his head. "You were one hot mama back then." Then his expression lightened. "And you made English class fun. I wasn't much of a reader but your class? I tried."

"Gee, I'm flattered." And she laughed. Back then she'd never minded when struggling students read Cliff Notes, as long as they participated in class.

The banter flew back and forth until waiters arrived, arms tiered with the tapas. The food on the small plates smelled so darn good. They picked up their forks.

"Hard to know where to start. But the sausage looks good." Carolyn sank her fork through a crisp casing.

"Now, let's take turns, Teach." When Brody winked at her over the banquet, the sausage almost lodged in her throat. Then he smiled and she swallowed. One by one, they tasted. He offered her a mussel. She offered him a clam. Wasn't long before they forgot which fork belonged to which plate.

"Such tiny plates and so much food. I have to catch my breath," she sighed at one point, pushing back. Now on her second margarita, she was getting mellow. Should she be on her guard? All that classroom talk had opened a gulf between them.

"What's up," he asked when he caught her staring.

"Nothing." Ducking her head, she played with a strand that had slipped from the claw clip.

He'd swung his chair around so they were side by side. "I love your hair like that." Brody's eyes wandered from her stray curl to her lips. Her scalp prickled and her lips plumped.

"Thank you." She dropped her hand into her lap.

"It's more like you."

"How do you know that?"

When his eyes narrowed, her breath tightened. "I know what I liked...*like*...about you."

No looking away. Their eyes dove into each other. Her body twitched from the impact and her mind spun. For a second there were no words, not the right ones anyway. They sat there staring, as if they spoke different languages. But their eyes? They translated just fine.

So maybe she'd just look. Brody was the essence of cool tonight. His blue shirt sleeves were folded up on tan forearms. How far did that golden skin extend? She imagined inches of skin she wanted to explore.

Yep, she really was in trouble. His gaze was impenetrable, as usual. "You are a sphinx."

Brody drew back. "Why do you say that?"

"I can't tell what you're thinking."

"A good thing right? Maybe I'm just cautious."

"Guarded. But I remember you as goofy. Wisecracks, that kind of stuff."

"Screamingly insecure is probably more like it." Reaching out, he brushed the corner of her lips with a thumb.

"Do I have food on my face?" She reached for her napkin. "What is it?"

"Nothing. I just wanted to touch your lips."

The comment spun her down like a warm July wave. Sent her

tumbling in mind-blowing directions until she could hardly breathe.

Meanwhile, he stayed cool. Brody's eyes roamed her face, a half smile dancing on his lips. "Didn't you ever wonder what students were thinking?"

"Not really. I didn't have time."

He laughed with lazy delight as he extended one arm around the back of her chair. Tipping his head to one side, Brody leaned closer and whispered, "It's a good thing you didn't know."

By that time the room was packed. The noise level had risen and she was glad. Glad he had to lean in close so she could hear. After that, their eyes took up the conversation.

A spotlight hit the stage. The noise dropped. A guitarist and three other men in black jackets took the chairs along the back of the stage. Flat black hats were tipped rakishly over their eyes. Fingers flicking against the strings, the guitarist played a throbbing flamenco rhythm. No one moved. Expectation held the entire room suspended. From the side, three female dancers appeared. They swirled onto the stage in floor-length costumes with tight red bodices and black ruffled skirts that cut up in the front. Fringed shawls hung over their shoulders, swaying with their movement.

"The real deal, right?" Brody whispered in her ear. She could only nod.

If she were at home right now, she might be sitting in the Mangy Mutt with Diana or Phoebe, enjoying a fish taco. The sense that her life was changing filled Carolyn with a jittery excitement and something else.

Foreboding. There was that foreshadowing again.

Time to concentrate on the dancing.

The show unfolded, a blur of color and rhythm, wailing voices and frenetic clapping, along with the stamping of feet.

"Do you know what they're saying?" She almost grazed his ear with her lips.

"Not really. Probably something about a lover killed with a dagger."

Carolyn smiled. "Or a lover who never returns."

"Or a lover who does return."

What? She cut him a quick glance. Brody's eyes were on the stage, fingers tapping the back of her chair. The roles had changed completely. Sitting there in the darkness, she struggled for balance. Was that the soft stroke of a thumb on her back? Her skin felt hypersensitive. She slid her margarita aside. No way did she want this to be about drinking or the music or the wildly romantic Santa Fe setting. No, she wanted this to be about Brody.

The dancing continued and the audience joined the rhythmic clapping. As they sat there together, the passion in the music transmitted to her body. Each sinuous sweep of a long, ruffled train became her, teasing Brody, wanting him. And he seemed to feel it too. The soft touches on her back stopped. His hand closed lightly over her shoulder. When he angled his chair closer, his leg touched hers and stayed there.

Her chest was heaving by the time the music ended.

As the last chord faded, she expelled a pent-up breath. The lights came up and the mood changed. Brody pulled away. Conversation and the clinking of glasses picked up.

He scanned her face. "Like it?"

"I've never seen anything like it. Thank you for bringing me." She was so glad she hadn't come with Howard and Alan that first night. This kind of emotional entertainment? She only wanted to experience it with Brody.

"I liked watching you." He whispered close against her neck.

"Why?" Lifting her eyes to his, she felt herself falling.

"You fascinate me."

Her mouth went dry. Thank goodness the waiter arrived. "Dessert?"

"You have to taste their flan," Brody said without batting an eye. "They make it themselves."

"Sounds good." She was in the mood for something decadently rich. Brody ordered the flan. But all the while he spoke to her, the girl was concentrating on Carolyn.

"What's the deal with her?" she murmured as the girl retreated.

"Who knows? So how's your grandmother enjoying your visit?" He was so good at changing the subject.

"We had a good time today. Shopping." The afternoon had felt so comfortable. "We've always had a special bond."

"She seems like a lot of fun. You're lucky your grandparents lived in the same city."

"I was. My father's parents had passed on, and my folks had a lot of social obligations. Fund raisers. Galas. They never trusted babysitters, and my grandparents were glad to have me visit for weekends in their River Forest home. They took me to the zoo, movies, out for ice cream. They were fun to be around."

"You're an only child?"

"Yes. And I wouldn't wish it on anyone. Did you say you have a brother?"

"Right. Braydon." He stretched his legs out under the table. "Without my brother, I might have ended up in my family's winery. I would have hated it."

Alan's words came back to her. "So for you, the family business wasn't security? Some guys would have loved it."

Brody's brow furrowed. She felt him struggling but didn't know why.

"When I was eight and Braydon was seven, our dad took off and came back here."

How astonishing. "Here? Santa Fe?"

He nodded. "This area, yes."

~•~

Trying to read her expression, Brody steeled himself. "My father lived in one of the pueblos. Or did live there before his death three years ago."

Brody hated pity. Carolyn's face was full of it.

"I'm so sorry. I never knew." She was processing and he let her. He'd learned to let silence open up.

"So you came back here to reconnect with him?"

"To reconnect with me." He laid the words down softly. A lot was on the line here, although Carolyn didn't realize that.

A tiny frown appeared between her delicate brows. He'd seen this look before. When a student in class made a remark with a new twist, Miss Knight would think it over. Then she'd ask a question. Their discussion might go on until the bell rang. It was one of the cool things about her. She really listened.

"Were you looking for yourself back then after college?"

The feeling of being understood swept through him. He felt a knot inside loosen. "Yes. Yes, I was." He was glad he was sitting close to her. The other diners seemed deep in quiet conversations except for one boisterous table of tourists.

"And did you find something? Your dad...did he help?"

A familiar pain twisted through him. "In a way."

He waved to the waitress. Carolyn nipped her lower lip between her teeth as if she were holding back the next question. Another familiar gesture. Only this time that look yanked a chain that ran right through his core.

After settling the bill, he pushed back his chair. "What do you say? Time to leave?" He'd had enough baring of his soul for one night.

When he'd driven her back to Santa Fe, he was doing a favor for a favorite teacher. When had things changed? The teasing smile, her sweet compassion, the relationship she had with her grandmother? The Miss Knight he knew back then was gone, but here was this woman. And he wanted more of her.

"Yes, I agree. It's time to go." She gave a kittenish stretch. "Although I am on vacation."

Just a few more days. That dug a hole in his gut.

"What?" She leaned closer.

"You're leaving Sunday, right? "

Was there regret in her quiet nod?

"Have you ever been to Museum Hill?"

She shook her head. "Not really."

"Would you like to go?" He didn't have to wait long.

Her face beamed. "I'd love it. The tour bus took us past it a couple days ago."

"Us? You and your grandmother?"

The blush was apparent even in this low light. "No, ah, Alan. That man you met? He was showing me around."

Oh, I just bet. No wonder his dad acted so funny, as if Brody were stealing a national treasure.

She stood up and he helped her with the shawl. Hand at the small of her back, he guided her to the front door. He couldn't blame the men whose eyes wandered her way. Carolyn was gorgeous and totally unaware of it. He liked that. But he gave a couple guys The Look. Their attention went back where it belonged.

Outside, the air held the cold edge of the mountains and she shivered.

"I should have brought the car." He ran his hands down her delicate arms.

"It's fine." She took his arm once they reached the sidewalk. "Let's walk. Clear our heads."

But it wasn't his head that was the problem. Putting a hand on hers, they moved in step together down Canyon Road. He could have strolled through the city all night with her. A slight limp told him her foot was bothering her. Her grandmother's gallery and the side street came up too soon.

She was quiet as they mounted the stairs to the casita. "Do you think your grandmother's home yet?" The casita looked dim inside.

"Who knows?" She gave a slight hitch of one shoulder. "There's so much I don't know about my grandmother, especially when it comes to Howard."

"A little mystery is nice."

"Maybe. Do you have your grandparents here? Your father's parents?"

The loss didn't get any easier. "Gone, unfortunately. Hey, don't look so serious." Taking her in his arms felt so natural.

Seeming content, she relaxed against him and tipped her head back. God, she was beautiful. And then she sighed through slightly parted lips.

Who could resist? Her lips were soft. He took his time. The first kiss was a tantalizing brush of his lips against hers. Yep, so damn soft. He drank in her sighs. Went back for more and then again. Felt the subtle shift of her body against his. Her arms wound around his neck. The kisses got wetter, longer. To save himself from embarrassment, he let a little air pass between them. But she wasn't having it. Shock riveted him when she pressed her curves into him, so soft and willing.

"Finally."

"Glad to hear it."

Glancing up, she wrinkled her nose. "I've wanted that for a while." She ran a soft palm down his cheek.

"Really?" *Wish I'd known.* "We've only known each other four days."

"That's how you see it?" Her features and voice sharpened.

But he didn't want her getting all analytical on him. "Okay. Maybe it's been ten years." This was different for him. He wanted to take it slow. But there was no safe way to explain. He could get all tangled up in his words and he wasn't taking that chance.

Her lips had found his neck, and his knees threatened to buckle. Her lips were swollen and her eyes heavily-lidded. He knew what an aroused woman looked like and Carolyn Knight? She was there. For him. Now *that* was a major turn on.

Edging toward the door, she smiled. He knew that mysterious tilt of her lips when she had something up her sleeve, like declaring a Gatsby Day. Who the hell knew what that was back then? Just her crazy idea. She'd waltzed into class, looking incredibly hot in a short beaded dress. Who could forget that feathered headband? All the girls showed up the next week with headbands.

But he liked this long, swishy skirt better. Carolyn unlocked the door. Warmth swirled out. There wasn't any question of coming in and Brody was glad. He pulled her to him for one more kiss. His body roared for more. "Good night, Teach."

"Night, Brody."

His body hummed like an electric wire all the way back to the curb.

Chapter 10

Church bells were ringing. So loud. Too loud. Why had she picked that ringtone for her phone? Carolyn woke up fuzzy-headed with longing. Brody had been in her dreams, all teasing eyes and sly humor. Hot kisses and roving hands. His phenomenal body and her own raging response. She pressed a hand to her forehead.

Yep. Feverish, for sure.

Early morning sunshine poured through the windows. The bells tolled again. She fumbled for her cell. "H-Hello?"

"You haven't called me." Her mother's crisp tone brought Carolyn upright.

"Mom. What's wrong?"

"You said you'd phone with an update after you arrived."

Carolyn fell back onto her pillow "It's only seven o'clock."

Silence. "Oh. Well, nine o'clock here."

"Not a problem." She rubbed her forehead.

"So how are things with your grandmother?"

"She's fine, Mom. No need to worry." Carolyn had to step carefully. "Mama V has made a remarkable comeback." *That includes a man and possibly sex.*

"Really? That's wonderful." Relief filled her mother's voice.

"It's such a worry having her out there."

"Yeah, she did great with her physical therapy. No wheelchair or walker needed anymore." The very idea almost made her laugh.

"Isn't that surprising? I called her physician and then her physical therapist, but they won't tell me a darn thing."

"And?" Carolyn yawned and stretched. She wanted to be back in those dreams.

"They wouldn't tell me anything." Outrage raised her mother's voice. "Some stupid rule blocks you from knowing about your own mother's health."

"Right. It's HIPAA, Mom."

"Yes, her hip. I just wanted an update."

"No, Mom. The stupid rule is called HIPAA. Don't ask me what that stands for. Something about patient privacy. But you can't just call up a doctor or a therapist and ask them to spill the beans about your relative. That's not allowed anymore."

"How inconvenient."

"Some people prefer privacy, even from their family."

"Utterly ridiculous." Her mother's irritation wasn't a complete surprise. This was the woman who'd rifled through her daughter's drawers in high school. Of course, she never found any evidence of drug use or wild sexual encounters. Although Carolyn understood her mother's concern, she was furious about the invasion of privacy.

"How is she keeping busy? Painting and working in the gallery, I suppose?"

Not really. Carolyn didn't think Howard was going away anytime soon. Brody's comments the night before helped her see that. Time to set some groundwork. She sure didn't want her mother flying off the handle with Mama V. "Actually, she's seeing someone."

"What do you mean?" Her mother's voice was a hoarse whisper. "A therapist?"

"No, Mama V is dating." By now, Carolyn was whispering too, in case her grandmother was awake.

"Dating! Since when?" The words exploded in her ear. Carolyn held the phone away and counted to five.

"He seems very nice, Mom."

"Nice! Probably a gold digger. My father would be furious."

"Don't you think Grandpa would want to see Mama V happy?"

"Well, she *is* happy, isn't she? At least she was the last time I saw her."

When was that? Carolyn thought back. Santa Fe and her mother weren't a good match. "My face looked like a roadmap," she'd sputtered after her last visit. "And I had constant nosebleeds."

Using their busy schedule as an excuse, her parents depended on Carolyn for any face-to-face with Mama V. Everyone liked it that way.

"The name, please?"

Oh, why had she even brought this up? Carolyn could picture the silver pen in her mother's hand as she overlooked downtown Chicago. "Haynes. Howard Haynes." And she smiled. Wait until Mom had her personal assistant look him up. Howard Haynes of Palm Beach and Santa Fe. She almost giggled. "So what have you and Dad been doing?"

While her mother ran through an exhausting list of activities, Carolyn responded with proper enthusiasm. So many boring galas or fetes, as some called them. To their credit, her parents supported these charities with more than just a phone call. They were true philanthropists. And they also helped organize them.

"You really should come over for the Spring Fling." Her mother named a Chicago event that included an auction, a dinner and a dance. Guests were usually over sixty and Carolyn would rather eat ground glass.

Come over. That meant from Gull Harbor. She wouldn't be here anymore. No more sopapillas or flamenco. No more Brody and his liquefying kisses. She clutched the covers. Feeling like Dorothy in the *Wizard of Oz*, Carolyn had been sucked out of Santa Fe by one comment, and she didn't like it.

"I'll check my calendar, Mom." Guilt tugged at her complacency. It had been a while since she drove into Chicago. Negotiating the Skyway and the Dan Ryan gave her hives the last time. She hated the traffic, not to mention the height.

"You could always take the train." Her mother often suggested Amtrak to help Carolyn deal with her "affliction."

"Maybe. I'll think about it."

"You have a birthday coming up, dear."

Holding out her bare left hand, she frowned. "I know, Mom."

"Your father and I, well..."

They wanted her married, providing grandchildren. "Please don't worry about me, okay?" Morning sunlight had crept into the room. Carolyn's stomach growled.

"Well, don't you think it's time you met someone? The right people, of course."

Carolyn's sigh was followed quickly by her mother's. They did the double sigh a lot. "I think I hear Mama V. Gotta run." She tried to make her tone brisk, as if her grandmother really needed her, which of course she didn't.

"Keep me updated," Mom said crisply, as if she were talking to her assistant.

"Sure, I will." She crossed her fingers. "Give Daddy my love."

"Of course. Bye, darling." The call ended.

Well, that was that. Carolyn set her phone on the nightstand. Rolling over, she cradled the extra pillow in her arms. Closing her eyes, she tried to recreate last night. Her lips tingled in response. Her thighs remembered the press of Brody's body against hers. Other parts of her took it from there. All systems were go.

But the pillow wasn't as muscled as Brody. Tossing it aside, she threw back the covers. Mama V wasn't in the shower yet. No noise from any area of the house. She'd better take advantage of the empty bathroom and grab a shower.

Twenty minutes later, Carolyn lolled on the back patio with her coffee. She took her time spreading orange marmalade on an English muffin. After ten minutes or so, the screen door opened and closed behind her. Her grandmother floated out in her purple caftan, carrying a breakfast tray. Whoa! That was a problem. Carolyn shot up to take the tray of freshly toasted muffins.

"Now, sit down. Relax." Her grandmother had always been so independent. "You don't have to worry about me."

Carolyn set the tray on the table. "Nonsense. Look at you. You're too gorgeous for this early in the morning." Howard was no doubt the cause of these new ensembles.

She glanced down at her gray track pants and t-shirt with a hoodie for warmth. Not exactly sex kitten material.

Her grandmother gave a coquettish shrug. "Can a woman ever be too beautiful, whatever hour?"

"You've changed. You know that?" Carolyn told her, sitting back in her chair.

"Change is good, right? Pass the marmalade, please."

Nudging the jar toward her, Carolyn smiled. "I meant change in a good way."

"I'm happy. Is that how I've changed?" Her eyes danced.

"And is Howard the reason?"

Setting down her butter knife, Mama V took a bite and chewed slowly, thoughtfully. "I don't think a man can make you happy, sweetheart. No one can. But you can be happier with a companion."

Carolyn glanced away. Was this what she'd been missing?

"How was your date with Brody?"

Such a subtle shift in topic. "Great. The dancers were wonderful."

A Cheshire cat smile creased Mama V's face. "Of course they are. How about Brody? I do like him."

"Me too." Right now, she had no words to describe Brody Wolf. Her body was practically screaming agreement. *Yes, yes, we like him. And we want more.* The descriptions she would have conjured up three days ago didn't fit. Not anymore. "Brody is fun. Sweet. Sensitive. Different." The last word held a note of wonder.

And hot. But she didn't want to go into that.

"If you mean he's different from when you taught him, of course he is." Three tiny finches hopped onto the pavers. Crumbling a toasted edge in her fingers, her grandmother scattered them. The birds went crazy.

Carolyn was still puzzling over Brody, trying to define their relationship. "When I think of how I matured in college, well, I guess Brody did too. I remember him as a goof-off. Now he can be funny but he's a lot more thoughtful. Mysterious, even." She had the strangest feeling that she knew only a part of his story.

"Really? Always good to have *some* secrets. Oh, I'll bet he was a dickens when he was a teenager." Mama V's chuckles died and she went into her business mode. "Wendy's covering the gallery today so I thought we might shop a little this morning and hit Tia Sophia's for lunch. Then up to Ten Thousands Waves."

"Up to..." The words lodged her throat. The center was situated high in the mountains.

Her grandmother patted Carolyn's hand. "Don't worry. It's not a mountain. Just a hill in the rocks. I've planned a special treat for us. But if you don't want to go, I'll understand."

"No, it's fine. Thank you. Sounds wonderful." Carolyn wasn't going to spoil it.

Her grandparents had always shown their love with exciting plans. They'd taken Carolyn to see *The Nutcracker* when her parents had been busy planning their annual Christmas Eve open house.

Her grandparents didn't just fill in the gaps, they made things wonderful for her. That hadn't changed, even though now it was just Mama V.

"Take your time. I'm going to get dressed." Humming, Carolyn took her dishes into the kitchen. Then she chose her clothes from the stash Diana had sent, settling on the torn jeans, a light white sweater and the leather jacket. The new boots were the final touch. Several times the night before she'd caught Brody staring at the boots. She'd chosen well. The tooling was intricate and the turquoise toes? The final touch.

Today she spent time on her eyes with a swipe of earthy brown eye shadow, an arc of ivory beneath each brow. Brody's earrings completed her western look. And it felt so right. Sweeping up the front of her hair with a claw clip, she let her newly-blonde hair fall softly to her shoulders. No braid. Yep, perfect.

Wandering the square with Mama V later, Santa Fe called to her from every shop window. Leather and suede, colorful embroidery and weavings, pottery and blown glass. The magic of the small town made her feel like she'd stepped into a different world. *Land of Enchantment*. Yes, it was.

Brody's world. While she shopped with Mama V, Brody was never far from her mind. How could he be? Leather, denim, boots. Every piece of merchandise would be better with His Hotness in them.

Better. Brody did everything better. She reached out for a brick wall to steady herself.

"You okay?" Her grandmother tugged on her sleeve.

Get it together. "Of course."

"Come on then." Her grandmother steered her into a shop filled with the rich smell of leather.

"But I don't need anything. Diana sent me all those clothes."

"Doesn't hurt to look around."

Sure. Okay. Her grandmother's impish expression didn't fool her. Purses hung from hooks on the wall, and the circular display racks held jackets, vests and even chaps. "Smells yummy, doesn't it?"

"Sure does." A muted aqua jacket caught her eye. Running her hand down the soft front panels, she enjoyed the feel of it.

"Try it on, Carolyn." As if to encourage her, Mama V slipped into a long western duster that swallowed her up. She looked comical but cute.

The aqua jacket felt light on her shoulders, fit perfectly and smelled wonderful. "I'm in love." When Carolyn twirled in the three-way mirror, her earrings swayed with her.

"Especially nice with the jeans." Tilting her head to one side, Mama V smiled and relinquished her oversized coat to the sales girl.

"Yes, but I don't need this." Carolyn couldn't stop touching it.

"You look fabulous in it." Then Mama V switched to her more practical approach. "Those Michigan winters get mighty cold."

"Oh, they do but I have plenty of coats."

Turning to the sales clerk, Mama V said quietly, "We'll take it."

Although she protested all the way to the register, Carolyn knew it was useless. Her grandmother never took no for an answer.

"I'd like you to enjoy your inheritance while I'm here to see it." Her grandmother produced a gold card.

The implications brought a lump to Carolyn's throat.

After circling the plaza a little more, they found a seat at Tia Sophia's. "I sure like your new wardrobe," her grandmother told her after they'd ordered.

"Diana's been a great addition to Gull Harbor. You'll have to meet her when you visit."

"Oh, I will. But I hope you'll visit here more often."

She covered her grandmother's knuckled hand with her own. "Me too. I don't know what's held me back. Maybe I have been too focused on my work. During June and July, I teach summer school and tutor kids, mostly freshmen. But they'd find someone else."

"We're all replaceable." Mama V stared off into the distance. For a brief second, tears glimmered in her eyes. Grandfather was not replaceable. Carolyn still missed him and her own eyes filled. What was it like to love so completely and then lose that person? She hoped one day to know that kind of deep love.

Total commitment carried risks. Life had taught her that.

By the time the waitress arrived with the food, they had lightened up and were on to other subjects. Mama V was telling her about the summer opera. "The theater is breathtaking. I do wish you could come."

Thinking back to when Howard and Alan had suggested the opera, Carolyn tensed. She wouldn't want any return trip to be misunderstood. "I'll think about it, Mama V." Playing with one of her earrings, she looked up to find her grandmother smiling. Quickly, she dropped her hand.

After lunch they stopped at Jackalope's for a quick tour through their unending out buildings. A flamenco CD caught her interest, and she quickly bought it while Mama V looked at furniture. The music would remind her of that night at El Farol with Brody.

Memories. Would that be all she'd have?

What more did she want?

No time to dwell on that as they hopped in the car, and her grandmother took off. Mama V jabbered all the way up the mountain, veering from one topic to another. Turning her head to one side, Carolyn closed her eyes so she wouldn't panic.

When they entered the main lodge of Ten Thousand Waves, her edginess from the ride was replaced by a curious sense of peace. They followed a girl to their room, the sun radiating off the stone path. Utter calm filled her soul. Once again, her grandmother was giving her a wonderful experience. "This is so nice. Thank you."

"Oh, we're just starting," her grandmother huffed. The upward path and the few stairs weren't easy for her. "Wait until you see."

Like the serene outdoor areas, their room held no fussy frills or heavy flowers. A single orchid arced gracefully from the side table. All of the furnishings were done with modern simplicity.

"Your massage appointment is at two o'clock," the girl said, turning to leave.

"Thank you, Irina."

As the girl left, Mama V squeezed her shoulders together. She looked excited as a child. "Pretty great, isn't it?"

"Different." Carolyn could book a massage in Michigan City or St. Joe, Michigan. But none of the facilities had this simple elegance. Shoulders settling, she realized she'd been tense. About what? Cripes, she was here on a vacation. But when she thought about Brody, every muscle in her body leapt to life. She was like that frigging orchid, reaching for him.

This was insane.

As she changed into her bathing suit, blue eyes came to mind and she shivered. Donning one of the fluffy white robes, she felt as if Brody's blue eyes were laughing with her, the way he had in high school when he'd done something goofy. But now, those sky blue eyes could darken to navy.

Now he wasn't always joking. Would she hear from him? What if he didn't call again before she left Sunday?

"Are you coming, Carolyn?"

Following her grandmother's voice, Carolyn wandered outside to two soaking tubs on the private verandah. Her grandmother was standing next to one, a small footstool set by the side of the tub. Her hair was protected in a pink shower cap, and she'd left her robe on a bench. "Could you help me, sweetheart?"

"Sure, Mama V. Of course."

Nothing is as humbling as helping your grandmother into a tub. Mama V definitely had trouble maneuvering. Although her bathing suit was beautiful, her scars were apparent. "You must think I'm a crazy old fool," her grandmother said, settling back in the water. "But I want to still enjoy everything that I can."

"I think you've got the right attitude, as long as someone is here to help you."

"Well, of course." Her grandmother had definitely visited the spa before and probably not alone. Off to one side a peaceful waterfall calmed the questions percolating in Carolyn's head. Howard was none of her business. She would just relax.

"Is the water toasty, Mama V?" She slid the robe from her shoulders.

"No it's not roasting. Just warm."

"Oh, I said..." But Carolyn buttoned her lips. Why make her grandmother feel bad? Obviously, something was going on with her hearing. But that could wait.

In no time, she was in the water, head resting on the curved lip of the tub. Birds flitted through the trees overhead.

"Isn't it wonderful?" her grandmother asked.

Seated in the warm water, Carolyn felt her muscles relax. "This is so different from any hot tub I've ever been in." A breeze rustled the needles of the pine trees, releasing a fresh, clean scent.

"Soaking is so relaxing. I guess that's how the Japanese do it."

She couldn't help it. Curiosity got the better of her. "So you've been here before?"

"Oh, yes." Eyes shut, Mama V tilted her lips into a smile. She must be remembering a wonderful experience. Maybe Brody was right about Howard.

"You came with Howard?"

"Sure did. His treat." The smile widened.

Okay, imagining Howard Haynes in one of these outdoor

teacup tubs brought on a fit of giggles.

"What?" With a splash, her grandmother sat up. Her bathing cap slid lower, and she jabbed at it with a wet hand.

"Nothing. It's just hard to picture my grandmother in this romantic place with her...beau."

"Why?" Her face puckered with hurt.

"Just not what I expected." She tried to coax her grandmother into seeing her point of view. "You know, I pictured myself helping you shop for groceries, cleaning up the house, maybe reading with you in the sunlight."

Her grandmother was laughing. "We can do that if you like. Sounds sweet but boring."

"No way." Carolyn slid deeper into her tub. "I'll take this anytime over cleaning house. It'll be a long time before I'm bobbing on Lake Michigan in an inner tube." The image didn't bring the usual welcome rush.

"Summer will be here before you know it," her grandmother said with her usual complacency.

"Weren't you nervous about moving all the way out here?" Carolyn just couldn't imagine it. "Santa Fe is wonderful, but you were so settled in Chicago."

Running her fingers across the top of the water, her grandmother studied the ripples. "I didn't want my life to end with your grandfather's death. He'd always encouraged me to keep growing. Sometimes I think he was preparing me."

"Grandpa was like that." Still, that took a lot of courage.

"You can't grow by doing the same thing day after day, even

when you like those things. You know, ice cream at Petersen's. There's always going to be another ice cream parlor." They both laughed. "Not that I ever anticipated meeting Howard. That wasn't it at all."

They relaxed in the warm water. The two of them always had a lot to talk about. Carolyn missed these quiet times together since Mama V had relocated. They shared so many great memories.

Before long, it was time for their massage. Carolyn helped Mama V from the tub. They both pulled on their robes and rubber-soled slippers. Then they followed the warm stone path to the massage area where two tables sat ready.

Two girls named Marisa and Adele took them through the drill. Only it was more a ritual. Then it was time for placing the warm stones. By then, the two of them were stretched out on their tummies. When Marisa placed the stones slowly along her spine, Carolyn eased out a sigh. Adele did the same with Mama V. In a short time, the manual massage began.

This could be a major turn-on, Carolyn soon realized, but not with your grandmother. The time passed so quickly, she even fell asleep while Marisa worked magic with her hands. When the massage was over, they found their way to their room. She couldn't remember when she'd felt this relaxed. It was hard to leave Ten Thousand Waves behind.

On their way back home, Carolyn's phone rang. It was Brody.

"Got plans for tomorrow?"

"Tomorrow's plans?" She glanced over at her grandmother.

"Don't look at me. Hope you don't mind, dear, but I'm busy

tomorrow."

Probably not true but Carolyn wasn't going to argue. "What did you have in mind?" Her active imagination offered suggestions involving Brody and bare skin. How crazy was this?

"We talked about Museum Hill. It might give you a better feeling for Santa Fe's history."

"I'm all for it." Somehow, everything sounded better with him.

"Ten o'clock?"

"Sounds good. Hey, don't you ever work?"

"Not when my favorite former teacher is in town."

The words sent heat spiraling through her. "So I'm really your favorite?"

"Oh yeah, Miss Knight." The words were a purr. "Definitely."

Her glance cut to the left. Thank goodness her grandmother couldn't hear well.

"See you tomorrow then. Ten o'clock."

The call ended. She tucked the phone into her bag.

"You know, your voice changes completely with when you talk to that young man," her grandmother said, mischief dancing in her eyes. Maybe laugh lines were worth having.

Carolyn felt the heady sensation of her life shifting.

Chapter 11

Brody stood on Carolyn's porch, head bowed and heart pumping. Damn. His stomach felt like he was on a carnival ride, feeling those crazy dips. Deep in his gut, today mattered. His hand was even shaking when he rang the bell.

When she answered the door, Carolyn's smile bathed him, warmer than sunlight. And the sun was blazing today. "Hey, Brody."

"H-Hey." That's all he could get out? She had that effect on him. Just looking at her, he felt overheated. How could a woman look so sexy in a plain white shirt?

Carolyn pushed open the door. "Come on in."

"Brody, is that you?" Mama V was sitting on the rattan sofa.

"Sure is." He couldn't help but smile. Her dress, or whatever it was, matched the cushions— bright pink and orange. And those oversized flower earrings? She was a trip. "Aren't you looking pretty today?"

While her grandmother blushed, Carolyn threw him an appreciative look. Sometimes he actually said the right thing.

"Carolyn tells me you're headed to Museum Hill today."

"Yes, ma'am. We are." His lips felt tight. *The moment of truth.*

"I love it up there," she said wistfully. "The view is fabulous. And of course the museums."

So the view was more important than the museums? What if Carolyn felt the same? His enthusiasm faltered. Maybe he had this all wrong.

Reaching into a closet, Carolyn took out a suede jacket. He helped her slip into it. It felt soft in his hands. "Something new?" She smelled of lavender.

"Yes, a gift from my grandmother."

"Soft." And cuddly. Carolyn looked totally hot in those torn jeans, plain white shirt, and then this soft, touchable suede.

"You braided your hair." The only benefit of that swept back style was that it emphasized the earrings he'd given her.

"Sure did." Then she added softly, "Not your favorite, I know."

He chuckled and she grinned, their minds filling in the blanks.

"Doesn't she look just beautiful?" her grandmother said.

"Gorgeous." Anticipation spiked the air. Being with Carolyn made him feel happy. They could be heading out to enjoy a simple sunset and he'd be satisfied. "Well, see you later then?"

"Have fun, you two." Mama V waved them away.

"Oh, we will." Face flushed, Carolyn led him to the door. Outside, she glanced up as they walked to the SUV in the bright sunlight. "Will you just look at this ? Not a cloud."

"We have a lot of sunny days. That's why everything is so dry. We need water." He was blabbing. Trying to fill the air with safe weather words so he wouldn't put his foot in his mouth. It would not be cool to say, *I want you, Carolyn Knight. Want you in the worst way.*

He didn't want the day to just be about that. When he opened the passenger door, Carolyn swung up with the grace of an antelope, looking so fine in those tight fitting jeans.

"Thanks for inviting me, Brody."

When she struggled with the seatbelt, he leaned over and helped. "There. All set." He backed out. "Don't want to lose you."

"Glad to hear it. I thought you'd forgotten all about me."

Was she kidding? "It's been hard to stay away." Then he saw her confused look. "I didn't want to be a pest. You know. You're here to visit your grandmother."

Her lips formed a luscious circle. "Oh."

It took a lot of self-restraint to back away. Head down, he circled the back of the car. The weather wasn't on his mind. "At least Mama V didn't give you a curfew," he said when he jumped up inside.

"Nope, that's far behind me. So tell me about these museums."

As they drove to Museum Hill, he filled her in somewhat. If you wanted to really get to know New Mexico, this was a great place to start. And he wanted the museums to speak for themselves. In ten minutes, they were there.

"Pretty impressive," she murmured as they parked in the lot. Stone steps led up to the structures. "The tour bus turned around down here so I never saw anything."

"What? Today we'll be going inside." She'd been with that wimp Alan. Nice enough but not good enough for her. Circling the car, it hit him. Was *he* good enough for Carolyn? Would Carolyn accept him and his complicated history? So much hinged on today.

Together they walked up the broad stone steps. He wanted to put his arm around her. Be closer to her the way they were coming back from El Farol. But in all fairness, he first wanted her to know more about him.

At the top of the stairs, she turned and he stood with her. This was one of his favorite views. Her eyes swept the countryside around them. "Kind of wild, isn't it?"

"Sure is." Maybe he was just imagining the appreciation in her voice.

She turned, her eyes darkening to swirling caramel. "Like you."

"Wild? Maybe that's why I love it here."

They studied each other. But he didn't want her to think of him like that. She was thinking of the old Brody again. "To be honest, Carolyn, my wild child days are over."

Her quick side-glance told him she may not believe him. Taking her elbow, he steered her toward the Museum of Indian Arts and Culture. "Okay if we start here?"

"Whatever you say." A strand of hair had worked loose from that damned braid. It danced at the corner of her lips. He couldn't help himself when he brushed it aside and kissed her. The kiss was just a teasing sweep, and he wanted way more. She swallowed hard, and he rocked his forehead onto hers. "Been thinking about you."

"Yeah. Me too," she whispered.

They both took a shaky breath. "Guess we should look at the museum," he finally said. She turned toward the sculpture garden. He took her hand, so small and dainty in his.

"Will you just look at that statue?"

"Like it?" He waited for her response, not wanting to blow this.

"Love it!"

Relief opened a small door. The huge metal piece was a warrior, machete in one hand and arrow in the other. But in front of the wide, low structure were other sculptures, many of Native American women. Carolyn took her time, admiring each one while he followed.

"Beautiful. Absolutely beautiful."

Hope prickled in his chest.

They went inside. "Hey, Brody," Kayla said, handing him the tickets. "How's it going?" She looked at Carolyn, obviously curious.

"Just fine." No way was he introducing them. Give Kayla a name, and by dinner time it might be bandied about town like yesterday's taco.

Besides, he didn't want to hurt Justine's feelings. She'd been a trouper about the whole thing. He didn't want her to think he'd been two-timing her. If he hadn't run into Carolyn, he might still be spending time with Justine. But that would be it.

And these feelings he had for Carolyn? Totally different from what he'd ever felt before. Different and precious.

Heading inside, they began the tour. Carolyn's comments as they passed the glass cases eased his anxiety. "Will you just look at the jewelry! Such craftsmanship!"

Unlike some women, she wasn't talking about the pieces as if she wanted to hang them around her neck. No, the reverence in her voice was all about the art. Her praise soothed his jittery stomach.

"Oh, Brody. These pots. How old are they?" Her enthusiasm continued in the next room. Stooping, she read the information posted with each pot.

"Why, the pottery carries history." She glanced up.

"Yep, it sure does. Ancestry." And he almost admitted it right there and then. But it wasn't the time. He wanted her to have the whole picture. They walked on.

The colorful woven blankets got her started all over again. The colors, the designs. She didn't miss a thing. And she seemed sincere. A while back, he'd brought a date here. But Kelsey hadn't appreciated any of it. She complained about the dust and her allergies.

Carolyn was different. Right now she was practically pressing her nose against the glass to see better and he smiled. "So these patterns have been passed on?" She turned back to him.

"Right. From one generation to the next until they were finally housed here."

"Wow. Some of these are huge." And she pointed to one that must have been three feet tall and just about as wide.

"Probably used for grain or water." This felt so weird. This time *she* was the student.

"And the ones with two openings?" She pointed. "They look special."

His heart started to pound, crazy as a wild pony. "Those are wedding vases. Some say the medicine man..."

Her eyes widened. "There actually was a medicine man?"

"Yes, there were wise men in each tribe who knew how to cure with herbs, performed sacred ceremonies—things like that."

"How amazing." She was like a little girl, hands clasped together.

"Probably so. The medicine man would pour in a love potion, or so the stories go. The bride and groom would both drink." He froze. Suddenly he could see the two of them, sipping from a vase like this. The mental picture shook him to the core.

Her lips parted in wonderment. Forget the pot. For a crazy moment he wanted to drink from those lips. "How beautiful." One hand went out, as if to touch it. When he tucked it back into his own, his heart began to beat again.

They kept moving. She asked questions and he answered. But all he wanted to look at was her simple beauty and that genuine spark of interest in her eyes.

"You know a lot about all this. I'm impressed," she said at one point.

"Yep." He glanced down at his boots.

"You're so modest." She teased him, coming closer until she tipped her face up. If eyes could spark, theirs did. Carolyn stumbled back. He caught her.

"I better watch where I'm walking."

"I'm keeping an eye on you."

"So I noticed," she said with a crooked smile.

Finally, they came to the area that gave Brody mixed feelings. Videos played and Native Americans recounted their experiences. What was the life of an American Indian like? Each interview provided another look at a painful past and their uncertain future.

Visitors came and went in the side room where the video played. Would she even be interested? Without hesitating, Carolyn slid onto one of the semicircular benches in front of the screen.

The stories took him back. He knew most of these people who talked about feeling deprived of their heritage. Displaced and wandering. He didn't know how that would sit with Carolyn. Leaning forward, she propped her chin on one hand. He gave her room. His father's people spoke about preserving the past so their children would understand and appreciate their heritage.

The moment came. An older man with a leathery, lined face came on. The name appeared on the screen as it had for the others. Lone Wolf. Brody started to sweat. He knew this interview word for word, but his skin prickled every time he heard it. His father told of a frustrated search for community, the depression that had led to alcoholism, the return to his pueblo that brought him some relief.

At the end, Carolyn swung around to face him "Brody? Lone Wolf. Is he related?"

"He's my father." And he waited.

Her face drained. Thank God no one else was in the room. She'd want to go home now. This was complicated. Definitely not what a girl from Chicago could accept. He started to rise. Her hand shot out. "Wait a minute. You're not going anywhere." This reminded him of the time he'd tried to sneak a bathroom break without asking. She'd streaked out the front door of the classroom and intercepted him in the hall. "You are not going anywhere, young man, without a pass."

Of course the whole class heard it.

"Talk to me."

He looked around. "How about lunch? We can talk in the restaurant."

"Sounds good. Sure." Looking dazed, she looped her bag over one shoulder.

Then she reached for his hand. He still stood a chance.

~.~

Her head filling with what she'd just seen and heard, Carolyn followed Brody outside. Visitors were arriving, checking out the sculptures. But Carolyn was sorting through her stuff. How had she missed all this when Brody was in school? She prided herself on knowing her students, connecting with them. But for Brody, well, she just hadn't.

The breeze lifted his hair when he wheeled around. God, he was gorgeous. "Still hungry?"

"Starving." Tantalizing aromas hung in the air. But she was hungry for more than food. Carolyn wanted to know more about the real Brody Wolf. And she wanted more than his kisses, which totally blew her mind.

A cafe was only a few steps from the museum. They stepped into the clatter of plates and the hum of voices. "Neat place." Like the museum, the restaurant had a new, modern vibe. Wood-topped tables filled the space. People were talking over full plates. The place felt alive.

When a waitress beckoned, Brody pointed to an empty table in the corner. Perfect. Carolyn had so many questions, and they were all personal. Why hadn't Brody told her this earlier, when he first mentioned coming back to Santa Fe?

The corner table was cozy. After they sat down, the waitress handed them menus. Strangely enough, the print blurred and she looked over at Brody. She was having trouble concentrating. He'd laid his menu down. "What do you usually order?" she asked as the waitress filled their water glasses.

"The chicken bowl on a cold day or the burrito. The cup of soup and half sandwich are good too."

"The soup and sandwich combo sounds great." She smiled up at the waitress. "And hot coffee, please."

Brody held up two fingers. "Make that two."

The waitress left and there they were, alone. Her gaze sought his. The eyes that could feel like an ice tunnel were now warmer than the teacup baths she'd enjoyed with Mama V. "I feel so stupid."

"Why?" A lock of dark hair fell over his eye, and he brushed it back.

"Because I didn't know. Because I never suspected."

He grinned. "Because you'd never seen a picture of a Native American with blue black hair and blue eyes?"

"Maybe. But it's more than that." She nodded outside. "Your obvious devotion to Santa Fe. I should have guessed."

"Yeah. That's what brought me back."

"To discover your history?"

"To find out who I really am."

"What about your brother?"

Brody tipped his head to one side. "Braydon's really into the winery. He had no desire to scare up lost ghosts. I think that's how he put it."

"Did he know your father?"

"Yes but I don't think he felt they had much in common."

Two steaming cups of coffee were slid onto the table. A little cream and sugar and she sipped, wondering how many questions she was allowed.

Meanwhile Brody leaned closer. She could see the green circle around each iris. "Don't look at me like I'm a homework assignment, okay?"

She set the coffee down. "Is that what you think?"

He nodded. "A little. Glad to answer any questions."

"Why? How? Like, how did your parents meet?"

"My mother's parents sent her to California to intern in a winery. My grandfather saw it as a rite of passage." Brody gave a dry chuckle. "If he had seen the outcome, he never would have suggested the arrangement. She met my father there."

"And he didn't approve?"

"Are you kidding? My dad wasn't at all what my grandfather had planned for his daughter."

"Probably really good-looking?" *Like you.*

"From the few pictures I've seen? Yes." His face twisted. "Not so much at the end. He was the strong, silent type. I'm afraid Mom filled in the blanks with what she wanted him to be, not what he was. They were mismatched from the start."

Carolyn almost laughed but it wasn't funny. Hadn't she done

that in the past with more than one guy?

The food arrived and she was hungry. After she'd finished her sandwich and soup, she circled back. "But they ended up together?"

"Right. Back then my dad was wild. That appealed to my mother. He was a laborer at the winery, everything my mother shouldn't want. His name was Maiitsoh, which means wolf. No one could pronounce it so he went by Mac and added Wolf for a last name. Sometimes he tried to fit in."

"For your mother?"

"Exactly. They fell in love and he made some concessions. For a while, anyway."

"And your grandparents?" Her folks would go ballistic.

"They went berserk. Then she went on a hunger strike. Game over. They gave in."

"Whoa. That's serious. So your parents married out of love?"

"Kind of. I was on the way."

"And then?"

Brody shifted in the chair. She hated to make him uncomfortable but wanted to know his story. And she had the feeling that he wanted to tell it.

"They never accepted him, not as a son-in-law. He worked in the vineyard. That's what he knew. Everyone thought he was a day laborer, and they treated him like it."

She recoiled. "How terrible."

"Then he made things worse. I think he broke under the strain of it all. Started wearing a headdress. People began calling him

Lone Wolf instead of Mac."

Carolyn tried to imagine what effect that would have on a child.

"By the time my father took off, my mother didn't shed many tears."

The empty look on his face tore her heart. "Oh, Brody. I'm so sorry."

"Maybe it was for the best." His jaw shifted. "My grandparents took care of us, and the rest is history. My mother lived in town during the week to put some space between us and her parents. They never let her forget her mistake."

"What a tragedy." No wonder he'd acted out at school.

His lips compressed. "We did okay. My grandparents meant well. They gave us the best education and made the situation livable for us. We were two mixed up little dudes. My grandfather passed away before my graduation from college and my grandmother, shortly after that. They never knew I'd headed back to New Mexico for my graduate work in architecture."

"To your father? Did you have a lot of contact with him after he left?"

"Not really. He was messed up pretty bad. Lived out in the mountains more than the pueblo. I made most of the contact. Braydon wasn't as into the ancestry search as I was." He gave her a bitter smile.

"And now?"

"My father died about a year after they produced that tape. Braydon and I gave them permission to use it. The story is true and it has to be told."

"But how crushing for you." If only she could soothe his pain.

His lapis eyes narrowed. "Let's not make this a pity party, okay?"

When she shopped with Mama V, they saw a lot of lapis lazuli stones, a beautiful dark blue that let in no light. She was looking at them now. "I'm sorry."

"Everything okay here?" The waitress had circled back.

"Yeah, we're good." He seemed so relieved. What had Brody expected from her? He struck her as very private and this was so personal. Right now Carolyn felt so close to him. He may not have room for pity, but she couldn't help wanting to heal his hurt.

"So why did you bring me here?" she said quietly. Carolyn wasn't going to assume she knew the answer.

"Because this is me." He opened both hands, palms up. "Not the boy you knew in Gull Harbor. Not some slick Santa Fe developer. This is who I am and it's complicated."

"Trying to scare me off?" The tentative look on his face turned her inside out. "I'm not going to cut and run, Brody, if that's what you're thinking. I do complicated well."

"Glad to hear it." Shoulders dropping, he smiled.

They finished their lunch and lingered. It was too early to head back. So they dawdled, sharing a piece of chocolate silk pie.

After the last mouthful, he put down his fork. "Want to visit the other museums while we're here, or I could show you my house?"

She'd had enough museums for one day. "I'd love to see your house. Did you build it?"

"Of course." The sparkle was back in the blue eyes.

The SUV was hot from sitting in the sun, and Brody pumped up the air. They didn't say much as they drove. "Is it far?'"

"Not at all, although everything seems distant out here." He took a deep breath. " All this space. A man can breathe. That's one of the things I love about it."

The streets were becoming familiar but not the hills. Once they left the city behind, the homes they passed felt isolated. "Are the adobe walls for privacy?"

"Yes, mainly. They're also part of the design. Why, don't you like them?"

"I just wondered. I've never been one for fences."

He tapped the brakes so fast, she was glad she was wearing a seat belt. "Wait a minute. You're thinking about that poem…"

Really? Maybe students had paid attention to her. "Yeah, the Robert Frost poem about mending fences."

Easing his foot off the brake, he seemed to be reaching back. "Wasn't that all about walling things in or walling them out. Am I close?"

"Close enough." They laughed together. By now, they were outside the city. "What do they call these bushes? I see them all over."

"Pinyon pines. They smell great. I have a fire pit."

"Can't wait."

They were climbing but the upgrade felt gradual. Pines clung to rock formations. Concentrating on the trees and bushes kept her from feeling the height. Cristo de Sangre remained in the distance.

Still, Carolyn's old fears felt so close to the surface.

Things were getting out of control. And she wasn't talking about her old fear of heights. Oh, no. This churning in her stomach had nothing to do with altitude.

Chapter 12

Deep breathing? Carolyn was fighting a losing battle by the time Brody pulled into a driveway. How high up were they?

"You okay?" Glancing over, he pushed a button on his rear view mirror. The gates swung open.

"Sure, it's just the height thing." She went to put a hand on her stomach, but it wound up on her heart.

"Sorry. I didn't realize it was that bad." He eased the SUV through the gates.

Yes, it's that bad, His Hotness. "Not that important. My fear of heights? Just my character flaw."

"Trust me, you don't have any flaws."

"Sure, right." Releasing her death grip on the door handle, she motioned to his amazing house. "Wow. Guess I should have expected this after seeing your project."

"Don't be too impressed. I'm glad you like it."

This was a whole new side of Brody. Architect and home owner, while she rented a bungalow in Gull Harbor. The wise cracks and ambling teen-age gait? He'd definitely moved beyond those.

And now she knew more about his journey. Their conversation

in the cafe replayed in her mind. A deepening respect added to the appeal of His Hotness. Brody parked and they got out. She followed him up shallow stone steps to massive double doors.

When he unlocked and pushed one open, cool air greeted them. This was a day of discovery. Any preconceived notions she'd had about Brody vanished once she stepped inside. Black leather and rough-hewn wood. A walls of windows with a kitchen island off to the left. "This is a man cave."

"Of course it is." Tossing his keys on a metal and glass side table with a neat industrial look, he saw her expression and laughed. "What did you expect? That it would look like my locker? Should I throw some dirty gym clothes on the floor?"

She had to laugh with him. "You got me there." Athletic shirts and shoes had always spilled from his locker, along with empty pop cans, barely used notebooks and dog-eared Cliff Notes. No more. That was all in the past. The worn leather furniture looked expensive and comfortable. A thick sheet of glass topped a gnarled wooden base, serving as a coffee table. Pillows in patterns like those in the museum were tossed here and there. She even saw bookshelves off to one side.

Now that was amazing. "Very masculine. Breathtaking."

"Which is it? Masculine, breathtaking or both?" he teased.

She met his dancing eyes. "You're still a stinker, Brody Wolf."

"And you're still h..."

"What?" She leaned closer.

But he'd slipped back into sphinx mode. With a shake of his head, he shed his jacket and reached for hers. When his hands cupped her shoulders, her skin heated.

"Hey, you're trembling."

"Am I?" *That would be a yes.*

Folding her jacket onto the sofa, he never broke eye contact. When he put his arms around her waist, she leaned forward until her forehead grazed his chin. He released a breath with a hiss.

Turning, he glanced toward the windowed wall, one arm still snug around her waist. "You okay with this?"

The scenery was beautiful. She nodded, although butterflies were having a heyday in her stomach. "Let's call this view desensitization."

He pulled her in front of him. Arms snug around her, Brody rested his head on hers. "Just don't confuse me with your mother."

"That's a deal." *As if I ever could.* Arching back into his heat, she felt safe.

His hands traveled to the base of her neck. "You're wound up tight. Am I making you tense?"

Very. "No."

Turning her, Brody tipped her chin up. "Liar." His eyes brushed her face.

"Okay, maybe a little," she admitted.

"Look, if this is too complicated, tell me. I'll understand. I unloaded a lot on you today." Brody blew out a breath. "And it's not pretty."

"I'm glad you told me." Did he think she was that shallow? "Your history is an important part of you."

But he didn't look convinced. "I don't want your pity."

"You're not going to get it, okay? We can't escape our pasts." Flattening one hand on his chest, Carolyn felt his heartbeat tick up. His open lips touched hers. She took that as an invitation. Her tongue swept in to meet his. They stoked the fire until heat crackled through her body.

"God, you taste so good," he whispered. Then he burrowed into her neck, the warm part, and kissed an erotic trail back to her lips, one kiss at a time. His Hotness was finding erogenous zones she never knew she had.

"Are you memorizing my freckles?"

"Yep," he said with a chuckle. "Getting to know them."

"I'm glad," she whispered. The teasing ended, and they both opened to a kiss that was wild, wet and hungry.

With a guttural moan, Brody worked his hands lower and edged her toward the sofa. She sank onto the soft leather and tightened her arms around him. By that time she was crazy excited and Carolyn was starting to like craziness.

"Oh, Brody, Brody." Her hands tunneled into his thick hair.

"Hmm. That feels so good." When he let his head fall back, she kissed the pulse point in the hollow of his neck. Her fingers started working. She really liked that hair.

"Gonna give me a scalp massage?"

She nibbled her way to his lips. "Maybe."

"Sure you're ready for it?"

"Are you?"

"Oh, yeah."

What were they talking about? He nudged her soft top up, one hand tracing her backbone while the other moved around to the front. With some innovative angling, the kisses continued. Wetter, rougher and oh, so hungry. She shivered.

"Are you cold? I know a room with warm quilts." Brody was breathing hard. So was she.

Still, she stiffened. "Um, I don't think so, okay?"

Caution froze his features. "So we're taking things slow?"

"For now."

"Setting boundaries. Like I'm not on your lesson plan." He half-closed his eyes. "So I scared you off?"

Now, she sure didn't want him to think that. "Brody, nothing you said turned me off. Everything has a time and a place."

His laugh held naughty suggestion. "God, I love it when you talk teacher. Now what page were we on?"

Was she confusing him?

"This page." Carolyn slammed into him with a kiss so hard she felt the ridge of his teeth. Oh, she may not be ready for bed, but she was more than ready for Brody Wolf. His hands turned her body to soft pulp while his lips made mush of her mind.

Before she knew it, she was grinding her hips into his. She couldn't help herself. When he moaned, she loved causing that response. Power pulsed through her.

"So…is this our dessert?" Those piercing blue eyes held a question.

"No. I mean, not yet." What was she saying?

"So the bell hasn't rung yet? Class hasn't started?" He was laughing at her. "Good thing you weren't this mixed up doling out homework. No one would have passed." He thumbed her lower lip.

Cripes, she had to clear her mind. "Shouldn't we talk more about everything you said today?"

"Like a heart-to-heart." His face turned to stone. "What's to say?"

"How do you feel about it? Your childhood, I mean."

"Oh, Teach...no, no, and no." He shook his head slowly. Her heart did a quick-step.

"But why? Family history is important."

"Yes, but it doesn't have to define us, does it?"

The words stunned her. He was right. "You might be a late bloomer," she told him, laying her head on his chest. "But you turned into an amazing man."

His chuckle rippled through her body. "What's the deal with the braid today, Teach? All knotted up, are we?"

Pulling away, she patted the tangled mess. "Feels like I'm falling apart."

"Right." His smile tilted. "Like you would ever let that happen."

"Not on purpose." She hated to admit it.

"You mind me rearranging this?" His fingers were already plucking at her hair.

Who could say no to this man?

Man, not a boy. "Nope. Go ahead."

He got busy. First, he slipped off her hair tie. Then he started on the french braid. She almost laughed at his expression, tongue caught between his teeth. As her hair came free, he let each strand trail through his fingers as if it were the eighth wonder of the world.

The intimacy tugged at her gut and lower. In the process, his muscled forearms grazed her body.

"How do women ever do this?" Looking super cute in his concentration, he kept working.

"We teach each other." When she shook her head, she felt the weight of her hair. Brody raked his fingers gently through the mess.

Did he realize how erotic this was? She felt incredibly turned on.

When he pulled back, his smile flattened. "What?"

"Nothing. Thanks." Drawing a line wasn't easy. She was going home Sunday and where did that leave them? She'd planned on spending Saturday, her final day here, with Mama V. Her attention fell onto his drafting table. "What's all this?"

~.~

"My latest project." Brody followed her to the mess of blueprints. Smoothing back the rolled edges, she pored over them. Concentration sharpened her features. Dang, if he didn't hold his breath. Felt like he was handing in his final exam, hoping he'd pass.

"All these are your work?" She studied the sizeable sheets one by one.

"Takes a lot of blueprints for a house like the one I showed you."

Her tall, slim body was bent like a paperclip over his plans, so beautiful with her butt in the air and hair cascading over one shoulder.

But she caught him gawking. Her eyes widened and he dropped his gaze.

Get it together. Stepping closer, he focused on the sketch. Trying to think of her as a client, he pointed. "Master bedroom." Now, why did he start there? He'd never begin there with any potential client. Fingers trailing over the paper, he moved on. "Two-story foyer. Family room to the right, kitchen to the left." Her eyes followed while he explained. She asked thoughtful questions, wanting to know why. Did everyone prefer to have the family room visible from the kitchen? So he explained the open concept. Pointed out the front and back stairs that he loved, the extra-large bathrooms and the oversized doors.

Talking her through the project, he felt his heartbeat return to normal. Well, almost. Each of her questions made him feel more proud.

"This is beautiful, Brody. So well thought out."

Women could tell him he had great eyes, a hot body—he'd heard it all. But Carolyn's questions? They hit him where he lived. Huge turn-on. But she wanted to go slow. Was she wiser than he was? In a couple days she'd be gone and he'd be a vacation memory. The timing wasn't right. His heart teeter-tottered between regret and hope. Then her eyes wandered back to his bookshelves.

"Brody, you amaze me." Stepping over to the shelves he'd had custom-made, she ran her fingers over the spines. "No way. *The Great Gatsby?*"

"And here you thought I wasn't listening."

Yeah, she recognized them all. Not only had he ordered some

of the classics she'd tried to teach him, but he had a ton of spy novels. "I eat these up like popcorn."

"So you go for psychological suspense?"

"Yep." God, he couldn't think when she fingered the covers like that. "Want to go outside?"

"Sure." She shoved his latest Baldacci book back onto the shelf. He led her to the enormous deck. "Are you okay coming out?"

She hung back. Brody tried to see it through her eyes. The deck dropped into nothing. At least, it looked that way. Sure, he'd put in metal cable railings, but he purposely didn't obstruct the view. Now he wanted an adobe wall, for her sake.

"Would you feel better sitting down?"

"Maybe." She looked so uncertain standing there. Behind a podium, she'd been master of room 207. Today? A shivery little girl. Reaching for one hand, he led her to a chaise. Settling onto the cushion, she glanced up with uncertain eyes.

"You're fine. I'm going to start a fire."

Hands gripping the arms of the chair, she watched him work with the logs. The fire caught, then she sniffed. "Pinyon?"

"You got it."

"Umm. Smells great." Clasping her hands over her tummy, she settled back.

Stretching out in the chaise next to her, he motioned with an open hand. "You're too far away."

Pushing up, she took his hand. He pulled her into the V between his legs and they snuggled. His body hadn't gotten the memo about keeping a safe distance. Brody hoped to hell he could keep his natural response in check.

To his delight, her slender frame relaxed against him. He kissed the top of her head. "You're safe with me, Teach."

"Yeah, right." When she twisted to kiss him, all bets were off.

Every kiss took him deeper. She knew him better than any woman ever had. He'd revealed so much to her, practically stripped naked, explaining his past. And he knew her. That story about the little girl at the amusement park? Turned him inside out. He wanted to be the man that made everything better for her. His body went into overdrive.

Carolyn pushed back. "What?"

"Maybe this isn't such a good idea." Restraining himself had hit the painful point.

Disappointment dimmed her face. "Really?"

"Teach, I'm not talking about this." A finger circled between them. "I mean you sitting here. Do you have dinner plans?"

"Yes, I do."

Was she going out with Alan? He wasn't about to ask. "I see."

The muscles worked in her throat when she swallowed. "My grandmother. I did come to visit her."

"Of course. Sure." He was horning in on her one-week visit. That felt great. And he'd hit her with a lot of stuff today. Maybe her acceptance was all in his head.

"Brody, that's it, really." She tugged on his shirt.

"You're sure what I said today hasn't turned you off?"

"No, I'm glad you shared that piece of yourself."

"Surprised?"

"Very. But not in a bad way."

Brody wasn't convinced. But he didn't want to give her up. A few kisses later, the sun was throwing long shadows over the deck. The logs in the pit had turned to embers.

"Guess I should go," she said.

When he pushed her up, she glanced back at the mountains. "Gee, I haven't felt anxious for at least ten minutes."

"Maybe I'm good medicine." He chuckled. "When are you going back?"

"Sunday."

His own disappointment reflected on her face. "School starts Monday."

"School." That one word put her back behind that podium. But he knew that he'd always remember her here. Just as she was now. The setting sun burnishing her face, the mountains that made her crazy soaring behind her.

"I wish I could stay."

He forced a laugh. "Right. Who knows where this could go?"

"Right. Who knows?" Suddenly, things felt awkward. Running her hands down her arms, she shivered.

"Well, better get you home then."

They walked back inside. He helped her on with her jacket. This all felt so final, and she looked preoccupied. Brody was all talked out.

When they reached the casita, he parked. Neither one of them made a move to get out.

Her phone rang and she dug it from her bag. "Hey, Sharon,

what's up? Everything all right?" Must be one of her friends. Carolyn looked so serious, and Brody got a little concerned until she smiled. "No way? Really? The pipes burst in the second floor boys' bathroom?" Her eyes swung to his.

Brody fought the chuckle rumbling in his gut. Oldest trick in the book.

"Oh, my gosh. Glenn must be furious."

Good thing she ended the call because he was laughing so hard, the caller could probably hear him.

Throwing him an almost triumphant smile, Carolyn said, "Do you believe it? The school's been flooded. Glenn's called off school next week while they fix the damage."

"Bad break, right?" But he felt crazy excited, and Carolyn had a feverish flush.

"Yeah." Slowly her eyes filled with suspicion. "That's happened before."

"Right. And my class did it," he admitted. "All the guys spread out and flushed toilets when the bell rang for study hall. It was epic. Mr. Rousey put us all on probation." His mother had been furious.

She chewed the corner of her mouth, like she was biting back a smile.

"That's gonna be one big insurance claim," he said.

"Guess so." Looking oh, so soft and sexy, Carolyn slid down in her seat. Started playing with her hair. "What'll I do with all that time?"

"Oh, I guess we'll think of something."

"I promised Mama V I'd spend tomorrow with her."

Carolyn's call from school had handed him a gift. Brody was feeling generous. "What about the rest of the week?"

"Whatever will we do?" She batted her eye lashes.

"You've got a good imagination. Consider this your homework assignment until Sunday." He reached for her.

Chapter 13

Time was on Carolyn's side. Saying goodnight to Brody had lost its sad edge since that call from school. "Mama V, are you home?" she called out, pushing the door closed behind her. "Sorry I'm so late."

Silence greeted her. Magazines overlapped in a row on the coffee table. Sofa pillows were fluffed and the afghan was neatly folded. Fading sunlight filtered through the skylights. The place felt empty, a ticking clock the only sound. Still, Mama V's car was out front.

When she saw a note on the kitchen table, she snatched it up. *Thought you might need a night off Mama V duty. Give me a call if you need anything. I'll be with Howard.* She'd left his phone number.

She'd been blown off by her grandmother. Dropping her purse in a chair, Carolyn chuckled. So Howard came first? Still, Mama V was a grown woman. She could do what she wanted.

When her church bells clanged, she scrambled for her phone. "Mama V?"

Silence. "Carolyn, it's me."

She slumped into a chair. "Mom. What's up?"

"Why do you think this might be your grandmother? Isn't she there with you?"

Her eyes skidded to the crumpled ball of paper on the table. "She might be at the gallery."

"But she isn't answering her phone."

"You called her?"

"Of course. That's how I know she's not answering her phone."

"Have you found out anything about Howard?"

"I did indeed." Each word was tightly compressed.

"And?" Were there any skeletons in his closet? For her grandmother's sake, Carolyn hoped not.

"Everything seems fine." She heard the long exhale of breath. "In fact, Howard seems to be well off. No concerns pop out. But what is he like, Carolyn? Give me your honest opinion."

Stuffy. Rigid. But she'd keep her opinions to herself. "He seems like a nice man."

"Carolyn Knight?" A warning note surfaced in her mother's voice. "If you have any doubts about him, please speak up."

She didn't want this responsibility. "Mama V has good judgment."

"Things change as we age."

We? Was Mom talking about herself too? Carolyn softened.

"She's fine, Mom," she said quietly. "I haven't seen her this happy in a long time."

"Really? Well, that's good." Relief flooded through her mother's words. Poor Mom. She probably did worry about Mama V. At least in the past, they had brunch together or Sunday dinner. Now they couldn't even do that. "Just keep an eye on her, all right, honey?" her mom continued, sounding increasingly worried. "She is older and she had that fall. I'm not there to check on her."

"Do you think you'll be coming out soon?"

"Nothing's on the calendar just yet." Papers rustled in the background. "I'm in charge of an auction next month. Your father and I have our duties." And she launched into a list.

"What about Myra? Can't you delegate some of that to her?" Sometimes her mom even had her assistant screen her calls.

"Yes, you're probably right. In any case I don't think I can come until at least July."

"All right then. Trust me." For years she'd wanted her mother to view her as an adult. Now she had no choice.

"She's in your hands now. Your grandfather would want us to watch out for her."

"And we will. But she's an adult."

"Who's not her self right now."

Carolyn's laugh came out as a snort. "Mom, I think she's back to being very much herself."

"If you say so, darling. I'm trusting you."

It was about time.

After the call ended, Carolyn wandered through the house. Some of the paintings were new. Mama V was experimenting with bold strokes and bright colors. Although her grandmother had been an art major, after marrying Grandpa, being a wife and mother kept her busy. But now he was gone and Mama V had turned to her art for comfort.

The phone rang again. "I told you I'd take care of it." Silence made her glance at the screen. Good grief. "Brody? Sorry, I thought you were someone else."

"Whoa. I wouldn't want to be that person. Who were you expecting?"

Her face burned. "My mother. Am I terrible or what?"

"Must have been some kind of conversation."

"We had a lot to discuss. Sometimes our conversations turn into arguments."

"My mother and I have our tense moments too."

"Oh, sorry. I forgot."

"She lives in Florida with her new husband and we're both busy. So we talk on the phone." How she envied his flat acceptance.

"Florida. I can't picture you there." He was a man who needed wide spaces, wild countryside. Santa Fe was right for him.

"Neither can I. Look, you might have plans with your grandmother this weekend. I'm just guessing here...how about Taos on Sunday?"

"Do you ever work?" The question was half teasing.

"Not when old friends are in town."

"Hah. So I'm moving up. No longer the former teacher?"

"Oh, you're moving up all right. I'm glad we'll have more time." His voice had grown bedroom soft.

She swallowed hard and whispered, "Me too."

He cleared his throat. "My thanks to the boys at Gull Harbor. I think I left those restroom blowup instructions somewhere in the locker room."

Probably the truth. "I'd love to see Taos with you."

"Great." He gave her a time. Sunday felt like a long way off. But it was all good. She wanted to think about all this. Her schedule had shifted. She had a refrigerator magnet that said "I dwell in possibility" taken from Emily Dickinson, her favorite poet. That's what this next week would be.

Looked like she'd be eating dinner alone, but Carolyn was glad. Never one for snap decisions, she wanted time to study every angle. Lunch felt like a long time ago so she got out the bread rounds, peanut butter and orange marmalade. Sitting at the table with her comfort food, Carolyn let her mind wander. Brody had changed things. She felt a little like that fairy tale where the prince awakens the girl with a kiss.

Her phone rang again. This time she looked at the caller name popping up on her phone. "Diana?"

"Yep. I'm doing a wardrobe check. Everything working out all right?

Taking tiny, sticky nibbles, Carolyn talked while she ate. "Don't know what I would have done without you. My elasticized pants and turtlenecks would not have cut it."

"I never knew how to break it to you. Pitch them. And how is he?"

Denying would be useless. "Great."

"Ah, so that's how it is." Her friend gave a sly chuckle.

"Diana, I don't know how it is."

"Okay. Details about this man, please."

But all she had was questions. "How can something feel so wrong and so right, all at the same time?"

Her friend's laugh rippled across the distance. "Oh, girlfriend, I know just what you mean. I never thought Will was wrong for me, but I was positive *I* wasn't right for him."

"Guess you settled that. How are the wedding plans coming?"

"Fine. When you come home, I want you to help me look for a dress. But enough about me. Why does Brody feel wrong for you when you have that dreamy note in your voice every time you say his name?"

"I was his teacher, for Pete's sake!"

"We've already been over that. Not a good excuse."

"Yes, well, he's not the goofy teenager I flunked back then. Now he has book shelves with some classics." She realized how difficult high school must have been for Brody. That brought a whole new perspective.

"So you've been in his house?" Diana didn't miss a trick.

"Just a quick visit. He lives in Santa Fe, Diana, and I live in Michigan. I'm not sure this is smart."

"You're getting ahead of yourself. See where your heart leads you."

Did Carolyn even knew how to do that?

"How convenient for you that the high school is shut down for another week," Diana said. "The whole town's buzzing about it."

"I suppose the kids are thrilled."

"More time to hang out at the Swirly Top, even though it's a wee bit chilly here. The parents are the ones grumbling while they grocery shop at Clancy's."

Thinking about the upcoming week with Brody, Carolyn gave a

sinuous stretch. "You're right. Now I have more time."

"Use it wisely." An impish note crept into Diana's voice.

"I don't know if I've ever felt like this."

"Then yes, you do need more time with him. I can't wait to hear all about it."

Getting up, Carolyn began stowing away the peanut butter and marmalade. "You're either a bad influence or a life saver."

"Can't I be both? Jump off that pier, girl! Splash around a little."

"I don't know how much splashing I'll do." But the comment got Carolyn thinking about Ten Thousand Waves.

"Don't worry about the future. I know that's hard for you."

"It's not easy. I do like my schedule." But Carolyn wanted a future. Somehow, what she had now didn't seem like enough. Ten years from now did she want to be wheeling her cart through Clancy's, buying frozen dinners for one?

They said good-bye. Carolyn made a cup of decaf and went outside. After setting her mug on the table, she stacked some wood in the fire pit. Thank goodness for the gas starter. Cuddling up with a blanket, she sipped her coffee and watched the logs catch fire one by one. The unmistakable scent of pinyon pine teased her senses.

She had to make good use of this extra week in Santa Fe. Opportunity could vanish like a wisp of smoke.

Chapter 14

A quiet rustling at the front door made Carolyn turn in time to see her grandmother creeping in the next morning. "Hi, Mama V."

"Good morning, dear!" her grandmother sang out, as if she'd just returned from the store. Her lilac tracksuit was the kind you'd wear to lounge around the house. Behind her, an overnight bag dropped to the floor.

Setting her coffee down, Carolyn wished her mom could see the excited flush in Mama V's cheeks. "Did you have fun?"

Her grandmother's eyes sparkled. "Why, yes. How about you?"

"Great date. The museums, you know." But she wasn't about to to go into the personal revelations that had helped unlock the mysteries of Brody Wolf. "Think you can put up with me for another week? A pipe broke at the school."

"Are you kidding? How wonderful!" With a lunge of lilac velveteen, Mama V enveloped her in a scented hug, "I'd love it."

"Me too. I'm so excited."

Pushing away, Mama V studied her. "Am I being a totally inappropriate grandmother?"

"That's not for me to say. Want part of my English muffin?" When her grandmother nodded, Carolyn handed half over.

Mama V slid onto the chair opposite but not without some effort. The more time Carolyn spent with her grandmother, the more she realized there were lingering issues that Mama V tried hard to conceal. "One more whole week," she said between bites. "Now if you were your mother." Here Mama V wagged a finger, as if she were Jacqueline Stanford Knight. "You'd ask me a million personal questions that were really none of your business."

Carolyn grinned. "Probably right. But I'm not my mother."

"Good, then I won't pump you for details either."

"There aren't any. At least, not yet."

"Ah, hah!" Her grandmother wiggled her eyebrows. "Hopefully there will be soon."

Okay, this felt weird. Girl talk with her grandmother. "Time will tell. What should we do today?"

"The gallery's always busy on Saturdays. Wendy called last night, and I could hardly hear her. She's picked up some kind of bug and I sure don't want her near the place."

When it came to Mama V and the gallery, Wendy could be very proprietary. Carolyn had always tiptoed around her, afraid she might mess things up. "I'd be glad to work at the gallery today." She loved the long, cool white hallways, the smell of oil paint and watching shoppers study the work.

After a quick shower, she sorted through her new wardrobe. How fun to have so many choices. The swirling skirt was perfect, as was the blousy peasant shirt. She wanted to look the role today. As a last touch, she piled on beaded necklaces, not caring if they matched. Of course, Brody's earrings dangled to her shoulders.

Catching the front of her hair up with a claw clip, she left the rest alone. No braid today. The look was very artsy fartsy, as Phoebe would say.

When her grandmother was ready, they walked arm-in-arm to the shop. Entering the gallery was like entering another world. On her earlier trip, Carolyn spent most of her time at the hospital every day. Before she went home to Gull Harbor, she'd set up Uber to take her grandmother to therapy at a nearby rehab facility. There had been no time for anything else.

Glancing at the walls today, Carolyn realized a lot had changed. Like most of the galleries on Canyon Road, the space had once been a home. One low-ceilinged room led to another, the work displayed on white-washed walls. What she saw today echoed the work in the casita.

"Such beautiful pieces," she said, as her grandmother snapped on the lights.

"Isn't it gorgeous? So many gifted artists."

"Are they all from Santa Fe?" She was stunned by a wide canvas with a grove of aspen trees turning gold, their slender trunks a white contrast.

"Gracious no. I get work from all over the country. Artists send me shots of their portfolio. I like to help out the new ones, especially."

Since it was only ten and the gallery didn't open until eleven, Carolyn had plenty of time to wander around. Starry nights, breathtaking vistas and mountain ranges of mauve and teal. The colorful abandon took her breath away.

Santa Fe was like that. Although Carolyn loved her position in Gull Harbor, this trip made her feel as if she'd missed something. Had she kept herself safe but limited with a career in one town? Unlike other professions, teachers rarely moved around for advancement. They stayed in one school. Their reputation grew. She loved teaching the younger brother or sister of a former student. Her career had been so satisfying.

At least, she used to feel that way.

When they reached the back office, her grandmother turned. "What is it?" She never missed anything.

"When did you change your style?" Carolyn swept a hand toward the riot of color on the walls.

That mysterious glint lit her eyes again. "Call it a next step or stage. I had to do something while I was recovering. The darker paintings? They're personal and stashed in the back. Didn't you take another step when you graduated from college?"

"That's different. I had to. I couldn't just go home and well, you know...."

"Live with your parents?" Mama V suggested gently.

"Right." She had never even considered it. Lake Shore Drive never felt like a home. Her grandparents' place in River Forest was home. Their cook Minnie always had banana bread baking or chicken and wild rice soup simmering on the burner.

"Sure, Mom and Dad offered to set me up with interviews at private schools. They had tons of connections. I wanted something different."

"So did I, sweetheart. So did I." Mama V took a seat at her

messy desk. In contrast to Wendy's neat reception area in the front room, here papers were heaped in slippery piles held steady by three coffee cups. Creative chaos. Must drive Wendy nuts. Carolyn smiled.

"You're fabulous." She bent to kiss her grandmother's cheek.

"I'm no such thing." Running one hand through her short wavy hair, she waved Carolyn away with the other. "Now walk around and see what we have so you can talk it up. Check out the back room. We're starting to carry pottery. You might like it after visiting Museum Hill. I've got some paper work to do before we open."

"Terrific. I'll just get caught up." Her new boots sounded on the hardwood floors as Carolyn swirled through the rooms. Sure enough, a back room was filled with pottery in all sizes and shapes. Some designs were traditional, like the ones she'd seen in the museum. Others had a more contemporary approach. In particular, a black bowl embedded with turquoise caught her eye. Corner cases held jewelry. Again, she could tie in the designs with what she'd seen that day with Brody.

This was the ancestry he treasured. The heritage that had caused him to walk away from Gull Harbor and everything familiar. How had he found the courage? Brody could have worked in the family vineyard with his brother. But he'd taken a different road. Her respect for him grew, along with her need to see him again.

Tomorrow felt so far away.

"Time to open the doors!" Her grandmother's voice shook Carolyn from delicious daydreams. "You take the front while I put on fresh coffee. I want people to feel at home."

Then Mama V was gone, her uneven steps more noticeable in the hallway where the floors had settled on a slight angle.

Carolyn was admiring the painting of the golden aspens when the bell behind her rang. Turning, she had to force a smile. "Hi, Alan."

"Morning. Hoped to find you here." Freshly shaven with hair slicked back, he looked so darned eager. Alan was such a nice guy. Polite and well-heeled. But not hot. Not a man who could stir a woman's soul, at least *her* soul.

He was no match for His Hotness.

"Helping out this morning?"

"Right. Wendy's sick." When she got up from the chair, Alan's eyes took in her long skirt and boots. Carolyn almost laughed at his surprise, but she didn't want to hurt his feelings. "You working in the shop today?"

"Yes, although James works with me on weekends. Dad does too, when he's not up here bothering your grandmother."

So that's how it was. "I don't think she minds."

"Guess not." His gaze flitted around the room, avoiding eye contact. "Say, I wonder if you have plans for tonight?"

"Oh, sorry, Alan. I do." Part of that was true. She did hope to spend time with her grandmother. Especially since she'd be gone all day tomorrow.

"When are you leaving?"

"Um, not for a while."

Like his father, Alan thought on his feet. "Well, how about

tomorrow then? Our shop's closed. We could make a day of it."

How amazing the difference one week could make.

Or one man.

Knitting her hands together, she perched on the corner of the desk. "Alan?"

His smile sagged. She felt terrible.

"You're such a great guy."

A frown drooped over that wilted smile. "But I just don't think we have that much in common."

"Hmm." While Alan's eyes shifted to his polished tasseled loafers, her thoughts drifted to Brody's work boots. "I see."

Carolyn felt like a teacher telling a student he'd flunked the course. Thank goodness her grandmother bustled into the room. "Oh hello, Alan." Her eyes circled between the two of them and bless her heart, she caught the whole scene. Carolyn watched various emotions play over her face, ending with sympathy for Howard's son.

"I'm on my way up to the Burnished Cup for coffee," Alan said, straightening. "Wanted to see if you ladies needed anything."

"Oh, aren't you sweet?" Mama V gestured toward the back. The scent of coffee lingered in the air. "But I've put some on. You're welcome to a cup."

"No thanks. Guess you're covered." The bright smile back in place, Alan edged toward the door. "Have a great day. Good seeing you both."

The blue door closed behind him, and Mama V turned to Carolyn. "He's not your forever guy, is he?"

"No, Mama V. He's not. Sorry."

"That's okay." Her grandmother did her cute nose wrinkle. "Might have made things a little sticky down the road. You never know. If Howard and I ever break up, that could be awkward."

The words knocked the breath out of Carolyn. "You are a woman of many surprises." But she felt relieved. "Can we have dinner tonight? You know, just the two of us?"

"Absolutely." Her grandmother squeezed her shoulders together. "Then you can tell me all about Brody."

Chapter 15

"Mama V, have you seen my new boots?" Barefoot, Carolyn stumbled down the hall from her bedroom. Where had she left them? After dinner at La Fonda the night before, they'd watched *The Notebook*, munching on popcorn and swiping at tears.

Her grandmother glanced up from the morning paper. "What suit are you talking about, dear?"

Maybe it was time. "Boots, Mama V," Carolyn said gently. "I'm looking for my new leather boots. Oh, there they are!" Stooping, she fished them out from under the sofa. Should she tackle the hearing issue now? It wouldn't get any easier. There were times when she really wished her mother were here. She tugged on her right boot, and then eased on her left. That foot was still tender.

Hands on her knees, she faced her grandmother. "Mama V, are you having trouble hearing things lately?"

Her grandmother's heart-shaped chin began to quiver. "Is it that obvious?"

This was so hard, but Carolyn had to be honest. "Yes, it is. I'm sorry."

"Howard has never said anything about it."

"Maybe he doesn't want to hurt your feelings?" Begrudgingly,

Howard won another point.

Her grandmother's left hand crinkled the newspaper. When had she stopped wearing her wedding ring? "I don't want him to know."

"But why? Doesn't Howard wear a hearing aid?"

"Oh, my goodness, no." Mama V was practically whispering. "He's quite a bit younger."

Well, hello. "Does that matter? Aren't hearing aids really small now? Maybe he wouldn't have to know."

"Oh, he'd notice. We're, you know… He'd notice." Ducking her head, she blinked furiously.

Carolyn wished she'd never brought this up. "If he doesn't have a hearing aid now, he will soon."

Mama V didn't look convinced.

"Will you consider seeing an audiologist?"

With a defeated sigh, Mama V nodded.

"Good. That's great." Jumping up, Carolyn circled the table and gave her grandmother a hug.

"You're such a sweetheart." Her grandmother gently patted Carolyn's hand. "Always worrying about me."

"I only want to see you happy."

"Oh, I am. I'm happy again."

Again. Meaning after Grandpa. Yep, maybe Howard wasn't such a bad guy after all.

Perched on the chair nearest the door, Carolyn waited for Brody. Her heart thumped wildly in her chest. They'd left a lot unfinished. Practically put it on the shelf because she was leaving.

Now she wasn't. Anticipation coursed through her veins, hot and sweet. She took another peek out the front window.

"Sweetheart, I think you might put a hole in my curtain if you pull it back one more time," her grandmother commented, dropping her eyes to the expensive rips in Carolyn's jeans. "I still cannot understand this fashion look. But, torn or not, you'd look fabulous in anything."

"That's just because you're my grandmother." Peace filled her heart. "Are you seeing Howard today?"

"Oh, maybe. Who knows?" Mama V was being evasive again. "Will you be home in time for dinner?"

"Oh, maybe. Who knows?"

Mama V broke into laughter. "Isn't this just the craziest thing?" She'd asked some rather pointed questions the night before at La Fonda. But Carolyn didn't have answers. Not yet. In the end, her grandmother simply said, "No use waiting, Carolyn. Whatever you decide, however you feel, don't put it off. That's my advice anyway."

Such simple words. But they felt complicated.

The knock at the door came as a relief. Analyzing stuff took a lot out of her.

She opened the door. Brody stood there, his brilliant blue eyes blazing against a dark tan. "No Stetson today?"

When he stepped inside, he brushed her cheek with a kiss, as if he did this every day. "It's in the car." The need to have his arms around her felt so primal. The glint in his eye? Maybe he wanted that too. Maybe he wanted even more.

Was she ready? Yes. She'd never felt more certain. And they were going to spend the day sightseeing?

"Hello, Brody," Mama V greeted him like an old friend. "So you're off on an adventure to Taos?"

"I guess." His eyes sought hers. "As much adventure as Carolyn is up for."

"Isn't that exciting?" Mama V clasped her hands together. "Don't forget the Millicent Rogers Museum. Fabulous collection of turquoise. I would have loved that woman."

"It's on my list. I think the two of you had a lot in common."

Carolyn had no idea what or who they were talking about. But Brody and her grandmother definitely hit it off. She grabbed her jacket from the back of the sofa.

"You ready?" His hand fell to the small of her back. She felt every fingertip.

"You bet. See you later?" She gave her grandmother a kiss.

"Will you be getting back late?"

Throwing Mama V a stern look, Carolyn said, "My grandmother loves to tease."

Brody chuckled. "Does Carolyn have a curfew?"

"For heaven's sake, no." Her grandmother brushed the question away. "Have fun."

Sure felt like Mama V had just given Brody free rein. As they left, Carolyn pulled the door shut. "The gallery's closed today. She probably has plans with Howard."

His gravelly laugh just about undid her. "Your grandmother is a trip."

"Yes, and sometimes I think she knows me better than I know myself."

Putting her sunglasses in place, she walked to the SUV. Brody opened the door and she got in. Everything in here smelled yummy and masculine…like him. She inhaled. When he climbed in, Brody seemed to fill the small interior. He was a man who shrank things down to size. Claimed things for his own.

But her mind was getting way ahead of herself. She snapped on her seat belt. "So we're going north?"

"We are. But we have some choices."

Hearing some hesitation in his voice, she turned to face him. "Like what?"

"We can take Highway 66 to Taos. Fast and easy. Of course the road gradually rises but you're not really aware of it."

"Yes." So this was a height thing.

"Or…" Here he paused. "We can take the High Road to Taos with spectacular views and little towns that aren't touristy. Some shops off to the sides. Rugs and pottery, stuff like that. Up to you."

This felt like a challenge. Diana's words came to mind. "Jump off that pier." Did Carolyn want to be hobbled by this irrational fear all her life? Even stepping into an elevator sent her stomach tumbling. "I vote for the high road."

"You sure?"

"Of course. I'm an adult." This wasn't the time to share how she'd gotten sick at the Omnimax during the Grand Canyon movie.

"Okay. We'll do it." Brody stepped on the gas. "How's the visit going with your grandmother?"

"Wonderful. I worked in her gallery yesterday."

He grinned. "Sell any high ticket items?"

"Two, actually. A gouache painting of the mountains and a modern metal sculpture. But the back room interested me most. She's carrying some pottery, blankets and native jewelry."

"I'll have to check that out."

"Made me think of you." Okay, maybe that was too honest.

He reached for her hand. "Glad to hear you thought of me. You've sure been on my mind." Warmth coursed through her veins like the expensive port her father drank after dinner.

She might wish she had some of that when they reached the mountains.

Brody went back to shifting when they turned off the main highway at the sign for Nambe Pueblo. "How did your father like living on a pueblo after being in Michigan?" Was the question too personal?

"There were issues." Brody's jaw shifted. "But they couldn't handle the drinking. He'd get violent, I guess. So my dad slept in the back of his pickup out in the hills."

"That sounds beautiful." What could she say?

Brody snorted. "Trust me, cold and lonely would be more like it."

"Sleeping under the stars, I mean. You surprise me." The hurt on his face surprised her more.

"I'm not like my father, Carolyn. No way."

"I know that." Now it was her turn to reach for *his* hand. Would he shake it off?

Instead, he squeezed her hand back. "I'd rather be in front of the fire in my own home instead of wandering around in the desert like a lone..."

"Lone wolf?" she offered, another piece of the Brody puzzle slotting into place.

The chin tightened further.

"Your own name offends you?" she said gently. "But there's such strength."

"And a lot of loneliness. Which is why I didn't take the whole name."

"In school you were always surrounded by friends."

"I like being part of a pack." Then he rolled his eyes. "Corny, right? Forget I said that."

She laughed. "Never. I'm going to remind you every day."

But she was getting way ahead of herself. They were in the left lane and Brody shot ahead. It was Sunday, without many cars on the road. Strictly a reflex, she braced herself and grabbed the door handle. His boot came up off the accelerator. "Didn't mean to frighten you."

She sighed. "Doesn't take much. I'm working on it."

They exchanged a smile. "You mean the teacher needs some lessons?"

"Maybe."

When he threw her that wicked smile, her tummy tightened. "Just maybe?" he teased. "I'm not a speed freak, even when there are no cars on the road."

"Duly noted." Her attention shifted to the landscape. Vast

stretches fell to either side. Homes were usually isolated, with maybe an outside pen for animals.

He cast a look to both sides. "Seems every time I drive up this way, more houses have sprung up."

"Mixed feelings?"

"As a matter of fact, yes." His forehead wrinkled. "I tell myself that one of the reasons I'm in the building business is to ensure that new structures complement the landscape. No white boxes along the road."

"That makes perfect sense. Your home is beautiful."

"Glad you like it. But not everyone can afford a house that size. We also build more modest homes. The Wolf Group has won awards for economical housing." He blushed, which was so darling. "Am I bragging?"

"Not at all. I'm proud of you." Oh cripes. She was back in the role of teacher.

Eyebrows raised, Brody slid her a look.

"Okay, I'm not proud of you."

He unleashed a gutsy laugh. "I shouldn't give you a hard time. But I have fun doing it. It's easy."

"Easy? You think I'm easy?" She was teasing but for a second he looked worried.

"Miss Knight, I'd never say that."

"Wait and see."

He sucked in a breath.

A sign for the High Road to Taos came up. Time for some deep breathing.

"You okay?"

She felt his eyes flick her way.

"No problems here." She was doing this. The road climbed. Carolyn hung on tight. Sometimes there was a shoulder and sometimes, not so much. State Road 98 was taking them through some rough landscape that was absolutely beautiful.

"There's a historic church up ahead," Brody said when they'd driven a while. "Want to stop?"

"Sure. Why not? I'm all for history."

~.~

Moments later he pulled into parking lot. "Pretty great, right?" He loved this church. It was surrounded by a walled courtyard with two worn wooden doors as a gate. A bell tower rose at each end of the church, a cross on each spire.

"Looks like a post card."

"People often come here to be healed." Brody took her hand as they walked to the doors. "At least that's the history of the church."

The sanctuary was dim and cool when they entered. Right inside the door was a baptismal font. Over to one side, a door opened and Brody headed toward it. He knew she'd appreciate what was inside. "You'll want to see this. This room is devoted to children." The walls were covered with pictures of children. The kind that made hash of your heart. To top it off, a pair of crutches leaned against the wall. Sharing all this felt special with her by his side.

"Kind of sad," she said, studying the photos.

"Hopeful too. At least I like to think that."

After a short stop in the gift shop, they went back to the car and drove farther up the road. They hadn't gone far when they reached a sign for Rancho de Chimayo Restaurant. "Hungry?" Brody asked.

"Starving." No hesitation on her part.

He loved the fact that she enjoyed food. So many women were on diets. Dates could become a guilt trip. "This place isn't fancy, but it is very cool."

"What does that mean?"

"You'll see." He hoped she'd like it. After parking the SUV under a tree, they headed inside. The restaurant had an old country feel to it. Brody asked for a table in the back where sunshine flooded onto a patio. Bright flowers, probably plastic, sat in the center of each table. Relaxed voices filled the air. After they ordered, he sat and studied her, so glad she was staying longer.

"What is it? Do I look terrible?" Her hand went to her hair.

"Sorry if I'm staring. You look fine. Perfect."

They gave each other a goofy smile. That was just the way he felt sometimes with her—goofy.

"Do you come here a lot?"

"When I have a job up in Taos. I try to leave early enough to drive the high road, either on the way there or coming back. It takes longer but the scenery is worth it." Sure, he'd brought a date here once or twice but it didn't mean anything. But with Carolyn he had to be careful. No way did he want her to think he had a string of woman. She seemed sensitive about that.

He'd been flattered by her questions in the car. Usually he didn't like to talk about his dad. But Carolyn's interest seemed genuine. At the same time, he felt cautious. He didn't like being compared with his father.

They both settled back in the sunlight falling through the huge glass panes. Being with Carolyn felt so natural. Her acceptance of his history brought a comfort level Brody hadn't felt with a woman until now. He enjoyed looking at her but wished she'd stop braiding her hair.

"A penny for your thoughts." Her caramel eyes swirled with curiosity, the way they had in class when she was teasing out a point.

"Total honesty?"

"Always."

"I'm wondering why you braid that beautiful hair. "

"I'll be right back." Carolyn left so fast that the woman at the next table threw him a dirty look, as if he must have done something wrong. Brody just turned his palms up and smiled. Maybe he shouldn't have said anything.

Or maybe not. When she returned, her hair fell past her shoulders, shining like gold in the sunlight. It would feel soft on his skin. That much he knew. "Your hair blows me away."

"Does it?" Flustered, she ran her fingers through the thick mass, and his own hand actually jerked forward. He was glad when the waitress arrived with the food. They ate in silence.

"You feeling okay so far?" he asked while they were eating.

"What do you mean?"

"The road?" He wondered if taking the high road had been a bad idea.

"Oh, I'm fine." But that shake of her head didn't seem casual.

Strictly as a diversion, he asked her about her parents. "Tell me more about your folks. They live in Chicago?"

"My parents are members of Chicago's high society, if there is such a thing. They do a lot of fund raising for good causes. Foundations. Galas. That kind of thing."

"Galas?" He was at a loss.

"Parties. Dinner dances where they raise funds for a cause. They go to tons of them."

Didn't sound like she approved. "So did you have to do that too while you were growing up?"

"No, they were for adults. That's why I spent a lot of time with my grandparents. Worked out great." Her shy smile came out again. "My father's parents died young so the Stanford side was all I had."

"Sounds like you grew up kind of lonely." He knew just how that felt. His younger brother had taken up all of their mother's attention—or what she had to give.

Their eyes caught and held. What passed between them was more psychic than said. That made him really uncomfortable. "Ready to move on?" He motioned to the waitress.

"Yep, you bet."

He settled the check and on the way out took her hand. That sense of comfortable companionship returned. It was amazing how right he felt with her. When they reached the SUV, he turned. The urge felt so strong. The need, so deep. "Carolyn?"

"Right here." She tilted her face up in a most inviting way. Of course he had to kiss her. Her lips tasted of tomato sauce. When she opened them, a jolt shot through him. He didn't need an invitation to go deeper. His arms tightened while he tasted. Carolyn's moan just about sent him over the edge. The tongue tangling got pretty intense when she molded her body against his. He could feel every curve through that soft denim.

And she could probably feel him. Her eyes widened. Pushing back, she grinned, looking pleased with herself. "Well."

He tried to get his breathing—and his body—under control. "Ready to ride?"

With a sigh, she settled against him. "Just give me a sec, okay?"

"Okay." He rocked her in the shade of that tree. *I could take this forever.* That thought blew him away. Being with her felt right. Like they fit together but could still be different people. The boisterous laugh of two couples leaving the restaurant broke the spell. Carolyn's arms loosened. He opened the car door and she got in.

Back on the road, he tried to keep her engaged as they climbed. By the time they got to Truchas, they were high in the mountains. Beside the road, the ground sheared away. He felt her tense. Heard her breathing change. She was struggling and he felt terrible.

Brody tried to see it through her eyes but failed. The mountains were exciting for him. So damn breathtaking. Maybe if he slowed down, she'd feel better. After all, there was no traffic behind them. But even after slowing to a crawl, he could hear her little gasps, see her white-knuckled grip of the car handle. Up ahead the road turned west. They'd be away from this edge and he was glad.

"Stop." Her hand gripped the wheel. "I want to try something."

"What? The incline is steep up here." They should have just taken the highway.

She was eyeing the road. "Can't we get out just for a second?"

Brody glanced at the narrow lookout area to the right. He felt fine with it but didn't want Carolyn to freak out. "You're the boss." He slowed to a stop. Walking around the car, he had second thoughts. Maybe this would only make things worse. But she'd asked him. How could he say no? Brody stumbled.

He could never say no to Carolyn.

That's how bad this was.

They hadn't even gone to bed together—and he sure hoped that's where this was headed—but he was already totally whipped. This had never happened to him before and it unnerved him.

Face pale, she eased out. When he took her arm, she was trembling. "I've got you, Carolyn."

The wind caught her hair and the curls danced. She looked crazy, eyes wide with terror. "Carolyn?"

"I'm fine." But her chest rose and fell like a netted bird. He got palpitations looking at her. A tree arched over them, and he slowly walked her to the trunk. Any anchor might help. A thin metal barrier curved with the road, more a warning than real protection. When her eyes found it, she turned paler. He didn't think that was possible. By now, he had both hands on her upper arms. She still was shaking. "I'm fine, just fine," she said, her breath coming in short, tight gasps.

"The hell you are. Can you breathe slower?" She was scaring him to death.

"I don't know how." Her eyes flew to his.

Miss Knight, the teacher who could take on a classroom of rambunctious senior boys, looked terrified. Seeing her fear just about broke him in two. "Let's try this. It might help." What did he know? Taking a breath in through his nose, he let it out slowly through his lips. He'd seen this somewhere on the Internet. She was nodding like a bobble-head toy. God, this was turning him inside out.

"Right. Sure. Okay." And that's just what she did.

"Let your eyes sweep the horizon," he said, pulling the words from someplace. Later he would wonder. "Breathe in, breathe out."

Below them the land rippled with hills and peaks studded with pines and cactus. She kept breathing, slower each time. Her death grip on his hand loosened. All the while, he kept encouraging her. "You're doing great, Carolyn. Doesn't it feel good?"

"I'm scared to d-death. But I'm going to beat this."

"Of course you are." If he were ever this terrified of anything, he'd try anything to get it under control. Brody had respect for what she was attempting.

"I have to do this," she gritted out between set teeth.

"You *want* to do it. You want to enjoy beautiful scenery." He sounded like a travel poster. *Santa Fe - the Land of Enchantment. The place to go to beat your fear of heights.*

Slowly, the stiff fear melted from her body. Color returned to her cheeks. He dropped his hands and looped one arm around her shoulder. She fit just right under his arm but kept one hand on his chest. He palmed it with his own. They smiled at each other like two kids playing hooky. Her eyes warmed to sherry. "This is wonderful, Brody. I feel better. Much better."

"Good." He couldn't begin to describe how he felt right now.

"My friend Diana told me I should do this." Color brushed her cheeks. "Except she said, 'jump off the pier.'"

He snorted. "Let's not be trying any of that."

"It was a metaphor, silly."

Not again. Brody shook his head.

"An implied comparison. Life is the pier." Then she frowned. "Oh wait. Life's the water. Fear is the pier."

Whatever. "Now *I'm* confused."

"Right. The water is life. I'm jumping in. That's the metaphor."

He had to go along with it. "Okay, Teach. Right. Meta For."

"Metaphor," she murmured, gazing over the beauty below.

"So you explained this when I was in your class?"

"Yep. You bet."

Brody pulled her tighter into his arms. "Think I was sick that day."

"Maybe you were in the bathroom again, killing time. Making me look bad."

"Ouch." Did he ever dream he'd be cuddling Miss Knight one day? Could he ever have imagined she would need him like this? Together they stared out over the land he loved, watching the shadows of clouds chase each other.

The world had never felt so right. When she angled her head, he kissed her. The meeting felt like more than lips. His heart was in that kiss. Would she freak out if he told her he loved her? The words formed on his tongue.

"Brody?" Breaking away, she licked her lower lip.

"Yep." Were they going to get into a literary discussion again? He steeled himself.

Lids lowered, she looked so sexy. "More please?"

It was as if she'd hit the release switch. Starting with her forehead, his lips roamed over her soft skin until they found her lips again. She settled in with a sigh. His former teacher was in his arms. A woman he'd adored and, truth be told, lusted after in high school was now whimpering with need. Every muscle in his body tightened.

Slowing down for the sideshow, a car passed. Carolyn buried her face in his jacket. Although it wasn't easy, he pulled away. "We don't want to end up on Facebook, do we?"

"You started it." She nicked his nose with the tip of a finger.

"Well, maybe I did." He ran a thumb over her smooth chin.

Ducking her head, she climbed back in the car, smoothing her hair. He couldn't help but laugh. In so many ways, Carolyn could be very proper.

But he knew a different side of her.

Then she turned to face the abyss again. His heart stopped. But if she felt nervous, she never showed it. Just yanked out the seat belt and fastened it. He closed the door, hurried around to the driver's side and got in.

"Carolyn?" His hand touched her back. "Everything okay?"

"Of course it is." She looked so pleased when she kissed him. "I'm fine. Isn't it beautiful?"

"Yes, it is. Wait a minute...is this a metaphor?" Was she talking about the spectacular view or their crazy kisses?

Throwing back her head, she laughed. "No, Brody. This is real life."

Damn, since driving was a lot easier than figuring this all out, he pulled away. Taking the left turn toward Taos, his mind moved ahead while her kisses lingered on his lips.

Chapter 16

When they reached the flatter highway, Carolyn felt embarrassed by her relief. Still, she'd done it. Today she'd conquered a fear that had terrified her since childhood. Could she have handled this without Brody? Perspiration glistened on his five o'clock shadow. The effort had wiped him out too. His deep breathing to slow her panic touched her heart in a place no one else had ever reached before.

Would conquering heights be this gut wrenching every time? She couldn't think ahead. Brody wouldn't be with her. The reminder made her slouch deeper in her seat.

He glanced over. "Hey, what brought that frown?"

She fiddled with the tear in her jeans. "Nothing really. Just thinking about how different everything is here." Tossing her head back, she focused her attention outside. They were passing gas stations and small motels, the kind you saw in old movies. Strip malls here were smaller than in the Midwest, with fewer stores.

"Different good or different bad?" His eyes fell to the rip.

Carolyn stopped her nervous hands. "Neither. Just different."

She'd forgotten how cautious he could be. Lounging in her classroom, he'd cock his head to one side when she called on him. Even back then, Brody had a sensitive side. Now she realized it may have been a defensive side. "Is that Taos up ahead?"

"Yep. I thought we'd park on the square, for starters. Are you up for another museum?"

She chuckled. "Yes. Are you?" Carolyn didn't know many men who liked to trek through the past. But Brody might be different. Maybe he had a reason. Ancestry seemed so important to him. He was a man piecing together his family history.

"Your grandmother wanted me to take you to the Millicent Rogers Museum."

"We don't have to do everything my grandmother says, Brody."

His grin widened. "Ah, teacher talk again. I love it."

Her cheeks flared furiously. He could be so maddening but so much fun, all at the same time. "I just meant, that might be nice."

He shrugged. "You'll love it. At least I think you will."

A man who knew what she would like. This was something new.

They'd stopped for the main traffic light and waited for it to change. Adobe buildings were everywhere, of course. But Taos felt different. The mountain town felt rougher. Like Brody. She grasped for Brody adjectives while they sat at the light. Hot. Funny. Real.

Real. The word rang in her head. Authentic. Brody had found out where he belonged. And the place where he fit in was sure different from where he'd been ten years ago. Back then he could be a clown one minute and a brooding teen the next.

Now he'd settled into a place where he could be himself. His comfort level was so obvious, she almost felt jealous.

The light changed. Traffic surged forward and they turned left. "The buildings are pretty much the way they were a century ago," Brody said while she craned her neck, taking in the small plaza with a gazebo.

The square was about the same size as Santa Fe's plaza. But there the comparison ended. Santa Fe's stores bustled, side streets shooting off in all directions. Taos looked contained. Quiet.

"This plaza was built to be defended," Brody said, pulling into one of the diagonal parking spaces. "They could barricade it if they had to, like a fort."

Feeling as if she'd stepped back in time, Carolyn got out and followed Brody onto the sidewalk that rimmed the plaza. "This town is a time capsule," she said. "I feel as if Gary Cooper or Clint Eastwood could walk out of a saloon any minute, guns in their holsters."

He chuckled. "I think you're right."

People relaxed on benches around the gazebo, enjoying the mild weather. One threw a frisbee for his dog to retrieve. Brody slung an arm around her shoulder. "Want to look around?"

"Sure. But I'm not much for shopping."

"A woman who doesn't like to shop? Didn't know there was such a thing." Pulling back in mock surprise, he kept his arm snug around her.

"You can wipe that smart-ass smile off your face," she said under her breath. Was he talking about past girlfriends?

He stopped. "What is it?"

"Nothing. Nothing." Carolyn kept walking. She didn't want him to think she was the jealous type. "A friend sent me enough clothes to last a while. I don't need to shop."

His eyes swept her with approval. "Is this outfit from your friend?"

"Yep."

"She has good taste. Leather is always good in the mountains."

"That's me. Wild West woman." Her mother would laugh to hear that.

Stopping, Brody peered through a store window. "Looks like the usual touristy stuff." But one store carried leather goods and they stepped inside. "Love the smell."

When he dropped his arm to enter the shop, she missed it. Ever since graduation, Carolyn had gotten used to traveling alone, visiting friends from school. Being part of a couple felt new to her. Different. Nice. Just for now.

She snuck a peek while Brody examined the jackets. Did this feel natural to him too? Checking out the purses and totes, she told herself not to read too much into this. That would be foolish. A few kisses and holding hands don't make a meaningful relationship. She followed him back out onto the square. In his boots and worn leather jacket, he belonged.

"What is it?" He turned to pin her with his piercing gaze.

"Nothing. Just enjoying the day." *Looking at you. Being with you. Feeling like a couple.* "Enjoying the day in a mountain town."

Her satisfaction must have been obvious. "You're so pleased with yourself."

"Today I am." She could drown in his eyes.

When Brody's tongue swept his upper lip, Carolyn wanted him so bad. Heat shimmered from the sidewalk. Maybe she would melt and become a puddle. He did this to her. And she cared for him, both the injured boy she'd taught and the strong man he'd become. But right now, the mindlessness of her feelings both unnerved and excited her.

"If we stand here much longer, we're going to make a scene," he muttered between set lips. "Want to go to the museum?"

"Yes. Sure." Why was going to a museum with Brody sexy? She wondered about it on the short drive up the highway.

"You're awfully quiet. Did I do something wrong?" Suddenly he was the teenager again. The guy who came to school with sleepers still in his eyes.

"Absolutely not. It's all good."

"Glad to hear it." His hand fell to her thigh and that felt good too.

Then his fingers found a rip in her jeans. She swatted at it.

"Cold?" he asked teasingly.

She shook her head. "Burning up."

"You should fix your jeans."

"You should mind your own business."

"Oh, I think I am." His look seared her. Taking his hand from her leg, she placed it firmly on the steering wheel while he laughed.

Brody had turned down a road, taking them off the highway. Around them, the area was flat and it felt as if the earth dropped away at the edges, except for the mountains soaring on their left. "The sky feels so big here," she said, ignoring her tumbling tummy.

"Are those the same mountains we see in Santa Fe?"

He gave them a jut of the chin. "Yep. The Sangre de Cristo mountains extend a long way. Pretty great, right?"

"Takes my breath away." She pressed one hand to her stomach.

Dust rose as they pulled into the parking lot. Turning off the car, Brody shifted to look at her, "Tell you what. *You* take my breath away." Those laser blue eyes, the color of a Taos sky, had turned Lake Michigan blue. Warm and welcoming. When he opened his arms, she leaned into them.

"These lips are becoming mighty familiar," she whispered after the third kiss or so. Not that she was counting.

"Glad to hear it." Cupping her chin in his hand, he smiled. "Let's go see the place."

Her knees felt wobbly when she climbed out.

Inside a receptionist greeted them. Of course there was a map, which Carolyn snapped up. "You've been here before?" she asked Brody.

"Yep, two or three times." They walked off to the right.

She hated the suspicion that crept over her.

Focus on the art.

She liked the way Brody worked through a museum. A little impatient herself, Carolyn would size up a room and spend time on things that caught her eye. Brody took the same approach. Sometimes they'd be shoulder to shoulder studying a Navajo pattern while Brody made comments. The boy was smart.

"You know a lot of stuff," she told him at one point.

"Stuff?"

"Good stuff." God, she loved that square jaw.

"What? Am I preaching?" He looked horrified.

"Not at all. It's just that, well, the shoe is really on the other foot, isn't it?"

He tugged her to him. No one else was in the room. "How does that shoe fit? Comfortable or not?"

Standing together like this felt like coming home. "Well, we just have to find that out." She could hardly breathe. His lips brushed hers. The tingling started. Casting a glance behind him, he nudged her against the wall.

"What if someone comes in?" she whispered, sinking into him.

"They'll have one more thing to talk about when they get home."

They pressed into a full body kiss. A few seconds later, she could hardly remember her own name. Placing one hand flat on his chest, she gently pushed him away. "We're going to shock the woman at the desk."

"I didn't see any surveillance screens."

"You're incorrigible."

He rolled his eyes. "There you go, using teacher words again."

"Well, you are."

"I think you like me that way."

What could she say? He was right. Approaching voices made her pull away. She straightened her jacket. Ran a hand over her hair. They moved on.

Silver jewelry gleamed in the next room. "What did you call these? There are so many of them." She motioned to a case heavy with necklaces, all variations of the same design.

"Squash blossom. Popular among Native Americans."

"They look like they might weigh a ton."

"Maybe you're too delicate for one. Maybe your neck is made for other things." But when he moved toward her, she scurried away. The voices still followed them.

Photos of Millicent Rogers stopped Carolyn short. A stylish blonde, the socialite looked very upscale. Maybe even snooty. Carolyn studied the photos. "She looks like a woman my mother would have lunch with."

Brody didn't look convinced. "A society girl? She looks a little like you, Carolyn."

Her heart contracted. "Do I look that aloof?"

"That's not what I meant. She's a beautiful blonde, just like you."

"You're delusional." But the words pleased her.

"You're too modest." The gallery was feeling too constrictive for her hammering heart. When she looked up at Brody, she forgot to breathe.

Breaking away before he could see desire radiating from her face, she stared at the next display. "Are these buttons?"

Bracing one arm over her head, he studied them. "Yep, pretty spectacular, right? The Indians didn't have much use for buttons until later. But apparently she had a quite a collection. All silver."

His body framed hers. She craved his heat in the worst way. And they were in a museum. Brody stroked her back absentmindedly, as if unaware that he was driving her crazy.

Would the exhibits ever end? The museum snaked back and forth until finally they were in a gift shop. Leaving the map there, they left. "You've taught me more about Indian culture than I ever knew before," she told him once they were back in the car.

"Native American," he said softly, shifting in his seat.

"Right. I'm trying to be politically correct."

"I know. Come here."

When he beckoned, she leaned in until his arms closed around her. Their kisses built to a new intensity. The more Brody revealed about himself, the closer she felt to him. A family came out of the museum, chattering away. Brody pulled away and started the engine.

"So. Hungry?" he asked, backing out of the spot.

"Starving." Her body howled for him, like the stuffed coyote they'd seen that day at the restaurant.

He lifted a brow. "Want to stop to get something to eat?"

"Food isn't what I have in mind." She was going to put that right out there.

Brody went into his sphinx mode, staring at the road ahead.

"Too bold?" That teetering feeling caught Carolyn off-balance again.

"There's no such thing, Teach. Not between us." His lips barely moved. The tension ran that high.

After conquering the height in Truchas, she wanted to throw herself off one more ledge, or pier. Whatever. Brody was that ledge. She wouldn't let herself worry about what came next.

She just wanted this. Now.

"My place?" He lifted a brow.

"Just what I had in mind."

They hardly spoke on the way back. "Is this a different highway?" she asked after awhile on the road. "We're not going through those small towns."

"We're taking the direct route."

"I like your thinking."

But she had to do more than lust on the way back. This trip had taught her a lot about herself. She was too controlling. Carolyn could see that now. A map and schedule person. Life wasn't like a day of classes, with time neatly divided for each subject. That approach hadn't served her well.

Here she was, thirty-two and single. Sure, she had a job she enjoyed. Teaching was fulfilling in a lot of ways. But she didn't want to be end up being sixty-five and single. An unclaimed treasure.

As they drove through the late afternoon, she could hardly keep her eyes off him. If a woman could feast on a man with her eyes, that's what she was doing. His Hotness. Bite by bite. "Hey, what's going on with you?" He caught her staring in the mirror.

"Nothing."

"We're about to change all that."

"Let's not overthink this."

"In the past week I've thought about it enough for both of us."

Chills had a heyday, scampering down her spine.

"What I'm thinking is purely instinct. Pure, raw instinct." He ran a hand down her thigh.

Her entire body hummed. "What's the speed limit here anyway?"

With a dry chuckle, he hammered down on the accelerator.

~.~

Gravel crunched beneath the tires when Brody pulled in front of his house. The drive had felt eternal, like taking his architecture finals. Beside him, he'd felt Carolyn's restlessness. He sure hoped that was excitement and not signs that she was having second thoughts. Why the hell had he suggested Taos today?

But who knows when a few kisses will turn to gut-wrenching need?

Jumping out of the SUV, he almost lost his footing. Not that he was in a hurry or anything. Carolyn wobbled unsteadily outside the passenger door. Her chest was heaving.

"Ready?"

Her long, steady look did nothing to calm him. Then she gave his shoulder a shy push. "Onward, cowboy."

Good God. Taking her elbow, he steered her to the door, jammed his key in the lock and shoved it open. Inside, he tossed his keys onto the side table and turned. Where to start? "Why do girls always wear so many clothes?"

"Always?" The look on her face froze the blood in his veins. "As in I've had so many women back here I've lost count?"

"That's n-not the way it was. Is." Hell, he could blow this whole thing right here. His heart hammered in his chest. No way did he want her to see him as a player. "Trust me, okay?"

The concern sharpening her high cheekbones eased. "Oh, Brody." With a sweet sigh, she fell against him, all warm curves and soft skin. Her arms encircled his neck. The jackets had to go. He hung them up on the floor. As he ran his hands up under the blouse, the feel of her skin almost undid him. When he tried to whisk the top up and off, he caught it on the gazillion chains around her neck. "I'm no good at this." He raised his hands, palms up.

"Oh, I think you are," she said with a slow, secret smile. One minute later, the necklaces were laid out on the coffee table. He helped her off with her boots and kicked off his own with a few hot kisses along the way. They unwrapped each other like Christmas packages. She was more exquisite, more delicately defined than he'd ever imagined.

"Do you know how many times I undressed you while I sat in class?"

"No way. You did?" She crossed her arms over her chest.

"Hey, I did it with respect, okay? I was just a boy back then."

"And now?" she whispered. Dropping her arms, she reached out to graze the angles of his body. Carolyn was driving him nuts.

"And now you'll see." Before his knees could buckle, he swept her up.

"Brody?" She gave a faint squeak.

"No more talking."

She was a woman of many words so that was a tall order. Hands cupping his face, Carolyn used her lips. He almost dropped her on the way to the master suite.

Up in his room, he laid her on the bed. Her eyes shifted to the mountains. The setting sun touched only the peaks. "Oh, my. How beautiful."

God, she looked like an angel. "Yes, you are."

She rolled toward him. "Brody, come." Her arms beckoned.

Chapter 17

Carolyn crept into the kitchen, the cold tiles curling her bare toes. In sleep pants and a hoodie, she needed caffeine bad. What time had she gotten in last night? Or had it been early morning? With any luck, Mama V would be at the gallery.

But her grandmother sat at the table, sipping coffee and throwing her a coy smile. "Good morning, sweetheart. Late night?"

"Kind of." Taking a mug from the cupboard, Carolyn grabbed the pot and filled her cup.

Mama V's shoulders shook. Was she laughing? "Brody's a nice young man," she finally managed to say between the giggles. "I like him."

"Me too." *Like him?* Last night had been amazing. Curling up on the hard kitchen chair, Carolyn longed for his big warm bed...and the man in it. He'd begged her to stay but she'd said no. Not this time.

"So I guess that smile means you had a good time. The museum was good?"

"The museum?" Carolyn tore her mind from broad shoulders, strong calves and everything in between. "Right. The museum. Lots of silver."

She'd never heard her grandmother snort through her nose before. Then Mama V cleared her throat and adjusted her pleased smile. "Yes, the museum does have lots of silver. Did you have dinner in Taos?"

"No, no. We, ah, came back."

Right. She came and came. Carolyn fought a silly smile. When she bit down on her lower lip, it yelped in protest. She'd never had sore lips before. Time to focus. Consider certain realities.

"But I'm only here for one more week." Even she heard the desperation in her voice. What was she doing?

Mama V set the newspaper aside. "Let me tell you, a good man is hard to find, Carolyn. And life? Well, you've got to live it as it comes. Grab it."

Her grandmother had given her tons of advice when Carolyn was growing up. When she lost the regional spelling bee in fifth grade, Mama V had reminded her that at least she'd made it to the finals and how great was that? When her hair turned out terrible for prom, Mama V came up with the idea of tucking blue violets in the wavy mess. She knew her way around any problem.

"But how do you know, Mama V? How can you know the person you're with today will be the same in ten, twenty years?"

Mama V's smile faded. "You're thinking of your father."

"Yes." Carolyn couldn't turn from the pain in her grandmother's eyes.

"Those years must have been so hard for you."

If Carolyn answered that question, she might start to cry.

Picking up a spoon, Mama V stirred more sugar into her coffee.

"Your dad was, is a good man. For a while he forgot the vows he'd taken. Thank God he came to his senses before he lost you both."

Carolyn had been so little then. "The silence was the worst. Sometimes they didn't talk for weeks"

"I know. It could be painful to be with them sometimes. They might have kept their marriage together for you, and then they came around."

The memories came spinning back. "We'd be out for dinner and a woman might brush past our table. A look would be exchanged. My mother's face would flush. When we got home, I was put to bed. They closed their door, but I could hear the raised voices."

"It's not always like that, Carolyn. Think of your grandfather and me. Many couples are happy. I'm afraid that your father acted on what he saw in his own family. Your grandfather and I should have recognized that weakness. But I doubt that we could have swayed your mother. She was obsessed with him. Loved him almost too much."

"She still does." Her mother's face lit up when Daddy walked into the room. And now, he looked only at her. But Carolyn didn't ever want to think about the past. Once had been enough.

Now Carolyn got up and circled the table to give her grandmother a tight hug. "Where would I be without you?"

"Well, you wouldn't be here in Santa Fe. That's for darn sure."

"No, I wouldn't." Carolyn took her seat again. Her imagination got to work. "Mama V, if you hadn't been brave enough to move out here, I'd be in Gull Harbor right now. Reading a book during my spring break. All my friends would be working." How bleak.

"But you're here, darling." Her grandmother tapped one manicured nail on the table. "And there's a reason why you're here. I truly believe that. Make the most of it."

"But what am I doing?" Her practicality was yanking the reins on her galloping heart. She had to protect herself. "Not only do we live in different states, Brody was a boy who went from girl to girl in high school. They probably sobbed their hearts out when he moved on."

Her grandmother frowned. "Not unusual for a teen-age boy, I would think. But he's a man now. And he's crazy about you. You'd have to be blind not to see that."

"Really, you think so?" Images from last night flashed through her head. Brody's eyes. His hands. His lips. His reassurance as she stood on that precipice. She glanced up to find Mama V laughing. "What?"

Wiping a tear from her eye, her grandmother said, "Nothing. Only I'm sure you feel the same about him. What woman could resist a man with that kind of charm?" She smiled as if she knew just how that felt.

"Is this how you felt with Grandpa?"

"Oh, yes. Definitely." But she seemed distant, detached.

Holy cripes. "And Howard. Howard too?"

Her shoulders lifted in a helpless gesture that almost had Carolyn rolling on the floor. "Trust me. Howard too," Mama V said. "Love can be just as crazy when you're older. But you have to open your heart. You have to let it in."

"Well, I am. I did." She couldn't even talk this morning. Her words got twisted. Love wasn't simple.

Her grandmother shook her head sadly. "There are no guarantees, sweetheart. Just choose wisely. Brody seems like a fine man. Time will tell, so why not give him that time."

What could she say? Carolyn regretted pulling her grandmother into a painful past.

But the perky smile returned. "Will you do me a favor, Carolyn? Enjoy this week, every minute of it. Think of it as a gift. Get to know Brody better. Have fun. You owe that to yourself."

"But Mama V, I came to see *you*. We should spend more time together while I'm here."

"No shoulds," her grandmother said with a stern shake of her head. "Don't worry about me. I'll be, well, busy."

TMI. But Carolyn felt relieved. "So am I cramping your style?"

Getting up to pop another English muffin in the toaster oven, her grandmother chuckled. "We'll just work around it. To be honest, I didn't realize how much time Howard and I had been spending together until you arrived. This is a learning experience for me too."

"Who'd have thought it?" Carolyn slid her coffee mug into the microwave to reheat it.

With her grandmother's advice in mind, she threw herself into the week ahead. Six glorious days. Laughing, she shared Mama V's words of wisdom with Brody.

"Smart woman." He grinned at her over his blue corn enchilada. They were having lunch at Tia Sophia's, their knees touching under the narrow table.

Like a couple, a small voice whispered inside. She shivered.

"What? What is it?"

"Nothing." She dropped her eyes to her chile rellenos. No restaurant came close to this in Michigan. "Gosh, I'm going to miss all this good food."

Brody made a choking sound.

"Hey, you okay?" *How did the Heimlich maneuver go?*

Then he swallowed. "All better. You're going to miss the *food*."

"I'm teasing." She nudged his knee with her own.

Her heart belonged to him now. The thought made her both happy and sad.

"What's up?" Reaching out, he played with her fingers. "What are you thinking about?"

With that shock of dark hair and those piercing blue eyes, what else could she think about? "You're too handsome for your own good. I'll always think of you like this."

His eyes clouded. "Why do I feel like you're sticking a note in a bottle, all set to toss it into Lake Michigan and say 'Bye, Bye, Brody.'"

He'd nailed it. "What a metaphor. Don't be silly."

"You're the one being silly. And it wasn't a metaphor. It was a statement. I think. Right?" He blinked, looking boyish and adorable. His lashes rivaled her own. She flushed, remembering how those lashes felt on her skin.

He leaned closer. "Maybe we should talk about the future."

"Why?" The last thing she wanted were promises he may not

keep.

"*Why?*" His chair creaked when he jerked forward. "Why not?"

The mood had changed. People were staring and she pushed her plate aside. The intensity in his eyes could be disturbing. "It's so nice today. Let's take a walk."

Brody sat back silently, and she felt disappointed that he gave up this easily.

The complications of their relationship loomed in her mind, like sand that slowly gathers width and height until it forms a dune. And this one was Mount Baldy gigantic. She used to watch kids scale that huge dune and wondered how they did it.

Once they were back outside, her fears eased. Later. They'd talk later. They strolled onto the square, following one of the diagonal paths. Casually dressed musicians played Beethoven beautifully. That was the amazing thing about Santa Fe. The effortless beauty. Drifting over to Palace of the Governors, they took another walk down the row of colorful blankets, waving to the gap-toothed man who'd made her earrings. He smiled when he saw them glinting in the sunlight.

"I'm taking up so much of your time," she told Brody when they wandered down a side street that led from the plaza. "Doesn't your work need you?"

"Don't worry about it, okay?" Brody backed her against a warm adobe wall. "I hire good people. They'll call if they hit a snag."

Glancing right and left, he smiled that reckless, crooked smile before kissing her senseless. Was he generating the heat or was it the sun on the adobe? The kiss was all lips, tongue and heat. A couple turned the corner. He backed off, took her hand and they moved on. It took a while to dial down the heat holding her body hostage.

As they wandered around the city, Brody pointed out places of interest. "Have you ever visited the Loretto Chapel?" He paused in front of a magnificent church, small in scale but beautiful.

"Nope. Never got to it."

"Come on." They went inside and he bought tickets for the tour.

Before she knew it, they were entering the empty church with a small group. Incense hung in the air and she sneezed. The Gothic arches and marble altar took her to a different time.

"Will you just look at those stained glass windows?" she whispered.

Speaking in an undertone, Brody threw out terms like *Gothic Revival, buttresses* and *helix-shaped staircase*. "How am I doing, Teach?" he paused to ask.

"I'm impressed."

Sunlight filtered through the stained glass windows, falling on the statues and gilded carvings. Their tour guide explained the magical legend surrounding the gravity-defying spiral staircase. A carpenter had appeared from nowhere. After the work was completed, he left just as mysteriously.

"And the people believe a miracle took place," the tour guide told them. "Right here."

"Can people be married in this chapel?" asked a young woman, clinging to her companion's arm.

The tour guide nodded. "We have weddings here at least once a week. From small intimate gatherings to a full house."

Okay, didn't need to know that. Carolyn shut her eyes, trying to block a mental image of Diana, Phoebe and the rest of the book group walking down this aisle in front of her.

"So it's that bad, huh?"

Her eyes fluttered open. Brody was staring at her. His expression was unreadable but the pulse jumped in his throat.

"What are you talking about?" Her voice rang hollow and he knew it.

"Time to leave."

And he was out of there. Horrified, she trailed behind him. Had the talk of a wedding spooked him? No way did she want him to feel pressured.

Next to the church, metal sculptures spun and creaked in the breeze. Brody barreled in among them. She was afraid he was going to knock one over. But that commotion was nothing compared to the fury in his eyes.

She had to make this clear. "Brody, really. I'm not picturing marriage. I loved the church, that's all."

Eyes blazing and lips twitching, he looked ready to rip her a new one. "Fine," he finally said. "Come on, let's get out of here." His head pivoted as if he were looking for an escape hatch. "Want to go back up to Museum Hill?"

"Not really."

She wanted *him*. Couldn't he see that? "Come on. Don't be so mad." She laced her fingers through his, although she had to pry them apart. "I'm sorry. I didn't mean anything."

Her wheedling apparently got to him. Reaching out, he played with her feather earring. "You're impossible."

She turned her cheek into his hand and kissed the palm. "So are you." A light flicked on in his eyes. The fun had returned.

"Come on. I'll race you back." And she was off, with him speeding behind her. She got to the SUV first but he pulled her into his arms. That kiss was medicine for both of them. "I don't ever want to fight with you," she murmured, tracing his lip line with a finger.

"That might be impossible." He tossed his head back. "Because you really make me mad. You have that power."

"Power?" *Really?*

He seemed to be considering that himself. "Scary, huh?"

Brody clicked the car doors open. Laughing, they hurled themselves onto seats warm from the sun. Thank goodness the drive to his house was short. The SUV almost took the gates off when they didn't swing open fast enough. Once in the courtyard, Brody parked under a huge aspen. Coming around, he yanked open the door and pulled her laughing toward the house. "I love it when you're like this, Teach."

Love. She bit it back.

Cripes, she'd almost said, "I love you, Brody."

Love and marriage. She'd really scare him off. Her laughter died. She'd scare herself too. This felt too early, too soon.

He must have seen something in her face. "What?"

"Nothing. You know what I want?" She whispered some

suggestions in his ear. His body jerked. The words had the effect of a cattle prod. This wasn't like her and he knew it. Heck, her own face was burning.

After fumbling with the lock, he pulled her inside. His kiss burned through to her backbone. She trembled while he undressed her. Then it was her turn to peel off the jacket, fumble with the buttons on his shirt, make her way down to his belt.

And all the time, he urged her on. "That's it, Teach. Be thorough. Let's dot the i's and cross the t's. What would a good metaphor be for this?"

"Peeling an onion," she supplied, kissing his chest.

"Ah, hah. You want to taste the onion too?"

"Right." She slid his belt from his jeans. "Your turn. Metaphor, please."

"Not now." He threw back his head.

"Yes, now." She was easing the zipper down, one metal tooth at a time. Then she stopped. "Let's hear it or else."

"Gee you're bossy, Teach." He was so cute when he got frustrated. And she was giving him a lot to think about. "Volcano! Eruption! Hell, I don't know."

"That's it. That's my A student."

Sweeping her up, he made tracks down the hall. "No more lessons."

That night when they made love, Brody was hot and sweet at the same time. She soaked up each comment and savored every word, pressing them into her memory like a prom bouquet.

But still, she would not stay the night. And she couldn't explain why.

Staying over felt like a forever thing. And they weren't at forever.

~.~

How would they spend these last days? Her mind shifted through touristy options when Carolyn lay in her bed later that night. No use trying to sleep. Then it came to her. Ten Thousand Waves. When she'd visited the spa with Mama V, she'd thought how fantastic it would be with a special someone.

One problem solved, she could finally get to sleep. The following morning, she picked up the phone. Ten Thousand Waves had an opening on Wednesday. "I have a surprise for tomorrow," she told Brody when he picked her up for lunch. "Mark your calendar. I've planned something special." She playfully put on X on his chest with her finger.

"Planning for us?" The corners of his lips tipped into a smile. "That's so sweet. I don't know what to say."

"And that's unusual."

"Are you getting sassy with me?" Eyes flashing, he pulled her into his arms.

"I think you're a boy who likes sass," she whispered.

"And I think you got that right."

Good thing Mama V was at the gallery. The kiss turned X-rated and involved some quality time on the couch. Finally, they left for lunch on the square.

"I'm taking Brody to Ten Thousand Waves," she told her grandmother when they both got back that afternoon. Although

Carolyn had wanted to take her grandmother out for dinner, she wouldn't have it. "You spend every minute you can with that man. You and I will have plenty of time for visiting. After all, there's always Skype."

"What do you know about Skype?"

"Wendy showed me how to use it. Brody will like Ten Thousand Waves. What man wouldn't? And so romantic." Her grandmother's knowing smile said it all.

But as she packed her things for that night, Carolyn hesitated. This was big. They would spend the night together. So much was at stake. She felt it in her tumbling stomach. But her hand moved higher to her heart. Yeah, right. She felt it there too. In fact, that's where she felt it most.

Where it could really hurt.

The sleeper shirt she was packing slipped from her hands to the floor.

Then Diana's encouragement came back to her. *Jump off that pier.* Maybe love was like that. Maybe it always involved risk. Diana had taken a huge chance with Will. She was plenty wounded at the time they met. Still, she got herself out there. Picking up the sleep shirt, she folded it, wishing Diana had sent her some sexy lingerie.

Carolyn had no time to shop. Besides, she wouldn't have it on long.

Chapter 18

The road to the lodge had been steep. Carolyn practiced deep breathing all the way. To her amazement, Brody caught her rhythm with his own inhaling and exhaling. That touched her heart more than she'd ever admit. Instead of clutching the door handle, her hands relaxed in her lap. The only distraction was Brody's broad chest expanding and contracting. Who needs roses or wine when your guy can deep breathe with you?

Her guy? Was he?

"What?" Brody asked when he caught her looking.

A giggle bubbled from her throat. "Nothing. You're just so cute when you do that."

"*Cute?*" His horrified expression made her laugh more.

"The breathing. Hey, you're helping me. I appreciate that." He'd probably be great at Lamaze. *Where had that come from?*

"What's up? You stopped breathing." He was so darn watchful.

"Nothing." She went back to breathing. Lamaze? Really?

The sign for Ten Thousand Waves came up and they took the turn. She felt a little nervous about his reaction. What if he didn't like it? They pulled into a parking place, and Brody leapt from the SUV. Watching the pines quiver in the mountain breeze, she wondered if this was a terrible idea. Was she pushing things?

When Brody opened the door and extended a hand, she took it and stepped out in her super cool boots.

Bending, he peered into her eyes. "Hey, what's up?" The man was too damned observant.

"What if you don't like this place?"

"Don't be silly. If you planned it, I'll like it." Folding his strong arms around her, Brody held her tight. She felt the beat of his heart. When he tilted her chin up, she smiled.

"Come on now, Teach. We'll have a good time."

"You can give them a grade for massage."

"Done. And you can grade me on what happens after the massage. I'm counting on this to be a major turn-on." His kiss soothed her.

Brody Wolf felt like her life's destination. She felt that soul-deep. Sliding her arms around his waist, she exhaled. Didn't get much better. Everything felt so right. But she wanted him to feel that too.

All the time she'd been teaching in Gull Harbor, had her former student grown into her soulmate? The one man who could make her feel alive? He might be a late bloomer, but he had matured. No more girls hanging around his locker. At least, she sure hoped so.

Hand in hand, they took the stone path and registered. Up here, the air smelled so clean, so fresh with the tang of pine. Then they followed the walkway to their room, and Brody carried their overnight bags inside. Their massage appointment was at one thirty so they skipped lunch for now. Instead of eating, they decided to try out the two soaking tubs that faced the hillside, so private and perfect.

"Kind of like the old outdoor hot tubs," he said with a lazy smile.

"But there aren't any spouts or jets. Just deep water. They're soaking tubs. Even my grandmother likes these."

"Well, Mama V is a happening chick. More older women should be like her." Hands on hips, he studied the two tubs. "Wouldn't one have been enough?"

"You don't like them?"

"Sure. They fascinate me."

"Liar." Although she was trying to connect with her inner vixen, Carolyn was having a hard time. Coming here with her grandmother was one thing. Bringing Brody was something else entirely.

"Why don't you use the bathroom to change, and I'll just slip into the pool?" His blue eyes circled from the tubs to her and back again. Like he was measuring the distance. Where had the raucous troublemaker from high school learned this sensitivity? Vixen or not, she wasn't comfortable parading out here in the nude or only in a towel. And he got that.

"Thanks. I like that idea."

After they'd stowed their few things in the drawers, she slipped into the bathroom to change. No bathing suits today. Now a fluffy white robe teased her skin. Every pore of her body felt super sensitive. Checking herself in the mirror, she pinned her hair on top of her head. "Show time, Miss Knight." And she smiled with appreciation at the woman she'd become this past week.

When she stepped out onto the tile floor, she cinched the robe tighter. Brody was already lounging in his tub, his muscled back to her, arms resting on the porcelain edge.

She tiptoed across the stone patio. "Don't turn around."

"I'll count to ten. One, two..."

Tossing her robe on the bench, she plopped into the tub so fast, the water lapped over. When he rocked his head back, his lazy smile promised mischief. "Pretty great, right?"

"More than great. And we get to soak for an hour before our massage."

"Right. Okay." Twisting, he crossed his arms on the lip of the tub, resting his chin on them like a little boy. But the glint in his eyes was anything but boyish. "Unless we can find something else to do. These two tubs are ridiculous."

While she laughed, Brody climbed from the tub in a heartbeat. Dear lord. He was an eyeful. Head lowered like he was up to no good, he came closer. Droplets dotted the floor. Her breath caught in her throat.

When he slid in behind her, water sloshed everywhere. His arms came around her. How she loved the slide of his skin on hers, the prickle of chest hair against her back. But when he began playing with her hair, she shook a warning finger. "Watch it. I don't want to have to dry it before our massage."

"Okay, Teach." He captured her finger and then claimed her lips. Clamped her closer until she could feel his need. Insane urges took control of her body and she went with the flow. Diana would approve. But this felt like so much more than the fling her friend had urged her to take.

"What?" He gently pushed her hair from her eyes. "Something wrong, babe?"

She shook her head, slowly tracing a wet heart on his chest. Probably annoying. Carolyn dropped her hand.

But Brody shifted restlessly. "Don't stop, Teach," he groaned.

This man could always make her smile. "You know how I feel about doodling."

"Right, but this isn't class, and I'm not school property. You're excused."

Yes, that was the Brody she knew…and loved.

"Just wondering. Maybe we're wasting time out here," she whispered as the hearts got bigger. He flinched when she nicked him with a fingernail. "After all, we have tonight for the tub."

"I like the way you think."

When she turned to face him, his eyes narrowed. "Maybe just a…"

"…quickie," she supplied.

"Yep, my thought exactly." After helping her out of the tub, he grabbed a towel from the bench.

"Let me dry you off." That spark in his eyes? Who needed a towel? He could burn the whole place down with one look.

"Your attention to detail is noteworthy," she whispered while he worked his way down her body, blotting and buffing

"Going to put that on my report card? 'Has skill with hands. Recommend shop class.' Maybe woodworking?" How he kept a straight face, she'd never know.

"Those comments are so grade school, Brody. High school teachers have conversations face-to-face on Parent-Teacher Night."

"Yeah, I remember. I was grounded for a month. Thanks."

By that time, he was working on her legs. "Sorry." Smiling, she tousled his hair.

"No, you're not."

Then she squeezed her eyes tight and grabbed his shoulders as he exhibited, well, even greater attention to detail.

"Okay, if there were comments on my report card, what would you have written? 'Brody needs to focus more?' "

"I think you've got that covered, mister."

Moments later, he proved it.

~.~

By the time the knock on the door came, they were both dried and wrapped in their robes. This Ten Thousand Waves idea had been great. Carolyn wasn't a woman who waited for the man to make the suggestions. Brody appreciated that.

Hell, he appreciated everything about her. But there was an invisible shield around her. Oh, she'd deny it. But Brody felt it. The distance she sometimes put between them made him crazy.

"Good afternoon, I'm Marcus, and this is Layla," the man said. Marcus had serious muscles. "We are here for your stone massages."

"And I will take Layla," Carolyn quickly said. Brody almost laughed. She wasn't comfortable with a man massaging her body.

Well, he didn't like that thought either. She would always have that prim and proper side. But in private, he knew firsthand it was a completely different story.

When the tables were set up, Brody and Carolyn stretched out on their stomachs, a towel covering their private parts. The tables were about a foot apart, wide enough so that Marcus and Layla could work and close enough that Brody could watch Carolyn. She shot him a shy smile. When he winked back, he enjoyed the telltale flush rolling over her features. When Layla began to lay the smooth back stones along her spine, Carolyn closed her eyes. Brody enjoyed watching her give herself up to the treatment.

Meanwhile, Marcus got busy. To his surprise, Brody found the hot rocks strangely erotic. The warmth eased into his core. This was pretty great and he needed it. Although he'd told Carolyn work was fine, the past week hadn't been easy, juggling his schedule.

But the time with her had been totally worth it.

This was it for him. Carolyn. Now and always. She was The One.

He'd never felt this certainty before. Brody sure as hell hoped she felt it too.

Thoroughly relaxed, they strolled into the restaurant later that evening. His legs felt like noodles. Once seated, he watched her study the menu. She had the habit of running one finger down the list, afraid she'd miss something. "What looks good to you?" she asked, looking so serious.

Resting his chin on one hand, he smiled. "You. You look good to me." She was a delight to watch.

Her eyelashes fluttered. How he'd loved getting her all flustered in high school. "How about you, Brody? What are you going to order?"

He dragged his eyes back to the Japanese listings. Raw fish was definitely not for him. "What is edamame?"

"Beans. Think big peas."

Ugh. "Do you have an answer for everything?"

She lifted those caramel eyes. "Nope, I don't."

Sometimes he could almost feel their thought transfer. Like now. They weren't talking about food anymore. "That's okay, Carolyn. We don't have to have the answer to everything. Not right now." That was all he could handle. Thinking of her leaving Sunday gave him heartburn.

After she'd asked the waiter a million questions, they ordered. Then they talked about everything and nothing. That's just how they rolled. Being with her was so easy.

"How's the steak?" she asked, after their meals arrived.

"Don't know yet. How do you work these chopsticks?"

"Practice. Like everything else." And she showed him. But his hands were too big and before long he traded the chopsticks for a fork. To his surprise, the meat was pretty tasty. "The steak's great. Can't pronounce it but I like it."

"Wagyu steak. It's tricky." Her nose wrinkled. She was wearing a greenish gauze blouse with holes in the shoulders showing just enough skin to pique his interest. And his interest didn't want to be sitting in a chair right now.

"How are your brussel sprouts?"

"Oh, yum." She speared one. What followed was the most sensual eating display he'd ever encountered. He nearly choked on his steak.

After her second attempt to lick a chopstick, he'd had it. "Please stop. You're making a scene."

"I'm just trying to be sexy." How could she say that and look so innocent?

"Okay. You've succeeded." Running a hand over his face, he groaned. "You're hopeless."

"I don't know what you mean."

Yeah. Right. He stared her down. "Yes, you do. Behave yourself."

Her face brightened. "Then my inner vixen's working?"

"Overtime. If you don't stop, we'll have to leave."

Ten minutes later, the waitress cleared the table and they ordered a different sake. He wasn't that interested in the plum wine but he needed time to set things straight.

"Carolyn, I don't think you're taking me seriously." There, it was on the table.

Her face drained of color. The muscle working in her delicate throat made him feel bad. But hell, he wanted this cleared up. "Look, here's the thing. We laugh and joke and."— he glanced around— "other things. But I love you, Carolyn."

Huge eyes stared at him from a face gone pale. "I love you too, Brody." Thank God their table was secluded.

The waitress approached with the sake. Sitting back, he waited until she left. The words still hung between them.

Brody pressed on. "So what? What's wrong between us? Sometimes I feel like you're just not here. Like I'm in this alone."

"That's my fault. It's just that…" She was choking on tears. So, he did really matter to her. But something was definitely not right.

"What? It's just what?"

A thin V appeared on her forehead. "For me this isn't a sake tasting, Brody." She waved a hand at the cups.

What the hell was she talking about? "I don't get it. Help me understand." Sometimes he thought they spoke different languages. "Is this another damn metaphor?"

When she nodded slowly, a single tear overflowed. "I guess." Damn. The tear ran slowly down her cheek. She made no move to blot it with her napkin. He was too dumbstruck to do anything.

"I'm not willing to be just another girl for two weeks." She was pressing her hands into her chest as if her heart might jump out at any time. He could feel an indentation in his own muscles.

"I'm not asking you to be just another girl, whatever that means. I'm asking you to give us a chance."

"Okay. All right." Then her face opened like one of the lilies that bobbed from pots in this place. "Because I do love you, Brody. I love you so bad."

When she closed her eyes tight, another tear squeezed out.

"Aw, Teach. You're killing me." He wanted to hold her. "Let's get out of here."

Chapter 19

Why did happy times fly by so fast? The rest of that week passed too quickly. Carolyn wanted to videotape it. Every second. Every kiss. Every word. When snow blanketed Michigan and the ice floes built up along the shore, she would have this week to remember. Where they were. What they did. Especially the times Brody told her that he loved her.

The L word traveled back and forth like the continuous loop of a love song. But they didn't talk about plans for the future. As much as she tried to let things unfold between them, Carolyn was a planner. She wanted to know their game plan. Maybe in Brody's mind they didn't have one.

When he came for dinner one night, Mama V cooked her famous pot roast with carrots in her slow cooker. With visible adoration, she watched Brody inhale the food. When he offered to help clean up, her grandmother threw her one of those *isn't he adorable* looks.

While the days counted down, Carolyn filled every moment with memories. But as she sat at the bar in El Farol with Brody that final Saturday night, it still wasn't enough. Musicians were setting up in the corner. Conversation flowed around her as she sipped a margarita. The two of them only paid attention to each other. God, how she loved him.

"Penny for your thoughts." He brushed her cheek with a finger.

"Nothing." She wouldn't whine, wouldn't beg.

So she waited.

Waited for "I'll come to visit you every month."

Or "I'm going to call you every night to say goodnight."

Facing quiet nights in Gull Harbor with crickets for company, she felt herself falling into a black abyss. Oh, she'd jumped off the pier all right, but right now she was floundering in the black waters below. Carolyn grabbed the edge of the bar and hung on.

"Sure you don't want anything to eat?"

She shook her head. "That would be a waste."

The band began a song that was bone-melting romantic. Leading her to the small dance floor, Brody took her in his arms as if he felt that way too. The lyrics sang about wanting someone's touch and finally finding it. Never wanting to let it go. She knew just how that felt. But until now, she hadn't known his name.

"I love you, Brody," she whispered, pressing her lips to his ear. "Love you so much it hurts."

"Oh, babe." His arms tightened around her. She felt his lips in her hair. Then he placed her right hand over his heart. "Feel that?"

She nodded. His heart throbbed under her fingers.

"Only beats for you."

Was this bliss or what? Carolyn wouldn't tell him the words were a cliché. For them, it was fresh and new. She tucked her head under his chin. How could she doubt his devotion? They'd work it out. This was real. She knew that in her bones.

The song ended. Reluctantly, they pulled apart. Brody threw some bills on the bar. "Let's get out of here."

But they never made it.

As they wound through the Saturday night crush, a girl separated herself from the crowd. Maybe she'd been there all along, watching them. Later, Carolyn wondered.

"Brody?" Gorgeous, she had long dark hair and a figure that turned every man's head. But her eyes sparkled only when they hit Brody.

"Hey, Justine." Turning, he smiled. "You look nice tonight."

Taking in the two of them, Carolyn just knew. Scenes from her childhood flashed through her mind. Her father had done it again. Hurt her mother with a careless fling. The walls closed in on her.

Familiarity thickened in the air. Gorgeous Girl stepped closer in her black stiletto boots. She ran red-tipped fingers up Brody's chest and slid an arm around his neck. "How've you been? Aren't you going to introduce us?"

A fireball of horror exploded inside Carolyn. Brody's expression shifted. His mouth opened and closed. Nothing.

Turning toward Carolyn, the stranger laughed, her voice flowing like dark molasses. "Hi, I'm Justine. Brody's last conquest. And you're...?"

"C-Carolyn." Her name was a whisper.

"My replacement, huh?" Pushing back her hair, she chuckled. "Woman of the week? Trust me, there's always next week."

"Stop it right there, Justine." Brody pushed away. Carolyn took off.

Veering around the two of them, she stumbled toward the door. Tears blinding her, she crashed into a man. He grabbed her elbows. "Hey, little girl. Slow down." Eyes bleary, he was having trouble standing. She slapped his hands away.

"F-Feisty." Swaying, he could hardly get the word out. "I like that."

"Get your hands off her." Brody's voice cut through the confusion. The man's attention faltered and she wrenched free. Shouts broke out behind her as she escaped, only this time it wasn't a food fight in the cafeteria.

Great. Just great. Grown men brawling.

Carolyn couldn't get out of there fast enough. Finally, she reached the door. The night had turned cold and she pulled her jacket tight. Thank goodness her grandmother's house was just down the road. Scurrying down Canyon Road in the darkness, she slipped twice but kept going. When Brody called her name in the distance, she picked up speed.

Justine? He'd never mentioned her. She wasn't a woman to be forgotten. The realization made everything so clear. No way could this thing with Brody be a long distance relationship.

He hadn't changed. There would always be other women.

And she'd been ready to throw away everything for him. In these last days, she pictured herself living here, close to the grandmother she adored. She loved this city, and the man who'd found himself here. Certainly Santa Fe needed teachers. What a dreamer. How foolish.

Now her thoughts mocked her. She kept running.

When she got to the casita, she missed a step and nearly fell. Taking out a key, she fumbled with the lock. Mama V was out with Howard, thank goodness. Inside, the house was quiet. A cold moon cloaked the room in blue shadows. Ripping off the suede jacket, she stumbled against the coffee table, cracked her shin and fell.

Somewhere along the way, her heart had broken.

Oh, Brody rang the bell again and again. Pounded on the door. She stayed huddled on the floor, arms locked around her throbbing leg. When he finally gave up and things were quiet again, she dragged herself down the hall, slipped out of her clothes and into bed.

"Let him explain," Mama V said to her the next morning after Carolyn had hiccupped through the whole sad story of the night before.

"Trusting Brody was a mistake. I should have known." She couldn't eat and her hands were jittery after two cups of coffee.

Alarm pinched her grandmother's features. "Sweetheart, how can you be so certain? Of course he's dated other people."

"That's the problem." She could still see Justine standing there. The self-assured woman was everything she was not. "Old lovers have a way of surfacing. Remember Daddy? Some men are just like this. I don't want it."

Brody may have sweet-talked her grandmother, but Carolyn wasn't having it. She'd seen what he was like in high school. Maybe she'd been too eager to believe he'd changed. Howard offered to drive her to the airport. Certainly not her first choice but her only option. Alan was mentioned but she quickly vetoed that idea.

Rushing around with final packing, she felt miserable. "Can we have this conversation later?" she asked her grandmother. Mama V nodded, her eyes sad.

Howard pulled up in plenty of time to get to the Albuquerque airport. Meanwhile, Brody blew up her phone with calls and texts. He wanted to take her to the airport so they could talk. *No way.* After texting him that she had a ride, she turned the phone off. Exchanging looks with Mama V, Howard took Carolyn's suitcase out to his car.

"Talk to you soon." She hugged her grandmother tight. Coming back to Santa Fe would always be painful now. How she hated that.

"Oh, I feel terrible about this."

"It's not your fault." Carolyn kissed her cheek. "I'll call you."

She left Mama V wringing her hands in front of the casita. Howard's tasteful, and no doubt expensive cologne, permeated the black Mercedes. Carolyn would probably reek of it for a week to come.

Numb with pain, she wished she could have it out with Brody. Throw a few vases and pound on his chest. But that wasn't her way. She felt stupid for letting this happen. Stupid and blinded by His Hotness. He was Brody Wolf. What had she been thinking?

Soon she'd be able to talk to Diana or Phoebe. More experienced than she was, they'd help her deal with this pain.

"I'm glad I have some time alone with you," Howard said when they were about halfway to the airport.

The poor guy. She hadn't said a word since they left Santa Fe. "Sorry, Howard. Guess I'm not very good company today."

He cleared his throat once. Twice. "I wanted to discuss something with you."

She shot him a wary glance. His hands wrung the steering wheel. This didn't look good. "About what, Howard?"

"Your grandmother." His forehead glistened with perspiration.

"Of course." Uneasiness spider-stepped down her spine.

"Did your grandmother tell you how we met?"

"No, I don't think she did."

Howard licked his lips. "We met in rehab. I'd just had a quintuple bypass and your grandmother, of course, was there for her hip."

Carolyn had no idea what a quintuple whatever was.

Howard continued. "We were both in a bad way. Neither one of us wanted to be there. I'd lost my wife two years ago and, frankly, things had been downhill since then. Of course, your grandmother still missed her husband."

Why had Mama V never told her this? Or had Carolyn been too busy with her own world to ask?

"One thing was clear to me. We were both survivors." They'd reached the outskirts of Albuquerque. "Some patients would drop out of rehab after one or two sessions. They'd give up. That could have been me, except for Vera. She came in like clockwork. In fact, I switched my schedule to be there at the same time. Your grandmother would never admit it, but she was having a hard time. So was I. Rehab wasn't easy. Still, we did it."

Her heart twisted. Every time she'd called, Mama V had assured Carolyn she was doing well. Rehabilitation was "a breeze."

"We'd cheer each other on. Crack jokes." He threw her a slightly embarrassed smile. "What do they say? The rest is history?"

"Howard, I had no idea."

"We saved each other, Carolyn. Sometimes I needed a good kick in the behind. And she needed me too."

She struggled to get her mind around this. "But Mama V always said everything was fine."

"She didn't want you to know." He hurried on, checking the highway signs for the exit. "Anyway. I love your grandmother like I was eighteen again. This might sound weird but I felt I should come to you..."

Her stomach sank. So her grandmother *was* sick. And of course, she wouldn't want Carolyn to worry. "Tell me."

Howard was struggling. "I'd like to ask for her hand in marriage."

"W-What?" If he had offered to fly Carolyn home on a magic carpet, she couldn't have been more stunned.

"I want to marry your grandmother. Marriage calls for certain formalities. I want to do right by her. You're the closest one in her family." While he took the exit ramp, she began to laugh. What a relief.

Howard looked stricken. "It's not funny, Carolyn."

"No, it's definitely not, Howard. I'm sorry. I'm so relieved." Just because her own life was a disaster, she didn't have to project chaos onto everyone else. "Do you know how my grandmother feels about this?"

Traffic became more congested. Howard edged into the lane marked Departures. "No, but I'll soon find out. That is, if you're okay with this?"

"Of course I am. I'm touched that you've asked. But I have no idea if she wants to marry again."

"We're pretty close, Carolyn, your grandmother and me. Oh, she keeps her secrets. Sure, she's older than I am, but I never let on that I know. And she has to do something about her hearing, although she tries to hide it. I'll deal with that." And he chuckled. "All the important pieces are there. We love each other, and we can work out any differences."

"I don't feel it's my place to grant permission, but it's sweet of you to ask."

She smiled to herself. Howard was definitely the man for the job. Her grandmother would probably need a sling for her left arm if she said yes. The engagement ring would be huge.

"Would you like me to take you to your gate?" The poor guy looked so relieved. "It would just take me a minute to park. I could help with your luggage?"

Not too long ago, she'd thought this man was insufferable. But he was really very sweet. "No. Definitely not." She'd misjudged him.

Disturbing thoughts washed over her. She'd been wrong about Howard. Was she also wrong about Brody?

"So then, you think..."

She'd gotten out of the car and so did Howard. They looked at each other over the roof of the gleaming black Mercedes. He looked uncertain.

"Go for it, Howard. You make my grandmother happy. I'll handle my mother."

"Oh, thank you." A handkerchief had appeared from somewhere, and Howard blotted his brow.

The dry wind must have blown something into her eye. Blinking furiously, she moved to the back of the car. "Now if you could just pop the trunk."

"Of course, Carolyn. And I hope things work out for you." Hauling her bag out, Howard said, "You know, Alan thinks the world of you."

Oh, great. So Alan was her plan B? She choked. One Haynes was more than enough in their family. "Thank you for the ride, Howard."

Shoulders straightening, he smoothed his navy sport coat. "It was nice getting to know you, Carolyn. I hope you'll come back soon." When he tried to shake her hand, she drew him into a quick hug. Howard wasn't her idea of a hero, but he was for Mama V. That was enough for her.

One quick wave and she swept through the huge glass doors. Her bag bulged with the clothes Diana had sent, and she made tracks for the check-in. The airport was filled with the excited chatter of happy passengers. She wasn't one of them. No, she was lugging a broken heart heavier than a steamer trunk. When she was halfway to the counter, a tall guy peeled himself from the wall. The broad set of his shoulders sent her heart plummeting. *Oh, please*

God, no. Brody.

Her eyes slid to the counter and back to his advancing figure, His Hotness in jeans and that Stetson. Well, she couldn't outrun him and scenes weren't her thing. Stepping aside, she let an older couple go ahead of her.

"Why aren't you picking up your phone?" He stood there, unshaven with reddened eyes but still heartbreakingly handsome.

This was where she'd run into him, and this was where they'd say goodbye. She'd always liked symmetry. But this moment was the denouement, not that Brody even knew what that was. This was the part of the book where things settle, the falling action. Ignoring the anxiety in her chest at the very thought of anything falling, she straightened.

"Nothing to say." She shifted in the boots that had worn a blister on her heel.

"You never asked about my past. I would have told you."

"That isn't it." But it really was. She threw her head back. "I was foolish to think you'd changed. Why would I want to hear about all the hearts you've broken? I'll never join that club. Do they meet at El Farol every Saturday night? Maybe play pool together in a back room?" Her words spilled out, rushed and cruel. She stopped.

His face paled. "That's not fair and you know it."

She dropped her head. Soon tears patterned her leather boots.

"Please, Carolyn. I love you."

Dashing shaking fingers under each eye, she wanted the floor to swallow her. "Right. Look, I have to check in or I'll miss my plane.

Just walk out that door, Brody Wolf, because I never want to see you or hear from you again. Ever."

Brody gave her a steady look, took her wrist and pulled her to the side. People passing threw them curious looks. "That might work with students, Carolyn. But not with me. I'm more than that."

"Are you?" She couldn't even look at him. Her nose was running too. Perfect. "Now stay. I have to leave."

"You haven't heard the last of me."

"Don't follow me, please. This is The End, in capital letters." She wrenched her wrist free. Looking down at her boots, she watched more tears spot the leather.

"You and I are not in a book, Carolyn." He bit off the words like that chewing tobacco guys seemed to like out here. "This is real life and I love you."

Turning, she walked away and he stayed put, damn him.

Of course, her luggage was now over the weight limit. The final straw. All those wonderful clothes and for what? The clerk threw out a horrifying figure, and Carolyn handed over her credit card. Pocketing her boarding pass, she dashed into the ladies room. The mirror told her she needed sunglasses. After rebraiding her hair so tight that she felt her eyes lift, she jammed sunglasses on her nose. Then she shouldered her tote and moved on.

Kicking off her boots at TSA, she placed them on the conveyor belt along with her tote. Pain pierced her like a meat hook. After picking up a small packet of tissue for the ride home, she plunked down in the waiting area. Across the way, a teenager was eating popcorn and the smell made her sick. Carolyn swore off popcorn for the rest of her life.

In the waiting area and on the return flight, people looked at her curiously. Who was the woman wearing the sunglasses inside? Someone famous?

No, someone stupid.

~.~

Thank goodness, school began again the next day. Because of the unexpected week off, there was so much to cover. Teachers and students struggled with the accelerated schedule. Carolyn welcomed it. Posters went up about prom. The thought of watching happy kids dance turned her stomach. When asked if she could chaperone, she put Glenn off. "I may have to go back to Santa Fe to check on my grandmother."

"Of course." Her principal had smiled with understanding.

Had Howard proposed? When would the happy announcement come? In the end, Carolyn decided not to alert her mother. There would be questions, and Carolyn just wasn't in the mood.

When Diana appeared at her door one night, she thought her friend had come for a recap. "Got a minute, stranger?" Beautiful Diana bustled in, her diamond engagement glittering on her left hand.

"Tea?" Carolyn asked, already heading into the kitchen area. These bungalows were so small. Former rentals, the one long main room ran from the living room to the kitchen, all visible from the front door. The T was completed by two bedrooms on either side. Filling two mugs with tea, she nuked the first one.

Diana slipped onto the stool. "We got some bad news today, Carolyn."

Something in her friend's voice made Carolyn turn. "Is this about Will?"

"No, it's Sarah." Tears brimmed in Diana's eyes.

A cold fist squeezed Carolyn's heart. "Her husband Jamie?"

"Right. Serving in Afghanistan." Carolyn and Diana had never met Sarah's husband. But a picture of Jamie in his uniform was taped to the register in the bakery. Any time they stopped for coffee, he was there.

"Jamie's not coming home."

"What? He decided to leave her?" After the past two weeks, abandonment was her first thought.

"I wish it were only that." Diana's face crumpled. "He stepped on a land mine." The painful story poured out and horror carved a hole in Carolyn's heart.

"Oh my God, Diana. What will Sarah do?" Sarah owned the Full Cup, a popular bakery and coffee shop that anchored Gull Harbor. Her mother helped her with the bakery and babysat for the two little boys. The family lived for their weekly Skype session with Jamie. He was supposed to be released from service this summer. Sarah had even gone on a diet recently. She called it her Jamie Juice Diet.

Diana shook her head. "What do you do when the love of your life dies? It's just so terrible. They were high school sweethearts. Can you just imagine?"

"No. No, I can't."

A member of the National Guard, Jamie had been activated almost two years earlier. Like many of the men in Gull Harbor, he wanted to serve.

"How is Sarah handling this?" The thought of Nathan and Justin growing up without a father sent a chill through her heart.

"Kate and Chili are over at Sarah's now."

Diana and Carolyn sat there, their tea growing cold. What more could they say? Her own problems seemed like nothing compared to this tragedy.

Finally Carolyn broke the silence. "What about your wedding? Everything coming along?"

"Everything's fine. And how about you? Did those clothes work?"

"They were fabulous. I can't thank you enough." Carolyn bit her lip. Conflicted feelings tore her apart.

"Oh whoa, wait a minute. That look on your face? What happened?"

This wasn't the time for details. "It just didn't work out." She had to create a yawn. Diana got the message, pushing off from the stool.

"Maybe later? I just wanted you to know about Jamie."

"Sure. Later. Thanks for coming over. Sorry but I just can't..."

"I get it." Diana gave her a tight hug. "I'll be waiting to listen when you're ready. Man, some days life just sucks."

"You got it." The sad news about Jamie spread from shop to shop, cottage to cottage. One of theirs would not be coming home. A memorial service would be held at the high school, often the case for graduates if the family requested it. The death plunged Gull Harbor into mourning, leaving no time for her own pain.

Just when Carolyn's spirits reached an all-time low, her grandmother called. "I have some news for you." She was practically singing and Carolyn smiled.

"Howard and I are engaged! What do you think of that?"

"Wow. That's wonderful, Mama V." She tried to inject surprise and excitement into her voice. "I'm so happy for you. When is the wedding?"

"Oh, we haven't set a date. It's all so new." She sounded flustered. Dropping her voice, Mama V whispered, "Honey, you should see the ring he gave me."

What a surprise. "Well, he is a jeweler."

Laughing with her grandmother felt strange, as if her face had forgotten how. It wasn't long after they hung up that her mother called. "Carolyn, did you know about this?"

She sucked in a deep breath. "Yes, I did but not for long. Look Mom, it's great. They're so happy together. I don't want to hear another word." She must have gone on for five minutes, singing Howard's praises. When she finally wound down, her mother didn't say anything.

"Mom? You still there?"

"Well, yes, dear. I was just going to say I've never heard her so happy. Your father and I are thrilled. I can't wait to see her ring."

"Me too." Rings. Weddings. Love.

A chasm opened up inside.

Carolyn didn't know if she could ever fill it.

Chapter 20

How much pain can a woman's heart hold? Sitting in the gym at Jamie's service, Carolyn studied his high school picture, posted at the front. She prayed that one of her students would never be recognized in a similar service one day. It was Saturday and the whole town had turned out.

In the front row, Sarah sat with her boys, so small and trying not to cry. On the other side of Justin and Nathan was her mother Lila and Jamie's brother Ryan. Behind them sat the book group. Carolyn was sandwiched between Phoebe and Diana, who had Will on her other side. In back of them, Kate sat with Cole, hands folded on her bulging stomach. Her sister Mercedes clutched Finn's hand. From there, the rows went on and on.

Tragedies like this made living in a small town so powerful. Everyone was there for Sarah and her family. The flag at the post office was at half-mast, and every storefront window held a Remember Jamie poster. In this town, people grew up together, held deep respect for their country and supported each other.

Kind of like the people in Santa Fe, from what Mama V had told her. At the slightest suggestion, Carolyn's thoughts circled back to Brody like homing pigeons. Misery seeped through every pore of her body. How long would it take to get over him? She'd embraced mourning Jamie as a fierce release. In her heart, she realized she mourned another death. The end of a dream.

Sarah had been so lucky to have Jamie. Carolyn remembered seeing them at Clancy's together, picking out groceries, doing that familiar shoulder bump and laughing together over what kind of potato salad to buy. They seemed totally in sync. Each time they welcomed a baby, Jamie passed out candy cigars. Sarah would always have those memories.

Carolyn wanted that. Yearned for that elusive perfect pairing that remained just beyond her reach. Or had she pushed it away? Was she keeping love at a distance for a ton of reasons, all of which began with her, not Brody? But why had he never mentioned Justine?

Jamie's brother Ryan gave a eulogy, although the poor guy had a hard time. Then Glenn spoke, talking about the boy who'd led the football team to victory and went on to lead a unit in Afghanistan. He spoke of integrity, respect and gratitude for this supreme sacrifice. An honor guard accompanied the flag-draped casket out the door, family and friends walking behind. There wasn't a dry eye in that gym.

Although she didn't think the day could get any sadder, it did. A cemetery can do that to you. While the funeral director folded up the flag and handed it to Sarah, taps were played. Those pure brass notes rose and resonated with the crowd, their right hands over their hearts. The vets all saluted. Then everyone went to Sarah's house. Carolyn didn't stay long.

At home, she shed her dress for jeans, a hoodie and flip flops. As a last thought, she put on the silver earrings from Brody. They gave her a comforting sense of connection. How she wished he were here to hold her. The day had been devastating.

Then she walked down to the beach. Once she reached the sand, she kicked off the flip flops and left them in the dune grass. The lake was feisty tonight. Huge gray waves crashed against the shoreline. Perfect for her state of mind. Bending her head into the wind, she walked. The wind tore at her braid until finally her hair streamed out behind her. Pooled around her neck, the hood was no match for this onslaught. Still, she kept going, pressing one foot after the other into the cold, wet sand.

No gulls circled tonight. They were huddled in clusters in the sea glass. The cold gradually worked its way up her legs. It would be at least a month before this hard-packed sand grew warmer. Gauging the lapline, she made her way along that rippled edge, leaving foot prints in the wet sand. Sometimes she ran across a stretch of tiny rocks, small but they could hurt. She took the pain.

Carolyn walked the shoreline until her legs felt wobbly and her face was numb. Regrets plagued her. Had she done the right thing? Or had she made a snap decision and hustled back into her comfort zone. Coming to a halt, she stared out over the roiling water. Moonlight danced along the tops of the shifting waves. Finally, she turned and made her way home. Her earlier footprints had been washed away. Life could be just that fleeting. First you had something and then it was gone.

That Monday she'd planned a movie for her sixth period class, which was right after lunch. No way could she discuss *The Great Gatsby* today. The echo of the funeral stayed with her. While she ran the movie, some of the kids nodded off. Of course, that reminded her of Brody. Glancing back at the chair where he'd sat, she could almost see him slumped there, head on one arm. That boy never stayed awake during any movie, whether it was *Grapes of Wrath*, *Jane Eyre* or *Hamlet.*

But he wasn't that boy anymore. Brody was that man. Fumbling, she slid open her drawer and reached for a tissue. Some of the kids closest to her noticed. One gave her a thumbs up. They probably thought she was crying for Jamie.

Brody had called several times. She let the calls go to voicemail. That night she weakened and listened to them, one by one. Talk about self-inflicted pain. When her mind tried to make sense of it, she couldn't.

Was Justine the only woman Brody had failed to mention? What would her response have been if he did? She didn't want name or phones numbers. They were probably all like Justine, young and attractive. Had he taken them to the museums? Had he shared his family history? Somehow she doubted it. That just didn't ring true in her heart.

Her grandmother called more often now, excited about her engagement and trying not to make a big deal out of it. "Can you believe that your mother has accepted this engagement?" she asked one time. "I thought she'd be mad as heck."

That did make Carolyn smile. "We're all happy for you."

"Oh, honey. You sound so sad. Is this about your friend's

husband? Or is it, well, more personal?" Okay, Mama V couldn't even say Brody's name.

"These aren't my best days. I'll admit that."

Her grandmother blew out a breath. This was so unfair. Carolyn felt as if she had chicken pox and shouldn't be infecting anyone else. "I'll just be glad when school's over this year. That's all."

"I hate the fact that you came to visit me and this happened."

Carolyn sighed. "Forget it. You're getting married, Mama V. This should be a happy time for you." Reaching deep into an empty well, she tried to be her old carefree but responsible self, asking all the appropriate questions.

Mama V and Howard would be married in July. They didn't want to wait. "Howard thinks waiting at this age can be dangerous," her grandmother had laughed. Well, he might have a point.

The July date was a relief. Diana was getting married in June and Carolyn didn't know how many weddings she could handle in one summer. Weddings led to babies. Kate was getting bigger every day, although she wasn't due until early fall. Couples and families were popping up all around her. Talking to her grandmother, she'd stretched out on her sofa, sipping tea. Now the hibiscus tea turned tinny in her mouth. "Gotta go, Mama V. Say hello to Howard."

"Honey, I sure will. And Carolyn? Could I ask you just one thing?"

"Of course. Shoot." She swung her feet off the sofa and sat up. Was Mama V going to ask her to be her maid of honor? Carolyn had mixed feelings about that.

"Do you mind if Brody calls me? Is it okay if I talk to him?"

Just hearing his name choked her. "Why would you want to do that?" Her voice came out scratchy, like it was being dragged across cut glass.

"He misses you, sweetheart. Wants advice." Her grandmother heaved a sigh that could have made sails billow out on Lake Michigan. "The truth is, I've been talking to him. I feel bad."

"You feel bad for *him.*"

"And you of course. But he doesn't understand this. Whatever this is." Her voice trailed off.

Carolyn couldn't explain. She let her head fall into one hand. "Mama V, you do what you want. But I have to go now. Prepare for tomorrow's class and all that."

"All right. But tomorrow is Saturday."

She crossed her fingers. An old habit when she fudged on the truth a little. "Diana and I have plans tomorrow. I have to make potato salad." What was she saying? Diana had gone away with Will for the weekend.

"All right then. Love you. Talk to you soon."

Outside her kitchen window, a lilac bush bloomed. The scent wafted in through an open window. But the lilacs weren't smelling sweet this year. Neither were the peonies or lilies of the valley. Nothing held the same charm for her anymore.

She spent the weekend trying to read the next book for book club. This was to be their first meeting after Jamie's death. At Sarah's bidding, they'd agreed to have a May meeting. Kate told them that Sarah had insisted. "She's going to march right on. All of us being together might be comforting for her," Kate had said. "She intends to march right on."

Maybe Sarah would be an inspiration.

On Tuesday night, Carolyn arrived at Kate's promptly at six thirty. She'd only read about five chapters of the book. There was only so much of the Civil War she could take. The heroine was jilted by a man early in the book. Carolyn hoped the woman won out but wasn't counting on it.

"Don't you look great?" Kate greeted her at the door of the A-frame that perched on the beach. A huge dog loped toward her.

"Priscilla, downstairs." Kate caught her collar. "Natalie!" Prissy, Cole's harlequin Great Dane, shot her a regretful look, her huge jowls trembling with excitement. *Gee, Carolyn. I really wanted to catch up with you.* She was just that kind of dog. Carolyn gave Prissy a good scratch behind the ears.

Natalie, Cole's daughter, ran up the stairs. "Now Prissy, don't you bother the ladies."

Members of the book club were arranged on the chocolate brown sectional in Kate's living room. Two rockers had been pulled over from the fireplace. Chili was missing but she was usually late. Book in hand, Sarah threw her a determined smile. The woman was amazing. A huge pitcher of sangria sat on the coffee table, along with a bowl of cucumber dip. Carolyn needed both, which was a surprise. She hadn't been eating much.

"We're starting the summer off early," Kate said, bringing a tray of glasses from the kitchen. "Did everyone read the book?"

A sheepish silence settled over the group. "I tried," Phoebe said. "But the salon's been so busy." She twirled a mauve curl around her finger.

"Me too" Diana chimed in. "But with the wedding planning and everything, I don't have much time."

They quietly put their books aside.

"How was your trip, Carolyn," Sarah asked just as she was heaping some cucumber dip onto her paper plate.

"Oh, great. My grandmother's getting married."

Chili arrived in time to hear the announcement, and a wild whoop went up. For the next fifteen minutes, Carolyn fielded questions about her grandmother and Howard. When the wedding would be and where. "The Loretto Chapel?" Kate said with the awe it deserved. "I've heard it's beautiful."

Yes, the Loretto Chapel. *Just shoot me*. Mama V had no idea of the pain that brought. Memories flooded back. Brody stood next to her in the saffron sunlight falling through the stained glass windows, her hand tucked in his. Grabbing a ruffled chip she scooped up a spoonful of dip, too busy crunching to talk. At least, that's what she wanted them to think.

"Diana tells me she sent you a bunch of clothes," Phoebe said, eyes snapping. "Hot mama, huh?"

Carolyn nearly choked. The room fell silent. Diana bit her bottom lip. Not everyone had gotten the full story about Brody.

She took her time swallowing. "The clothes were great. Did you help pick those out, Phoebe?"

The hairdresser nodded. "So how did that go, Carolyn?" But Phoebe must have seen Diana shaking her head. When Carolyn tried to sip her sangria, she spilled it down the front of her white turtleneck.

"Oh, now." Leave it to Sarah to be the first to reach for her and give her hand a squeeze. "You don't have to tell us if you don't want to."

But if she couldn't tell this group, then who could she tell?

Bolstered by an encouraging nod from Diana, she said, "I ran into a former student in the airport."

She had their attention now.

"Is he single?"

"Did you always like him?'

"What does he look like?"

Questions bombarded her. Standing on the lip of her story, she felt the vertigo return. This time there was no Brody to calm her. No strong arms to anchor her.

But hadn't she handled it all alone before?

Carolyn took a deep breath. "That first year I taught at Gull Harbor, Brody was a senior taking my lit class. He was a royal pain. Probably one of those late bloomers. And boy, had he bloomed."

Chuckles circled the group. Looks were exchanged. All eating stopped.

"He'd been the class clown. In fact, I flunked him first semester. Couldn't even pass a quiz. Never came prepared."

But here words failed her because now Carolyn knew the reason why he'd done so miserably in school. "As it turned out, he had family problems."

The group clucked in sympathy. "He's a lot younger than me of course. At first I couldn't take him seriously."

Hah, that was a laugh. He had her at banana cream pie.

They all seemed to be doing the math in their heads.

"Chica? Porque no?" Chili held up four fingers. "Four years, no? That's nothing."

The others seemed to agree. There was a general nodding of heads, the whole group leaning forward so they wouldn't miss a word.

"So what's he like now?" Phoebe wiggled her eyebrows.

His Hotness, His Hotness, His Hotness. The words spun through her mind.

"Well, he's changed. Matured. And he lives in Santa Fe now." But she didn't go into his Native American background. That topic was so complex.

"But you, ah, hit it off? I mean, when you were nursing your grandmother?" Phoebe had no shame.

Carolyn took a sip of sangria. "That's the joke. My grandmother's fine. She didn't need my help at all. She'd been having a hot time with a man she met in rehab, for heaven's sake. Howard's now her fiancé." She played to the crowd. That set off a volley of cheers that brought Prissy upstairs again, afraid she'd missed something. Close on her heels, Natalie corralled the big dog. "Prissy, the ladies are making a lot of noise, but Dad says to just ignore them." Then the two of them were gone. Curiosity rippled in the air while the women drank, nibbled and feasted on a story more interesting than cucumber dip.

Phoebe waved a finger. "I think you are holding something

back."

No wonder all the women flocked to her hair salon. Phoebe had a way of ferreting stuff out. Therapy mixed with a shampoo and set. Carolyn's defenses began to crumble like the potato chip mashed in her fingers. This group knew her too well. "This isn't for all Gull Harbor to know," she said, with a pointed look in Phoebe's direction. "But yes, we went out. He showed me the town and we, ah, spent time together."

The situation must have shown on her face. But looking around she didn't see pity, just concern. After all, these were the women who backed each other no matter what. "Girlfriend, I think you fell in love." Phoebe stretched out the last word seductively, until it sounded like luv.

"Yes," she whispered. "I guess I did."

Kate had strategically placed a box of tissues on a side table, although they certainly hadn't been intended for Carolyn. Reaching over, Sarah snapped off two sheets and handed them to her. The gesture itself unleashed a bucket of tears. There was no laughter now. "But he, he wasn't telling me the truth."

Lips pursed and fists clenched. These were fighting women. "What lies did he tell you," Diana said, with a wary glance. After all, a lie had led her to Gull Harbor.

The confusion of the past weeks tumbled in Carolyn's mind. Desperate, she grasped at threads to weave them into the deception she'd experienced at El Farol. "It was what he didn't say that hurt."

A collective intake of breath sucked the air from the room. Outside dark clouds scudded over a moonless sky and thunder rumbled in the distance. "What didn't he say?" Sarah asked, in the softest voice ever. Of course, hers was a voice that would forgive a man anything.

"There was a woman." Heads began to nod. "That final night we went to a bar that meant something to us. They had flamenco. At least, it was special to me." She was setting the scene, and her book group hung on every word. Chili's fingers moved as if attached to a pair of castanets.

"And what happened that final night?" Kate leaned forward. Her first husband had been unfaithful. She knew. She'd realize. Carolyn's eyes clung to Kate's. "A woman approached us. She was young and so beautiful, you guys. Long dark hair. Body to die for. I could just tell they'd been together. And she confirmed it. Came right up to us."

"Bitch. What did he say? Brody?" Diana's eyes had narrowed. These girls were on her side.

"He said hello. Of course later he insisted that was all in the past." His phone messages had been emphatic. "How can a woman like *that* be really over?"

"Maybe it was," Diana interrupted. "Every single man dates, Carolyn."

"Of course they do. Unless they are a padre." Chili jumped right in.

The tide had turned. Carolyn struggled for words. Didn't intuition count for anything?

As if sensing her confusion, Diana changed the topic and started to talk about the wedding dress she'd found at Second

Hand Rose. Relieved, Carolyn sank back. Wedding dresses. How would she make it through this summer?

Since Diana had brought her and Phoebe, they drove home together. "I'm still a little confused about this," Diana said after they'd said good-night to Phoebe. "So did you and Brody have a discussion after this other woman showed up? Did you talk it all out? She might just be jealous because he ditched her."

Carolyn watched the occasional car headlights approach and then zoom past. "Diana, honestly, I don't know what we said. The point is, I didn't know anything about her. The situation reminded me of my dad. And I can't go there again. Other women."

"I never knew that about your father," Diana said slowly. "How awful."

"Yes, it was. And for a lot of reasons, my parents stayed together. Worked it out. And I think they've been happy. But I'll never forget the lies and arguments during those years."

"But that was your parents, not you and Brody. Carolyn, I've never heard you as happy as you were in Santa Fe."

"That's another thing, Diana. Another reason why that would never work out. He's in Santa Fe, and I'm in Gull Harbor."

"Forget the place, for now" Diana's eyes swung her way. "Do you love him?"

"Yes, yes I do. And I hate what happened. Lately, I've been wondering..."

"...if you jumped the gun?"

She nodded. Terrible but true. Regret curled around her like the dust of Santa Fe, refusing to be shut out.

"You know, Carolyn. I love you like a sister. But teachers sometimes have an attitude. You are so used to everyone listening to you. Maybe you should do a reality check. Don't bury a good relationship with the bath water. Be sure what of what you're saying."

Okay that was a whopper of a mixed metaphor but Diana did have a point.

Chapter 21

Brody had to do something. Work had become impossible. There'd been a complaint that his mind wasn't on the job when his guy installed the wrong french doors. He couldn't afford to lose a client like Frederick Knowles. But he also couldn't afford to lose Carolyn.

Maybe he already had. He felt raw with worry and was taking it out on his crews. If he kept this up, no one would work for him. Food nauseated him and he couldn't sleep. When he did, his dreams all focused on Carolyn. She was on a boat, sailing away. Or getting on a plane, waving goodbye. It was bizarre and driving him nuts.

She wouldn't answer her phone, and he was getting tired of talking to her grandmother. The feeling was probably mutual.

"What are you going to do about my granddaughter?" Vera had asked during their last chat, as she called them.

"I don't want to make the wrong move. Push her further away."

Mama V's *tsk, tsk* made him smile. "Well, Brody, she's in another state. How is that going to solve anything?"

Time to bring in the A team. He looked up Hippy Chick and called, hoping Diana Prescott wouldn't hang up on him. When he explained who he was, she stopped him. "Hold it right there,

Brody. I know who you are and what you've done."

He almost passed out. "But I haven't *done* anything."

"It's about the other women."

"But there aren't any." Damn this was frustrating. "Not since Carolyn came into my life."

"Then you better get a move on." Diana chuckled. "You've got some explaining to do. And I think this has to be face to face."

That night he bought his plane ticket.

~.~

The last week of school arrived. Carolyn graded exams and turned in final grades. The kids cleaned out their lockers and left. The halls were quiet. Busy in her room, Carolyn was boxing stuff up.

Summer stretched before her, long and uncertain. When summer school was mentioned, she didn't volunteer. Although in the past she often worked part time in Clancy's deli from June through August, she told them she had other plans. Big lie.

She wanted to do something different this summer. Experiment. Take some chances. Plans were still shaping up. Mama V had mentioned a visit, and Carolyn was getting up the courage to go back, face Brody and settle things. Because they sure weren't settled now. She thought about him, dreamed about him. Her body longed for him, and so did her heart.

Forgetting him was a full time job.

Taking posters and pictures from her bulletin board left her dusty. Some had been there for years. Definitely time for a change. Setting her boxes aside, she walked briskly to the teachers' lounge to wash her hands. The tiled halls echoed with silence. When she returned, she went right to her desk and continued clearing it off. The dried straw arrangements? Waste basket. Her neat pack of lesson plans? She rolled them up tightly and stuffed them in the can. The desk pad where she'd doodled Brody's name? She traced the mindless scribbling with one finger. The letters were etched on her heart. And her heart was hurting.

A throat cleared. She jumped. Her eyes flew to the sound in the back.

"Can I help with anything, Miss Knight?"

Okay, she was going crazy. Right now, she could see Brody in that last row, long legs stretched out to the side. If this didn't stop, she would have to see a shrink.

But when her hallucination almost couldn't squeeze his hips out of that desk, she realized it was really him. "Too damn small for me." Brody just about upended it.

"You-you don't fit." She walked to him, taking baby steps. "Not anymore."

"Nope, guess not." Looking shame-faced, he scratched the back of his head. She longed to cradle it in her hands. Feel the dark lengths slide through her fingers. "I mean, I don't fit here in these chairs."

"I can see that." They met halfway.

The question in his eyes squeezed her heart. Seemed like they both had one thing on their minds. Their words overlapped.

"I'm sorry."

"I've been an idiot."

He opened his arms. She fell into them. "You look terrible but wonderful." God, he felt good. Laying her head on his chest, she breathed in his blue sweater. For her it smelled as good as the most expensive cologne in the world. She'd know that scent anywhere.

"Have you been eating?" He ran his hands down her arms and frowned.

"No. You?" Brody was looking leaner than ever.

He shrugged. "Look, I should have told you about Justine. But I was afraid you wouldn't understand."

She thought back. "Yeah, you were probably right. So you'd been dating her?"

His eyes grew wary.

"That's not a trick question, Brody. You can tell me."

"That ended when you and I started feeding each other coconut cream pie."

"It was banana. Kiss me."

"Yes, ma'am." He lowered his head.

"Don't call me that, please," she whispered against his lips.

"Okay, Teach." He stifled her protest with hungry lips, hands cupping her face. "God, I missed you."

The slight tremor of his body convinced her this was true. But she had to clear this up. "I should have understood, Brody. But I was terrified that other women would come out of the woodwork."

"I know. Diana told me."

"She did?"

"Ah, huh." He closed in for another kiss, angling his head just right. This was more action than room 207 had ever seen. "So I guess it had to do with your dad, and I'll take it up with him when we meet."

She swatted at his hand. "You will not. That's over. My parents' marriage is doing fine and let's keep it that way."

Uncertainty clouded his eyes. "Are *we* over, Carolyn?"

"Oh, I hope not."

His whole body seemed to release. "Look, I can't live without you."

"I wouldn't want you to. But how will we work this, the two different states and everything?" She wanted the suggestion to come from him.

"How flexible can you be?" He shot her a questioning glance, as if he might not like the answer.

"Try me. If my grandmother could start a new life, then so can I. Now don't freak out, but I didn't sign a contract for next year. I thought I'd do some substitute teaching in Santa Fe. See what the high schools have to offer."

If she ever wondered if that suggestion might freak him out, his grin convinced her otherwise. "Are you kidding? That's great. You amaze me."

"That's for us to find out. My grandmother's delighted since after her wedding, she's moving in with Howard. I can live in her casita."

"I have a better idea."

"Oh, really." They were nose to nose, breathing with the same rhythm. "What's that?"

"Why don't you live with me?"

"Maybe. But I'll have a whole summer off. What'll I do with all that time?"

"I have lots of ideas." His eyes turned sultry with suggestion.

"Oh, I'll just bet you do." She traced his cocky grin with a finger. He would always be a handful. She wouldn't have it any other way. "In fact, some of those activities might deserve extra credit."

He lifted a dark brow. "Enough to raise my grade?"

"Just might." She liked talking nonsense with him.

"You mean, someday I might move from boyfriend to husband?"

She sucked in a breath. "Let's take things slowly, okay? After all, you just moved from my late bloomer to boyfriend. Our new chapter is just starting."

Drawing back, Brody smiled. "That chapter stuff. Is that a metaphor?"

His Hotness was too adorable for words. And he was hers. "Yes, it is," she murmured as she kissed him. "And for this story, *our* story, you won't need the Cliff Notes."

THE END

Coming Home to You

All books in the *Man from Yesterday* series stand alone. You won't be lost if you dive right in for a visit to Gull Harbor. A lot of my readers have commented they want these girls for friends! The first book in that series is *Coming Home to You,* and an excerpt is below. Returning to Gull Harbor to help her mom, Kate Kennedy runs into her high school crush, Cole Campbell. She had her issues with him, and prom was one of them. But Cole's had his own challenges over the past few years. His daughter Natalie and Prissy, their Great Dane, are only too eager to tell Kate all about it. It's so hard to stay mad at Cole when Kate's falling in love with his daughter and that dog. You can find *Coming Home to You,* usually FREE in ebook format, on Amazon, Barnes and Noble, iBooks and Kobo.

Chapter 1

The thumping started when Kate Kennedy reached Greta's Gifts on Red Arrow Highway. Cheese curls churned in her stomach as she tapped the brakes. Almost home but something was wrong with the kayak strapped to her roof. Gravel crunching beneath the tires, she pulled into Greta's and parked. The sun bounced off the hood of her SUV, but a cool May breeze bathed her face when she cracked open the door.

Welcome to Michigan. Her eyes felt grainy from fourteen hours on the road, but she was home.

Stretching, Kate breathed in the lake, damp and beachy. The tightness in her shoulders eased. Pine trees caught a high spring gust and the familiar rustle made her smile. Her stomach gurgled. Not much to eat the whole ride from Boston except peanut butter and jelly, plus bags of cheese curls washed down with coffee.

Looking up, she exhaled. At least she hadn't lost Gator, her green kayak. A red security tie flapped in the breeze. Must have lost the other strap along the way. Kate scrubbed her face with hands shaking from all the caffeine. A semi roared past, kicking up dust. She tugged up the zipper on her hoodie.

"Doggone it, Gator."

The kayak slid a bit farther. Too bad she'd left her small kitchen stepladder in the Boston condo, along with a lot of other stuff. When she yanked the remaining red band, it fell away in her hand. One frustrated shove and Gator retaliated, smacking her square in the chest before clattering to the ground. The pain bent Kate over like a paper clip. She almost didn't hear the door slam behind her.

Blinking furiously, she pulled herself up, grateful for the sunglasses. No way would anyone see Kate Kennedy cry. A man ambled toward her in work boots, worn jeans, and shoulders that tested the seams of a beat-up jean jacket. That walk looked familiar and her heart kicked up a beat. He wore aviator sunglasses, so no telling for sure. A black and white dog hung out of the pickup, Great Dane ears pricking forward. Big muzzle, big dog.

"Need some help?"

Yep, it was him. Kate's legs weakened. "No, I'm fine."

His eyes shifted to the kayak on the ground. "Doesn't look fine to me."

She fisted her hands on her hips. "I'm fine. And so is Gator." Her chest throbbed.

Blue eyes swept like a July wave over the tops of his sunglasses. "Gator?"

She swallowed. "My kayak. Seemed appropriate."

"I see."

But Cole Campbell had never understood why Kate wanted all her belongings named and in their proper place. Shoot. They'd been on the high school debate team together, and he didn't recognize her? Maybe it was her recent drugstore dye job. She'd had brown hair in high school. Now she ran a hand over blonde hair, crisp from two days of neglect.

He swayed back on his heels, a Good Samaritan with second thoughts. The two empty seats of the kayak stared up at them. "Lucky you didn't lose it on the road. Could have smashed into another driver. You need to batten it down."

"Thought I did. It was dark when I loaded it."

"Try doing it in the daytime. You could kill somebody."

"I left at midnight."

"Midnight?" He lowered the glasses and his eyes darkened.

Her chin came up. "Highway's quiet at night. Just the truckers."

"Exactly. Truckers. You think that's safe?"

None of his business. "I've, ah, probably got some rope in the back." She seriously doubted it.

"I'll be glad to help." Cole's attention shifted to her jeans. The corners of his lips lifted. "You saving that for something?"

Kate looked down. A cheese curl was caught in her crotch and she batted it away. No time for games. Especially not with him.

His eyes flitted from her to Gator and back. A stern mask slipped into place. Cole's teenage acne had left faint pockmarks that definitely didn't detract from his macho appeal.

Was he going to help her or not? Her chest throbbed. Could this day get any worse? The boy she'd lusted for in high school didn't even recognize her. Kate's throat closed. Nothing like feeling forgettable.

In two thrusts of his muscular arms, Cole had Gator back in the rack on top of her SUV. Disgusting how easy he made it look, but it gave her time to enjoy the view. Cole Campbell had definitely left "gawky" behind.

"Thank you."

Wheeling around, he caught her staring and grinned. "Got that rope?"

Her face burned. "Sure. I'll get it. Let me just check Bonita."

"Bonita?" He tilted his head.

"My car." One glimpse of the pretty blue SUV on the lot and she knew it was Bonita.

"Sure. Right."

Popping open the back gate, Kate launched herself into the tightly packed boxes and bulging trash bags. Her rear end felt big as a helium balloon.

"Finding anything? I might have something in the truck."

Feeling him hovering, she tried to squeeze her butt tighter.

When she heard the scratch of his boots, Kate thought maybe he was leaving. Her disappointment surprised her. After all, she wasn't at her best. If you're going to run into an old flame… well, a man you wanted to be your old flame… a girl should look hot, not sweaty.

Kate was sweaty. And not in a good way.

Finally, she climbed out empty-handed. Cole was ambling toward her with a roll of heavy gauge rope.

"That looks serious." Her mother wouldn't even be able to get a clothespin around this sturdy stuff, although she'd probably try.

"Want to stand on the other side and catch this?"

"Sure." *I'd hold anything for you. Like my breath.*

While Cole tossed a length of rope over the kayak, his dog watched from the pickup with mild interest. Grabbing the rope, Kate threaded it back and he knotted it securely. "First, I like to tighten the bow and then the stern."

"You kayak?"

Whipping out a Swiss army knife, he cut the rope. "Way too much work. I sail."

Of course. She pictured an elegant yacht skimming Lake Michigan. Samantha McGraw would be rubbing her tan body against his. Kate didn't need the instant replay. Had enough of that in high school.

Cole worked with calm efficiency, the way he'd handled Student Council or Debate Club.

Oh, yeah. He'd handled their debate group just fine.

When he turned back, his eyes went to her hair. Smiling, Cole whisked something from the mess. Her breath left her body.

Maybe she was just tired.

Or maybe she was desperate for a man's touch.

He handed her a cheese curl. "You missed this."

"Great. Thanks." She jammed it in her jean pocket and then felt stupid. Was she going to press it in her high school scrapbook?

Kate slammed her back gate shut.

Cole's eyes rested on the Massachusetts license plate. "Passing through or coming for the summer?"

"That depends." He still didn't know her? She edged toward the driver's door. "Thanks for your help."

Cole cocked his head to one side, like he was listening to her voice. "Sure. No problem."

"Got to get to an appointment." Maybe a shrink. She opened the driver's door so fast she almost cracked herself in the mouth.

"Ah, huh. Well, good luck."

"Right. Thanks." Kate needed more than luck this trip. Without looking back, she peeled out and did a U-turn on Red Arrow. In bad need of a friendly face, she headed into town.

Driving toward Gull Harbor, Kate passed the ice cream parlors, restaurants, galleries, and gift shops that lured tourists. Some looked closed, and she hoped that was just seasonal. Winters could be hard on businesses, and this economy didn't help any.

Clancy's grocery store sat at the main intersection of Whittaker and Red Arrow, just next to Dressel's drugstore. Kate ducked into the grocery, grabbed a cart, and zipped through the aisles, snapping up basic necessities like OJ, milk, bread and cheese curls. Stopping at the deli counter, she picked up some sliced turkey and cole slaw. Should hold her for a while.

After stowing the bags in her trunk, Kate glanced across the street. The Full Cup sign swung above the frosted glass door. A cheese crown called to her from Sarah's shiny clean case. Hardly any traffic on Whittaker in early May and she sprinted across the two lanes. Kate pushed open the door of the bakery and breathed in the scent of warm, fresh pastries. No need to begin sensible eating now. Sour cream donuts, almond braids, cheese crowns and frosted brownies were neatly arranged behind the glass.

Freshly perked coffee perfumed the air with a hint of hazelnut. Definitely not the roadside stuff. Everything about the place looked the same, just the way Kate liked it. Her irritation eased. Would it be a cheese crown or a brownie? Kate was still deciding when Sarah whirled through the swinging door to the back, patting her brown curls. "Why, Katie Kennedy. Back so soon?"

"Couldn't stay away from your cheese crowns."

"I know. Me too." Laughing, Sarah wiped her hands on the apron around her ample waist. Miss Congeniality, hands down.

"Everything good? Boys and Jamie doing all right?"

Sarah had married Jamie Pickard, her high school sweetheart now serving overseas. They had two little boys.

"Yep, as far as I know. One cheese crown coming right up." Sarah handed over the largest pastry on the tray. She nodded toward the tables at the window. "Got time to chat? Coffee's free."

"Sounds like a plan." That run-in with Cole after all these years had left Kate's head fuzzy. She just wasn't ready to see her mom yet. After pouring a cup of hazelnut coffee, she slid onto one of the wire-backed chairs.

Sarah settled across the table with a sigh. "Your mother will be glad to see you."

"So you know about the second stroke?" No secrets in this town. Today that felt good.

"How's she doing?"

"The therapists say she's improving."

"She'll be tickled to see you." Supportive to the bone, Sarah always had your back.

"Picked up groceries and thought I'd stop here." Kate's grin felt shaky. "Kinda tired. I started out late last night."

"A woman on the highway alone at night?"

"Cole Campbell already told me that was stupid."

"You're in touch with Cole?" Sarah's eyebrows lifted into her curly mop.

Kate brushed the crumbs from her jeans. "My kayak came loose, and he stopped to help."

"Really? Always so helpful. Cole's a mover and shaker here in town."

"Samantha must love that." Kate had heard Cole and Samantha married right out of college. By that time, Kate had been dating Brian for three years. High school friends pairing up had been old news.

But with Cole? Okay, the news gave her a twinge or two.

"They split up." Sarah stirred more cream into her coffee. "It's been tough for him the last few years. He has custody of their daughter."

Cole Campbell, a single father? "Thought the mom always got the kids. Does Samantha live around here?"

"Nope. California, from what I hear. Anyway, Cole wants to move Gull Harbor ahead." Sarah glanced at the street outside. "Make some changes."

"Things look just fine the way they are." Kate took another bite of the sweet cheese.

"We've had a rough few years, Kate. Shops have closed or changed hands. Michiana Thyme was sold. Did your mom tell you?"

Kate shook her head, struggling to swallow. She always bit off more than she could chew. "Nope. She might be a little out of touch now." Craning her neck, Kate stared down Whittaker at the combination gift shop and diner on the main corner. Been there forever. Now it was sold? Her contentment at being home unraveled around the edges. "I was looking forward to their stuffed French toast."

"And I would have been right there with you, not that I need it. Loretta retired and moved to Florida to be near her son William. No one wanted to take on the store."

"What's going to happen to the place?"

Sarah lifted a shoulder. "Town meeting pretty soon. Cole bought it. He's got plans. Your mom never said anything? She's always been so involved in Gull Harbor."

"She will be again. I have no doubt."

Sarah's eyes softened. "She'll be so glad to see both of you."

"Mercedes can't come. Too much going on with her company."

At least that had been the excuse. Kate didn't need to spell it out for her old friend. Eons ago, her older sister had borrowed an outfit from Sarah. The fluffy teal sweater and pants had been so pretty. After go-karting with friends, Mercedes returned it with oil stains. Never said a thing about it. Kate had been so embarrassed.

Just another page from the book of Mercedes Kennedy. "I'm hoping Mercedes will be able to come soon."

"You Kennedy women are strong. Almost didn't recognize you, Kate. Like the blonde hair."

"What was I thinking? Crazy, right?"

"Maybe you need more crazy."

"Don't know if I'm ready for that." But change was bearing down on her, whether she liked it or not. This two-block street was all Kate had ever known in Gull Harbor. They'd hung out here at the Swirly Top, eaten Loretta's special orange ricotta stuffed French toast at Michiana Thyme and grabbed pizza at Touch of Italy. All the local kids got part-time jobs in the shops during the summer. "I want it to stay just the way it is."

"I don't know if that's possible, Kate."

Her coffee had turned lukewarm. The cozy hazelnut flavor was gone and a chill stole through the glass window. "Boy, it's cold. When will spring get here?" Kate pulled her jean jacket tighter.

"We had a long winter." Sarah gave her a wry smile. "The ice floes didn't melt until just a couple weeks ago. Beach is going to be wide this year. Hope people can afford to rent cottages."

By Memorial Day, families would be bustling from store to store with bulging shopping bags. At least, that's the way it used to be. "How's your business?"

"Not bad. Course I have been taking more day-old pastries to the soup kitchens. Might as well have someone enjoy them, right? Gonna be here for a while? I'm sure the girls would love to see you. You probably have to get back, though. Husband, job, and all that."

Kate sucked in a slow breath, not quite ready to share the news. "So much depends on Mom's condition. I'm freelancing now, you know. Healthcare blogs."

"Right, you told me the newspaper had a layoff." A silence stretched until Sarah carefully swept crumbs off the table and into a napkin. "Well, then. You always liked to read, Kate. Come to our book group."

"Anybody I know?" Last thing she needed was a bunch of strangers asking questions.

"Chili and Carolyn Knight, who teaches at the high school."

"Chili? Don't think I would have passed Spanish without her." Chili would quiz Kate about verb conjugations until she could recite them in her dreams. "Carolyn? You mean Miss Knight? Still single and teaching at the high school?"

"Yep and then Phoebe and Diana. Both new to the area. You'll enjoy them. Phoebe has a hair salon and Diana opened Hippy Chick, a clothing store. Kind of cute."

Being with other women, people she didn't know sounded good. "Maybe. Thanks for mentioning it."

Sarah looked pleased with herself. "Good. We're meeting next Wednesday. My house at seven."

Whoa. "But I haven't read the book."

"'Bridges of Madison County.' I'll get it to you next week."

"Oh, I can wing that one." An old favorite, the novel was packed up in the garage of the condo, waiting for a destination address.

The door to the kitchen slammed open, and two little boys tumbled out, barefoot with t-shirts untucked. "Mom, Mom!" the first little guy called out, running to Sarah. "Nathan won't share!"

"Mine! These are my dinosaurs!" The other boy clutched some plastic figures to his heaving chest. The unruly hair marked them as Sarah's children.

"Double trouble." Sarah stared them both down. "Justin and Nathan, can't you say hello to Kate?"

The boys looked like they might consider it.

"Hello."

"Hi."

Sarah laid one hand on each boy's shoulder. "Where's Grandma Lila?"

Justin poked one finger back toward the kitchen. "Making something."

At that moment, a silver-haired woman appeared in the doorway, looking tired and more than a little frustrated.

"Sarah, I tried but they're bored." When Lila threw up both hands, white flour flew. "Hi, Kate. Good to see you."

"Boys, we're going to learn to share or your father will be very disappointed." Sarah wagged one finger before turning back to Kate. "Their daddy is a very brave soldier." The last was obviously said for their benefit.

"You must be so proud of him," Kate said. With his polished Italian loafers and weekly hair styling, Brian wouldn't have dreamed of going over to the Middle East. "Was Jamie in the reserves?"

Sarah nodded. "Called up, but he would have volunteered

anyway. I've got a ton of chores ready when he gets back."

Kate checked the time. "I should get moving. Guess I'll take a cheese crown for my mom."

Shepherding the two boys toward their grandmother, Sarah bustled back behind the counter to retrieve Kate's cheese crown. "Mom, I think it's nap time."

Both boys howled.

Waving away Kate's money, Sarah squeezed her hand. "Oh, don't be silly."

"I'll see you…"

"Next Wednesday," Sarah supplied. "My house. Seven o'clock."

"Right." Slotting something on her calendar felt good. Almost banished the embarrassment from running into Cole Campbell.

After all, wasn't he the one who should be embarrassed?

Continue reading this book on Amazon, Barnes and Noble, iTunes or Kobo!

Other Books by Barbara Lohr

Windy City Romance series

Finding Southern Comfort

Her Favorite Mistake

Her Favorite Honeymoon

Her Favorite Hot Doc

The Christmas Baby Bundle

Rescuing the Reluctant Groom

The Southern Comfort Christmas

Man from Yesterday series

Coming Home to You

Always on His Mind

In His Eyes

Late Bloomer

About the Author

Barbara Lohr writes heartwarming contemporary romance. A flair for fun and subtly sexy love scenes is her trademark. In her *Windy City Romance* series the women are based in Oak Park, Illinois, a western suburb of Chicago. However, these girls get around. Readers enjoy jaunts to Tuscany, Guatemala and Savannah. The *Man from Yesterday* series is based in Gull Harbor, Michigan, where close high school friends welcome newcomers with equal warmth. The charming small beach town actually exists but under another name.

Family often plays a role in Barbara's stories. "No woman falls in love without some family influence, either positive or negative." Dark chocolate is her favorite food group, and yummy food often figures in her work. Barbara lives in the South with her husband and a cat that insists he was Heathcliff in a former life. Sign up for her newsletter by going to her website. Friend her on Facebook or connect on Twitter! She loves to hear from readers.

For more information on the author and her work, or to sign up for her newsletter, please see:

www.BarbaraLohrAuthor.com

www.facebook.com/Barbaralohrauthor

www.twitter.com/BarbaraJLohr

A Word from the Author

Many thanks to Romance Writers of America, a group whose members are generous with their knowledge base. The loops and forums of writers who address writing and publishing issues are invaluable to me.

To my readers, thank you! Your appreciation and support warm my heart. To my Street Team, you rock! Special thanks to Kay Crocker, Pam Mitchell, Debbie Sutherland and Jane Whitmeyer for their excellent proofing skills. To my growing Read and Review team, love you guys! Keep responding to my newsletters and be sure to enter my giveaways. I sure appreciate your interest and hope to continue to write books that take you on "journeys of the heart," as one of you mentioned.

Thanks to Kim Killion for covers that package my work perfectly. I look at those covers and think, yes, my characters could walk right off that page. And the same to Chris Hall, my editor. After untold hours of working on a manuscript, your suggestions and insight are invaluable.

For my daughters Kelly and Shannon, keep those reading lamps on over your beds. For us, reading has always been a tie that binds. My grandchildren Bo and Gianna bring me such joy and of course pop up in Mama B's novels. To my husband Ted, words aren't adequate to thank you for your love and support, especially when my computer crashes and you provide tech support. May we have many more wonderful years together with trips to Leopold's for ice cream.